D1261401

MANHATTAN IN REVERSE

MANHATTAN IN REVERSE

Peter F. Hamilton

SUBTERRANEAN PRESS 2012

First U.S. Edition

ISBN
978-1-59606-440-9

Subterranean Press
PO Box 190106
Burton, MI 48519

www.subterraneanpress.com

Table of Contents

◆

Dedication

To all the Friday-night-down-the-pub boys, past, present, and future. Whose whimsical flights of fantasy go a great deal further than anything in this book.

Introduction

I'M NOT THE MOST prolific of short story writers. I do enjoy the form, but novel writing takes up most of my time these days. Consequently I get to write about one a year, if I'm lucky.

This, then, is a collection of all my short stories written since 1998, when the last collection, *A Second Chance at Eden* was published. Looking through them I'd be the first to admit they're not particularly short, with the exception of "Forever Kitten", which was written for the excellent *Nature* magazine, and had to be kept to less than 1000 words. I can do it, but that's a rare event. Very rare.

The rest have all been published in various anthologies or magazines, apart from "Manhattan in Reverse", a story featuring the detective from my Commonwealth universe, Paula Myo, which was written exclusively for this collection. I also took the opportunity to revise "Footvote", bringing it slightly more up to date. A strange thing to do with an SF story set in the alternative near-past, but I couldn't resist.

Peter F. Hamilton
Rutland, 2011

WATCHING TREES GROW

◆◆◆

ONE
OXFORD, ENGLAND AD 1832

IF I WAS DREAMING that night I forgot it the instant when that blasted telephone woke me with its shrill two-tone whistle. I fumbled round for the bedside light, very aware of Myriam shifting and groaning on the mattress beside me. She was seven months pregnant with our child, and no longer appreciated the calls which I received at strange hours. I found the little chain dangling from the light, tugged it, and picked up the black bakelite handset.

I wasn't surprised to have the rich vowels of Francis Haughton Raleigh rolling down the crackly line at me. The family's old *missi dominici* is my immediate superior. Few others would risk my displeasure with a call at night.

"Edward, my boy," he growled. "So sorry to wake you at this ungodly hour."

I glanced at the brass clock on the chest of drawers; its luminous hands were showing quarter past midnight. "That's all right, sir. I wasn't sleeping."

Myriam turned over and gave me a derisory look.

"Please, no need to call me *sir*. The thing is, Edward, we have a bit of a problem."

"Where?"

"Here in the city, would you believe. It's really the most damnable news. One of the students has been killed. Murdered, the police seem to think."

I stopped my fidgeting, suddenly very awake. Murder, a concept as difficult to grasp as it was frightening to behold. What kind of pre-Empire savage could do that to another person? "One of ours?"

"Apparently so. He's a Raleigh, anyway. Not that we've had positive confirmation."

"I see." I sat up, causing the flannel sheet to fall from my shoulders. Myriam was frowning now, more concerned than puzzled.

"Can we obtain that confirmation?" I asked.

"Absolutely. And a lot more besides. I'm afraid you and I have been handed the family jurisdiction on this one. I'll pick you up in ten minutes." The handset buzzed as the connection ended.

I leaned over and kissed Myrian gently. "Got to go."

"What is it? What's happened?"

Her face had filled with worry. So much so that I was unable to answer in truth. It wasn't that she lacked strength. Myriam was a senior technical nurse, seeing pain and suffering every day at the city clinic—she'd certainly seen more dead bodies than I ever had. But blurting out this kind of news went against my every instinct. Obscurely, it felt to me as though I was protecting our unborn. I simply didn't want my child to come into a world where such horror could exist. *Murder.* I couldn't help but shiver as I pulled on my shirt, cold fingers making a hash of the small pearl buttons. "Some kind of accident, we think. Francis and I have to investigate. I'll tell you in the morning." When, the Blessed Mary willing, it might be proved some ghastly mistake.

My leather attaché case was in the study, a present from my mother when I passed my legal exams. I had been negligent in employing it until now, some of its fine brass implements and other paraphernalia had never even been taken from their compartments. I snatched it up as if it were some form of security tool, its scientific contents a shield against the illogicality abroad in the city that night.

I didn't have a long wait in the lobby before Francis's big black car rolled up outside, crunching the slushy remnants of last week's snowfall. The old man waited patiently whilst I buckled the safety restraint straps around my chest and shoulders before switching on the batteries and engaging the gearing toggle. We slipped quietly out onto the cobbled street, powerful yellow headlamps casting a wide fan of illumination.

The apartment which Myriam and I rent is in the city's Botley district, a pleasant area of residential blocks and well-tended parks, where small businesses and shops occupy the ground floors of most buildings. The younger, professional members of the better families had taken to the district, their nannies filling the daytime streets with prams and clusters of small excitable children. At night it seemed bleaker somehow, lacking vitality.

Francis twisted the motor potentiometer, propelling the car up to a full twenty-five miles an hour. "You know, it's at times like this I wish the Roman Congress hadn't banned combustion engines last year," he grumbled. "We could be there in half a minute."

"Batteries will improve," I told him patiently. "And petroleum was dangerous stuff. It could explode if there were an accident."

"I know, I know. Lusting after speed is a Shorts way of thinking. But I sometimes wonder if we're not being too timid these days. The average citizen is a responsible fellow. It's not as if he'll take a car out looking to do damage with it. Nobody ever complains about horseriding."

"There's the pollution factor as well. And we can't afford to squander our resources. There's only a finite amount of crude oil on the planet, and you know the population projections. We must safeguard the future, we're going to spend the rest of our lives there."

Francis sighed theatrically. "Well recited. So full of earnest promise, you youngsters."

"I'm thirty-eight," I reminded him. "I have three accredited children already." One of which I had to fight to gain family registration for. The outcome of a youthful indiscretion with a girl at college. We all have them.

"A child," Francis said dismissively. "You know, when I was a young, in my teens in fact, I met an old man who claimed he could remember the last of the Roman Legionaries withdrawing from Britain when he was a boy."

I performed the maths quickly in my head. It could be possible, given how old Francis was. "That's interesting."

"Don't patronise, my boy. The point is, progress brings its own problems. The world that old man lived in changed very little in his lifetime—it was almost the same as the Second Imperial Era. While today, our whole mindset, the way we look at our existence, is transformed every time a new scientific discovery drops into our lap. He had stability. We don't. We have to work harder because of that, be on our guard more. It's painful for someone of my age."

"Are you saying today's world makes murder more likely?"

"No. Not yet. But the possibility is there. Change is always a domino effect. And the likes of you and I must be conscious of that, above all else. We are the appointed guardians, after all."

"I'll remember."

"And you'll need to keep remembering it as well, not just for now, but for centuries."

I managed to prevent my head from shaking in amusement. The old man was always going on about the uncertainties and dangers of the future. Given the degree of social and technological evolution he'd witnessed in the last four hundred years, it's a quirk which I readily excuse. When he was my age the world had yet to see electricity and mains water; medicine then consisted of herbs boiled up by old women in accordance with lore already ancient in the First Imperial Era. "So what do we know about this possible murder?"

"Very little. The police phoned the local family office, who got straight on to me. The gentleman we're talking about is Justin Ascham Raleigh; he's from the Nottingham Raleighs. Apparently, his neighbour heard sounds coming from his room, and thought there was some kind of fight or struggle going on. He alerted the lodgekeepers. They opened the room up and found him, or at least a body."

"Suspicious circumstances?"

"Very definitely, yes."

We drove into the centre of Oxford. Half past midnight was hardly late by the city's standards. There were students thronging the tree-lined streets, just starting to leave the cafes and taverns. Boisterous, yes; I could remember my own time here as a student, first studying science, then latterly law. They shouted as they made their way back to their residences and colleges; quoting obscure verse, drinking from the neck of bottles, throwing books and bags about...one group was even having a scrum down, slithering about on the icy pavement. Police and lodgekeepers looked on benignly at such activity, for it never gets any worse than this.

Francis slowed the car to a mere crawl as a bunch of revellers ran across the road ahead. One young man mooned us before rushing off to merge with his laughing friends. Many of them were girls, about half of whom were visibly pregnant.

"Thinks we're the civic authorities, no doubt," Francis muttered around a small smile. "I could show him a thing or two about misbehaving."

We drew up outside the main entrance to Dunbar College. I hadn't been inside for well over a decade, and had few memories of the place. It was a six storey building of pale yellow stone, with great mullioned windows overlooking the broad boulevard. Snow had been cleared from the road and piled up in big mounds on either side of the archway which led into the quad. A police constable and a junior lodgekeeper were waiting for us in the lodgekeeper's office just inside the entranceway, keeping warm by the iron barrel stove. They greeted us briskly, and led us inside.

Students were milling uneasily in the long corridors, dressed in pyjamas, or wrapped in blankets to protect themselves from the cool air. They knew something was wrong, but not what. Lodgekeepers dressed in black suits patrolled the passages and cloisters, urging patience and restraint. Everyone fell silent as we strode past.

We went up two flights of spiralling stone stairs, and along another corridor. The chief lodgekeeper was standing outside a sturdy wooden door, no different to the twenty other lodgings on that floor. His ancient creased face registered the most profound sadness. He nodded as the constable announced who we were, and ushered us inside.

Justin Ascham Raleigh's accommodation was typical of a final year student—three private rooms: bedroom, parlour and study. They had high ceilings, wood panelled walls dark with age, long once-grand curtains hanging across the windows. All the interconnecting doors had been opened, allowing us to see the corner of a bed at the far end of the little suite. A fire had been lit in the small iron grate of the study, its embers still glowing, holding off the night's chill air.

Quite a little group of people were waiting for us. I glanced at them quickly: three student-types, two young men and a girl, obviously very distressed; and an older man in a jade-green police uniform, with the five gold stars of a senior detective. He introduced himself as Gareth Alan Pitchford, his tone sombre and quiet. "And I've heard of you, sir. Your reputation is well established in this city."

"Why thank you," Francis said graciously. "This is my deputy, Edward Bucahanan Raleigh."

Gareth Alan Pitchford bestowed a polite smile, as courteous as the situation required, but not really interested. I bore it stoically.

"So what have we got here?" Francis asked.

Detective Pitchford led us into the study. Shelving filled with a mixture of academic reference books and classic fiction covered two walls. I was drawn to the wonderfully detailed star charts which hung upon the other walls, alternating with large photographs of extravagant astronomical objects. A bulky electrically powered typewriter took pride of place on a broad oak desk, surrounded by a litter of paper and open scientific journals. An ordinary metal and leather office chair with castors stood behind the desk, a grey sports jacket hanging on its back.

The body was crumpled in a corner, covered with a navy-blue nylon sheet. A considerable quantity of blood had soaked into the threadbare Turkish carpet. It started with a big splash in the middle of the room, laying a trail of splotches to the stain around the corpse.

"This isn't pretty," the detective warned as he turned down the sheet.

I freely admit no exercise in self control could prevent me from wincing at what I saw that moment. Revulsion gripped me, making my head turn away. A knife was sticking out of Justin Ascham Raleigh's right eye; it was buried almost up to the hilt.

The detective continued to pull the sheet away. I forced myself to resume my examination. There was a deep cut across Justin Ascham Raleigh's abdomen, and his ripped shirt was stained scarlet. "You can see that the attacker went for the belly first," the detective said. "That was a disabling blow, which must have taken place about here." He pointed to the glistening splash of blood in the middle of the study. "I'm assuming Mr Raleigh would have staggered back into this corner and fallen."

"At which point he was finished off," Francis said matter-of-factly. "I would have thought he was dying anyway from the amount of blood lost from the first wound, but his assailant was obviously very determined he should die."

"That's my belief," the detective said.

Francis gave me an enquiring look.

"I agree," I stuttered.

Francis gestured weakly, his face flush with distaste. The sheet was pulled back up. Without any spoken agreement, the three of us moved away from the corpse to cluster in the doorway leading to the parlour.

"Can we have the full sequence of events, please?" Francis asked.

"We don't have much yet," the detective said. "Mr Raleigh and five of his friends had supper together at the Orange Grove restaurant earlier this evening. It lasted from half-past seven to about ten o'clock, at which point they left and separated. Mr Raleigh came back here to Dunbar by himself around twenty past ten—the lodgekeepers confirm that. Then at approximately half past eleven, his neighbour heard an altercation, then a scream. He telephoned down to the lodgekeeper's office."

I looked from the body to the door which led back out into the corridor. "Was no one seen or heard to leave?"

"Apparently not, sir," the detective said. "The neighbour came straight out into the corridor and waited for the lodgekeepers. He didn't come in here himself, but he swears no one came out while he was watching."

"There would be a short interval," I said. "After the scream he'd spend some time calling the lodgekeepers—a minute or so."

"People must have been using the corridor at that time," the detective said. "And our murderer would have some blood on their clothes. He'd be running, too."

"And looking panicked, I'll warrant," Francis said. "Someone would have seen them and remembered."

"Unless it was the neighbour himself who is the killer," I observed.

"Hey!" one of the students barked. "Don't talk about me as if I'm a piece of furniture. I called the lodgekeepers as soon as I heard the scream. I didn't bloody well kill Justin. I *liked* him. He was a top chap."

"Peter Samuel Griffith," the detective said. "Mr Raleigh's neighbour."

"I do apologise," Francis said smoothly. "My colleague and I were simply eliminating possibilities. This has left all of us rather flustered, I'm afraid."

Peter Samuel Griffith grunted in acknowledgement.

I looked straight at the detective. "So if the murderer didn't leave by the front door..."

Francis and I pulled the curtains back. Justin Ascham Raleigh's rooms looked inward over the quad. They were in a corner, where little light ventured from the illuminated pathway crossing the snow-cloaked lawn. Mindful of possible evidence, I opened my case and took out a pair of tight-fitting rubber gloves. The latch on the window was open. When I gave the iron frame a tentative push it swung out easily. We poked our heads out like a pair of curious children at a fairground attraction. The wall directly outside was covered with wisteria creeper, its ancient gnarled branches twisted together underneath a thick layer of white ice crystals; it extended upwards for at least another two floors.

"As good as any ladder," Francis said quietly. "And I'll warrant there's at least a dozen routes in and out of Dunbar that avoid the lodgekeepers."

The detective took a look at the ancient creeper encircling the window. "I've heard that the gentlemen of Dunbar College do have several methods of allowing their lady friends to visit their rooms after the gates are locked."

"And as the gates weren't locked at the time of the murder, no one would have been using those alternative routes. The murderer would have got out cleanly," Francis said.

"If we're right, then this was a well planned crime," I said. If anything, that made it worse.

Francis locked his fingers together, as if wringing his hands. He glanced back at the sheet-covered corpse. "And yet, the nature of the attack speaks more of a *crime passionelle* than of some cold plot. I wonder." He gazed back at the students. "Mr Griffith we now know of. How do the rest of these bedraggled souls come to be here, Detective Pitchford?"

"They're Mr Raleigh's closest friends. I believe Mr Griffith phoned one as soon as he'd called the lodgekeeper."

"That was me," the other young man said. He had his arm thrown protectively, round the girl, who was sobbing wretchedly.

"And you are?" Francis asked.

"Carter Osborne Kenyon. I was a good friend of Justin's; we had dinner together tonight."

"I see. And so you phoned the young lady here?"

"Yes. This is Bethany Maria Caesar, Justin's girlfriend. I knew she'd be concerned about him, of course."

"Naturally. So do any of you recall threats being made against Mr Raleigh? Does he have an equivalent group of enemies, perhaps?"

"Nobody's ever threatened Justin. That's preposterous. And what's this to you, anyway? The police should be asking these questions."

The change in Francis's attitude was small but immediate, still calm but no longer so tolerant. And it showed. Even Carter Osborne Kenyon realised he'd made a big gaffe. It was the kind of switch that I knew I would have to perfect for myself if I ever hoped to advance through the family hierarchy.

"I am the Raleigh family's senior representative in Oxford," Francis said lightly. "Whilst that might seem like an enviable sinecure from your perspective, I can assure you it's not all lunches and cocktail parties with my fellow fat old men doing deals that make sure the young work harder. I am here to observe the official investigation, and make available any resource our family might have that will enable the police to catch the murderer. But first, in order to offer that assistance I have to understand what happened, because we will never let this rest until that barbarian is brought to justice. And I promise that if it was you under that sheet, your family would have been equally swift in dispatching a representative. It's the way the world works, and you're old enough and educated enough to know that."

"Yeah, right," Carter Osborne Kenyon said sullenly.

"You will catch them, won't you?" Bethany Maria Caesar asked urgently.

Francis became the perfect gentleman again. "Of course we will, my dear. If anything in this world is a certainty, it's that. I will never rest until this is solved."

"Nor me," I assured her.

She gave both of us a small smile. A pretty girl, even through her tears and streaked make up; tall and lean, with blond hair falling just below her shoulders. Justin had been a lucky man. I could well imagine them hand in hand walking along some riverbank on a summer's eve. It made me even more angry that so much *decency* had been lost to so many young lives by this vile act.

"Thank you," she whispered. "I really loved him. We've been talking about a long term marriage after we left Oxford. I can't believe this...*any* of this."

Carter Osborne Kenyon hugged her tighter.

I made an effort to focus on the task in hand. "We'd like samples of every specimen the forensic team collects from here, fibres, hair, whatever," I told the detective. The basic procedures which had been reiterated time and again during my investigator courses at the family institute. Other strategies were invoked by what I saw. I lowered my voice, turning slightly away from the students so I could speak my mind freely, and spare them any further distress at this time. "And it might be a good idea to take blood samples from people in the immediate vicinity as well as any suspects you might determine. They should all be tested for alcohol or narcotics. Whoever did this was way off balance."

"Yes, sir," the detective said. "My team's already on its way. They know what they're doing."

"That's fine," Francis said. His look rebuked me. "If we could also sit in on the interviews, please."

"Certainly."

THE OXFORD CITY POLICE station was less than a mile from Dunbar College. When Francis and I reached it at one o'clock there were few officers on duty. That changed over the next hour as Gareth Alan Pitchford assembled his investigator team with impressive competence. Officers and constables began to arrive, dressed in mussed uniforms, bleary-eyed, switching on the central heating in unused offices, calling down to stores for equipment. A couple of canteen staff came in and started brewing tea and coffee.

The building's Major Crime Operations Centre swung into action as Gareth Alan Pitchford made near continuous briefings to each new batch of his recruits. Secretaries began *clacking* away on typewriters; detectives pinned large scale maps of Oxford on the wall; names were hurriedly chalked up on the blackboard, a confusing trail of lines linking them in various ways; and telephones built to a perpetual chorus of whistles.

People were brought in and asked to wait in holding rooms. The chief suspects, though no one was impolite enough to say it to their faces. Gareth Alan Pitchford soon had over thirty young men and women worrying away in isolation.

"I've divided them into two categories," he told the Operations Centre. "Dunbar students sharing the same accommodation wing; physically close enough to have killed Raleigh, but for whom there is no known motive, just opportunity. And a batch of his closest friends. We're still waiting for the last one of them to arrive, but I gather the uniform division has now located him. First off, I want the doctor to collect blood samples from all of them before the interviews start; if this is a drug or alcohol induced crime we'll need to be quick to catch the evidence."

Standing discreetly at the back of the room, I watched the rest of the officers acknowledge this. It was as though they were willing that to be the solution. Like me, they didn't want a world where one normal, unaffected person could do this to another.

"Wrong approach," Francis muttered quietly to me.

"In what way?" I muttered back.

"This slaying was planned; methodically and cleverly. Drugs or alcohol implies spur of the moment madness. An irrational act to which there would have been witnesses. You mark my words—there won't be a fingerprint on either the knife or the window."

"You may be right."

"When Pitchford starts the interviews, I want us to attend those with Justin's friends. Do I need to tell you why?"

"No." It was at a time like this I both appreciated and resented the old man's testing. It was an oblique compliment that he thought I had the potential to succeed him eventually; but it was irritating in equal proportion that I was treated as the office junior. "Whoever did this had to know Justin, which means the friends are the only genuine suspects."

"Glad to see all those expensive courses we sent you on haven't been totally wasted," Francis said. I heard a reluctant note of approval in his voice. "The only other suspect I can think of is a Short. They don't value life as much as we do."

I kept my face composed even though I could not help but regard him as an old bigot at heart. Blaming the Shorts for everything from poor harvests to a tyre puncture was a prejudice harking back to the start of the Second Imperial Era, when the roots of today's families were grown amid the Sport Of Emperors. Our march through history, it would seem, isn't entirely noble.

The interview room was illuminated by a pair of hundred watt bulbs in white ceramic shades. A stark light in a small box of a room. Glazed amber tiles decorated the lower half of the walls, adding to the chill atmosphere. The only door was a sturdy metal affair with a slatted grate half way up.

Peter Samuel Griffith sat behind the table in a wooden chair, visibly discomforted by the surroundings. He was holding a small sterile gauze patch to the needle puncture in his arm where the police doctor had taken a sample of his blood. I used my pencil to make a swift note reminding myself to collect such samples for our family institute to review.

Detective Gareth Alan Pitchford and a female stenographer sat opposite Mr Griffith whilst Francis and myself stood beside the door, trying to appear inconspicuous.

"The first thing which concerns me, obviously, is the timing of events," the detective said. "Why don't you run through them again for me, please?"

"You've heard it all before," Peter Samuel Griffith said. "I was working on an essay when I heard what sounded like an argument next door."

"In what way? Was there shouting, anything knocked about?"

"No. Just voices. They were muffled, but whoever was in there with Justin was disagreeing with him. You can tell, you know."

"Did you recognise the other voice?"

"No. I didn't really hear it. Whoever they were, they spoke pretty quietly. It was Justin who was doing the yelling. Then he screamed. That was about half past eleven. I phoned the lodgekeepers."

"Immediately?"

"More or less, yes."

"Ah, now you see, Peter, that's my problem. I'm investigating a murder, for which I need hard facts; and you're giving me *more or less.* Did you phone them immediately? It's not a crime that you didn't. You've done the right thing, but I must have the correct details."

"Well, yeah... I waited a bit. Just to hear if anything else happened. That scream was pretty severe. When I couldn't hear anything else, I got really worried and phoned down."

"Thank you, Peter. So how long do you think you waited?"

"Probably a minute, or so. I...I didn't know what to do at first; phoning the lodgekeepers seemed a bit drastic. I mean, it could just have been a bit of horsing around that had gone wrong. Justin wouldn't have wanted to land a chum in any trouble. He was a solid kind of chap, you know."

"I'm sure he was. So that would have been about, when...?"

"Eleven thirty two. I know it was. I looked at the clock while I was calling the lodgekeepers."

"Then you phoned Mr Kenyon straight away?"

"Absolutely. I did have to make two calls, though. He wasn't at his college, his roommate gave me a number. Couldn't have taken more than thirty seconds to get hold of him."

"What did you tell him?"

"Just that there was some sort of trouble in Justin's room, and the lodgekeepers were coming. Justin and Carter are good friends, *best* friends. I thought he'd want to know what was going on. I'd realised by then that it was serious."

"Most commendable. So after you'd made the phone call to Mr Kenyon you went out into the corridor and waited, is that right?"

"Yes."

"How long would you say it was between the scream and the lodgekeepers arriving?"

"Probably three or four minutes. I'm not sure exactly, they arrived pretty quick once I got out into the corridor."

The detective turned round to myself and Francis. "Anything you want to ask?"

"No, thank you," Francis said before I could answer.

I have to say it annoyed me. The detective had missed points—like had there been previous arguments, how was he sure it was Justin who screamed, was there anything valuable in the room, which other students had been using the corridor and could confirm his whole story? I kept my silence, assuming Francis had good reason.

Next in was Carter Osborne Kenyon, who was clearly suffering from some kind of delayed shock. The police provided him with a mug of tea, which he clamped his hands around for warmth, or comfort. I never saw him drink any of it at any time during the interview.

His tale started with the dinner at the Orange Grove that evening, where Justin's other closest friends had gathered: Antony Caesar Pitt, Christine Jayne Lockett, and Alexander Stephan Maloney. "We did a lot of things together," Carter said. "Trips to the opera, restaurants, theatre, games...we even had a couple of holidays in France in the summer—hired a villa in the South. We had good times." He screwed his eyes shut, almost in tears. "Dear Mary!"

"So you'd known each other as a group for some time?" Gareth Alan Pitchford asked.

"Yes. You know how friendships are in college; people cluster together around interests, and class too, I suppose. Our families tend to have status. The six of us were a solid group, have been for a couple of years."

"Isn't that a bit awkward?"

"What do you mean?"

"Two girls, four men."

Carter gave a bitter laugh. "We don't have formal membership to the exclusion of everyone else. Girlfriends and boyfriends come and go, as do other friends and acquaintances; the six of us were a core if you like. Some nights there could be over twenty of us going out together."

"So you'd known Justin for some time; if he could confide in anyone it would be you or one of the others?"

"Yeah."

"And there was no hint given, to any of you, that he might have been in trouble with somebody, or had a quarrel?"

"No, none."

"What about amongst yourselves—there must have been some disagreements?"

"Well, yes." Carter gave his tea a sullen glare, not meeting the detective's look. "But nothing to kill for. It was stupid stuff...who liked what play and why; books, family politics, restaurant bills, sports results, philosophy, science—we chewed it all over; that's the kind of thing which keeps every group alive and interesting."

"Name the worst disagreement Justin was currently involved in."

"Bloody hell!"

"Was it with you?"

"No!"

"Who then?"

Carter's hands tightened round the mug, his knuckles whitening. "Look, it's nothing really. It's always happening."

"What is?"

"Okay, you didn't hear this from me, but Antony likes to gamble. I mean, we all do occasionally—a day at the races, or an evening at a casino—just harmless fun, no big money involved. But with Antony, it's getting to be a problem. He plays cards with Justin. He's been losing quite heavily recently. Justin said it served him right, that Antony should pay more attention to statistics. He was a legal student, he should know better, that there is no such thing as chance."

"How much money?"

Carter shrugged. "I've no idea. You'll have to ask Antony. But listen, Antony isn't about to kill for it. I know Justin, he'd never allow it to get that far out of control."

"Fair enough," the detective said. "Do you know if Justin had anything worth stealing?"

"Something valuable?" Carter appeared quite perplexed by the idea. "No. We're all students. We're all broke. Oh, don't get me wrong, our families support us here; the allowance is adequate for the kind of life we pursue, but nothing more. Ask Antony," he added sourly.

"I wasn't thinking in terms of cash, possibly an heirloom he kept in his room?"

"Nothing that I ever saw, and I've been in there a thousand times. I promise you, we're here only for our minds. Thoughts are our wealth. Which admittedly made Justin the richest of us all—his mind was absolutely chocka with innovative concepts. But nothing a thief could bung in his swag bag." He pantomimed catching a thought, his beefy hands flapping round his head.

"I thought Justin was an astrophysicist," Francis said.

"He was."

"So what ideas could he have that were valuable?"

"Dear Mary." Carter shot Francis a pitying look. "Not industrial ideas, machinery and trinkets for your factories. Original thoughts. Pure science, that was his playground. He was hinting that he'd come up with one fairly radical notion. His guaranteed professorship, he called it."

"Which was?"

"I haven't got a clue. He never really explained any of his projects to us. Justin could be very conservative, in both senses. The only thing I know is, it involved spectrography...you know, picking out the signature of specific elements by their emission spectrum. He was running through a collection of photographs from the observatory archives. I could help him a little with that—spectrography is simple physics. We were speculating on how to improve the process, speed it up with automation, some kind of electromechanical contraption. But we never got past a few talks in the bar."

"Did he write any of this project down?" the detective asked. "Keep notes, a file?"

"Not as far as I know. As I said, a fanciful speculation in its early stages. Talk to any science stream student and you'll get something similar; we all have our pet theories that will rock the universe if they're proven."

"I see." The detective dabbed the tip of his pencil on his lips. "How long had Mr Raleigh and Miss Caesar been an item?"

"Oh, for at least a year. Bout time too, they'd been flirting ever since I knew them. Bit of a relief when they finally got it together, know what I mean? And they were so well suited. It often helps when you're friends for a while first. And they're both bright sparks." He smiled ruefully. "There. If you want a qualifier for our group, I suppose that's it. We're all top of the league in what we do. Except for dear old Chris, of course. But she's still got the intellect. Gives as good as she gets every time."

Gareth Alan Pitchford rifled through his notes. "That'll be Christine Jayne Lockett?"

"Yeah. She's our token artist. The rest of us are science stream, apart from Antony; he's law. Chris dropped out of the formal route after she got pregnant. Loves life in the garret. Thinks it's romantic. Her family don't share the opinion, but she gets by."

"What is your field of study?" Francis asked.

Carter glanced up, surprised, as if he'd forgotten the two of us were there. "Nuclear engineering. And a hell of a field it is, too. Do you know the Madison team in Germany is only a few years from building a working atomic reactor? Once that happens and we build commercial reactors to generate electricity, the world will never burn another lump of coal ever again. Isn't that fantastic! It's the science of the future." He stopped, apparently in pain. "That's what Justin and I always argued about. Damn!"

"Justin disagreed with you about atomic power? I thought he was an astrophysicist."

"He was. That's why he disagreed. Damn silly star gazer. He kept insisting that fusion was the way forward, not fission. That one day we'd simply tap the sun's power directly. What a beautiful dream. But that was Justin for you. Always went for the high concept."

"Can you tell me roughly what time you got the phone call from Mr Griffith telling you something was wrong?" the detective asked.

"That's easy enough. It was just after half past eleven."

"I see. And where were you?"

Carter's face reddened slightly. "I was with Chris in her studio. We went back there together after the meal."

"I see. Was that usual?"

"Sometimes I'd go there, yeah. Nothing unusual about it."

"What exactly is your relationship with Miss Lockett? Her number was the first which your roommate gave to Mr Griffith."

"We have a thing. It's casual. Not serious at all. Is this relevant?"

"Only in that it gives you and her a definite location at the time of the murder."

"Location..." His eyes widened. "You mean an alibi."

"Yes. Providing Miss Lockett confirms it."

"Bloody hell, you're serious, aren't you?"

"Absolutely. So tell me what you did after receiving the phone call from Mr Griffith."

"I went straight to Dunbar. Hailed a cab. It took about twenty minutes. They'd found the body by that time of course. I think you were there yourself by then."

"I probably was."

"You said you went straight to Dunbar college from Miss Lockett's studio," I said. "When did you call Miss Caesar?"

"As soon as I got to Dunbar. The police were everywhere, so I knew it was a real mess. I used Peter's phone before I went into Justin's room."

"Where was she?"

"At her room in Uffers...Uffington College."

"And she arrived straight away?" Gareth Alan Pitchford asked.

"You know she did. You were the one who let us in to Justin's rooms, remember? Uffers is only just down the road from Dunbar, it's less than four minutes' walk away. I expect she ran."

"Okay." The detective closed his notebook. "Thank you very much. We'll need to talk to you again, of course. I'll have a car run you home."

"I'll stay, thanks. I want to be with the others when you've finished interviewing them."

"Of course."

It was Antony Caesar Pitt who followed Carter into the interview room. By that time it was close to three o'clock in the morning. A Caesar family representative came in with him; Neill Heller Caesar. Younger than Francis, dressed in a very expensive grey business suit. There was no way of telling what an inconsiderate hour it was from his deportment; he was shaved, wide awake, and friendly with the police. I envied that ability to insinuate himself into the situation as if his presence was an essential component of the investigation. Another goal to aim for. People like us have to be as smooth as a beach stone.

The world calls us representatives, but negotiators would be more accurate. We're the deal makers, the oil in the cogs of the Roman Congress. Families, that is the big ones like mine who originated from the Sport of Emperors, can hardly venture into physical conflict when we have a dispute amongst ourselves. Violence is going the same way as Shorts, bred out of our existence. Instead, you have us.

Families have their own internal codes of behaviour and conduct, while the Roman Congress provides a framework for overall government. So when two families collide over anything—a new invention, access to fresh resources—people like Francis and Neill Heller Caesar sit down together and thrash out an agreement about distribution and equal rights. Two hundred years ago, when the Americas were opened up, the major disputes were over what territories each family should have to settle, which is when our profession matured. These days, the big quarrels mostly concern economic matters—inevitable given the way the whole world is hurtling headfirst into scientific industrialisation.

But representation of family interests also goes right down to a personal individual level. To put it in First Era crudity, we were there that night to make damn sure the police caught whoever killed one of us. While Neill Heller Caesar was there to ensure his family members weren't pressured into confessing. Unless of course they were guilty. For all our differences, no family would tolerate or cover up for a murderer.

Neill Heller Caesar shook hands with both of us, giving me an equal amount of respect. As flattery went, I have to admit he scored a partial success.

"Hope you don't mind my sitting in," he said pleasantly. "There are two of our flock involved so far. Best to make sure they conduct themselves correctly now. Could save a lot of time later on. I'm sure everyone wants this appalling incident cleared up as soon as possible. My condolences, by the way."

"Thank you," Francis said. "I'm most gratified that you're here. The more people working on this investigation, the faster it will be solved. Hope you can manage the crowding. I don't believe this room was built with such a large audience in mind."

"Not a problem." Neill Heller Caesar sat down next to Antony, giving the young man a reassuring smile. Antony needed the gesture. He had obviously had quite a night; his tie was unknotted, hanging, round his collar, his jacket was crumpled, and there were several stains on the fabric. Apart from that he came over as perfectly average, a short man with broad shoulders, who kept himself fit and healthy.

"You had dinner with Mr Raleigh and your other friends this evening?" Gareth Alan Pitchford asked.

"That's right." Antony Caesar Pitt's voice was strained, attempting defiant contempt. He couldn't quite pull it off, lacking the internal confidence to make it real. He searched round his jacket pockets and pulled out a silver cigar case. Selecting one of the slim cigars and lighting it was another attempt at conveying calm nerves. He took a deep drag.

"I understand the dinner finished around ten o'clock. Where did you go after that?"

"To some friends."

"And they are...?"

"I'd rather not say, actually."

The detective smiled thinly. "I'd rather you did."

Neill Heller Caesar put a friendly hand on Antony's leg. "Go ahead." It was an order more forceful than any the detective could ever make.

Antony exhaled a thick streamer of smoke. "It's a club I go to occasionally. The Westhay."

"On Norfolk Street?"

"Yes."

"Why were you there?"

"It's a club. Why does anyone go to a club?"

"For a dance and a pleasant evening, usually. But this is different. People go to the Westhay, Mr Caesar, because there's an unlicensed card game there most evenings. I understand you're a gambling man."

"I enjoy a flutter. Who doesn't? It's not as if having a game with friends is a major crime."

"This is not the vice division; I don't care about your personal shortcomings, I'm investigating the murder of your friend. How long were you there?"

Antony chewed the cigar end. "I finished just after one. They wiped me out, and believe me you don't ask for credit at the Westhay. It's strictly cash only. I walked back to my college and your constables were waiting for me. But look, even if I give you the names of the guys I was playing with it won't do you any good. I only know first names, and they're not going to admit even being there."

"That's not your concern right now, Mr Pitt. I gather you and Mr Raleigh played cards on a regular basis."

"For Mary's sake! I wouldn't kill Justin over a couple of hundred pounds."

The detective spread his hands wide. "Did I say you would?"

"You implied it."

"I'm sorry if that's the impression you received. Do you know of anyone who had any kind of dispute with Mr Raleigh?"

"No. Nobody. Justin was genuinely a great guy."

The detective leant back in his chair. "So everyone tells us. Thank you, Mr Pitt. We will probably need to ask you more questions at some other time. Please don't leave the city."

"Sure." Antony Caesar Pitt straightened his jacket as he got up, and gave Neill Heller Caesar a mildly annoyed glance.

One of the station's secretaries came in as Antony left. She handed a clipboard to Gareth Alan Pitchford. His expression of dismay deepened as he flicked through the three flimsy sheets of paper which it held.

"Bad news?" Francis enquired.

"It's the preliminary forensic report."

"Indeed. Where there any fingerprints on the knife?"

"No. Nor were there any on the window latch. The site team is now dusting all three rooms. They'll catalogue each print they find."

"And work through a process of elimination," Francis said. "The only trouble with that is, the prints belonging to all Justin's friends will quite legitimately be found in there."

"That's somewhat premature, isn't it?" Neill Heller Caesar said. "You've no idea how many unknown prints they'll find at this stage."

"You're right, of course."

I could tell how troubled Francis was. I don't know why. He must have been expecting negatives like that in the report: I certainly was.

"You have a problem with it?" Neill Heller Caesar asked him.

"No. Not with the report. It's the way Justin's friends are all saying the same thing: he had no enemies. Indeed, why should he? A young man at university, what could he have possibly done to antagonise someone so?"

"Obviously something."

"But it's so out of character. Somebody must have noticed the reason."

"Perhaps they did, and simply aren't aware of it."

Francis nodded reluctantly. "Maybe." He gave the detective a glance. "Shall we continue."

Interestingly from my point of view, Neill Heller Caesar elected to stay in the interview room. Maloney didn't have any family representative sit in with him. Not that the Maloneys lacked influence; he could have had one there with the proverbial click of a finger. It made me wonder who had made the call to Neill. I scribbled a note to ask the police later. It could be guilt, or more likely, anxiety.

Alexander Stephan Maloney was by far the most nervous of the interviewees we'd seen. I didn't consider it to be entirely due to his friend being murdered. Something else was bothering him. The fact that *anything* could distract him at such a time I found highly significant. The reason became apparent soon enough. He had a very shaky alibi, claiming he was working alone in one of the laboratories in the Leighfield chemistry block.

"Number eighteen," he said. "That's on the second floor."

"And nobody saw you there?" Gareth Alan Pitchford asked, a strong note of scepticism in his voice.

"It was quarter to eleven at night. Nobody else is running long-duration experiments in there right now. I was alone."

"What time did you get back to your rooms?"

"About midnight. The college lodgekeepers can confirm that for you."

"I'm sure they will. How did you get back from the laboratory to the college?"

"I walked. I always do unless the weather is really foul. It gives me the opportunity to think."

"And you saw no one while you were walking?"

"Of course I saw people. But I don't know who any of them were. Strangers on a street going home to bed. Look, you can ask my professor about this. He might be able to confirm I was there when I said I was."

"How so?"

"We're running a series of carbon accumulators, they have to be adjusted in a very specific way, and we built that equipment ourselves. There are only five people in the world who'd know what to do. If he looks at it in the morning he'll see the adjustments were made."

"I'd better have a word with him, then, hadn't I?" the detective said. He scrawled a short note on his pad. "I've asked all your friends this question, and got the same answer each time. Do you know if Justin had any enemies?"

"He didn't. Not one."

There was silence in the interview room after he left. All of us were reflecting on his blatant nerves, and his non-existent alibi. I kept thinking it was too obvious for him to have done it. Of course not all the suspects would have alibis: they didn't part after their dinner believing they'd need one. Ask me what I was doing every night this past week, and I'd be hard pressed to find witnesses.

Christine Jayne Lockett bustled into the interview room. I say bustled because she had the fussy motions that put me in mind of some formidable maiden aunt. When she came into a room everyone knew it. When she spoke, she had the tone and volume which forced everyone to listen. She was also quite attractive, keeping her long hair in a high style. Older than the others, in her mid twenties, which gave her a certain *air*. Her lips always came to rest in a cheerful grin. Even now, in these circumstances, she hadn't completely lost her bonhomie.

"And it started out as such a beautiful day," she said wistfully as she settled herself in the chair. Several necklaces chinked and clattered at the motion, gold pagan charms and crucifixes jostling against each other. She put a small poetry book on the table. "Do you have any idea who did it, yet?"

"Not as such," Gareth Alan Pitchford said.

"So you have to ask me if I do. Well I'm afraid I have no idea. This whole thing is so incredible. Who on earth would want to kill poor Justin? He was a wonderful man, simply wonderful. All of my friends are. That's why I love them, despite their faults. Or perhaps because of them."

"Faults?"

"They're young. They're shallow. They have too many opinions. They're easily hurt. Who could resist the company of such angels?"

"Tell me about Justin. What faults did he have?"

"Hubris, of course. He always thought he was right. I think that's why dear Bethany loved him so much. That First Era saying: 'differences unite'. Not true. She's a strong willed girl as well. How could a strong person ever be attracted to a weak one—tell me that. They were so lucky to have found each other. Nobody else could win her heart, not for lack of trying you understand."

"Really?" Gareth Alan Pitchford couldn't shade the interest in his voice. "She had admirers?"

"You've seen her. She's gorgeous. A young woman of beauty, complemented by a fiercely sharp mind. Of course she had admirers, by the herd."

"Do you have names?"

"Men would ask to buy her a drink every time we went into a tavern. But if you mean persistent ones, ones that she knew... Alexander and Carter were both jealous of Justin. They'd both asked her out before she and Justin became lovers. It always surprised me that they managed to remain friends. A man's ego is such a weak appendage, don't you think."

"I'm sure. Did this jealousy last? Were either of them still pursuing her?"

"Not actively. We were all friends, in the end. And nothing I saw, no wistful gazes, no pangs of lust, would cause this. I do know my friends, Detective Pitchford, and they are not capable of murder. Not like this."

"Who is, then?"

"I have no idea. Somebody from the First Imperial Era? One might still be alive."

"If so, I've not heard of them, but I'll enquire. Do you know if Justin had antagonised anyone? Not necessarily recently," he added, "but at any time since you knew him."

"His self-confidence put a lot of people off. But then all of us have that quality. It's not a characteristic which drives someone to murder."

"Mr Kenyon claims he was with you after the dinner at the Orange Grove. Is this true?"

"Perfectly true. We went back to my apartment. It was after ten, and baby-sitters are devilishly expensive in this city."

"The baby-sitter can confirm this?"

"Your officers already took her statement. We arrived back at about quarter past ten."

"And after that? You were together for the rest of the night?"

"Right up until Carter got the phone call, yes. We drank some wine, I showed him my latest piece. We talked. Not for long, mind you. We hadn't even got to bed before he dashed off." Her fingers stroked at the book's leather cover. "What a dreadful, dreadful day."

Gareth Alan Pitchford glanced round at all of us after Christine left, his expression troubled. It was as if he was seeking our permission for the interview we all knew couldn't be avoided. Neill Heller Caesar finally inclined his head a degree.

Bethany Maria Caesar had regained some composure since I saw her in Justin's rooms. She was no longer crying, and her hair had been tided up. Nothing could be done about her pallor, nor the defeated slump of her shoulders. A sorrowful sight in one so young and vibrant.

Neill Heller Caesar hurriedly offered her a chair, only just beating me to it. She gave him a meek smile and lowered herself with gentle awkwardness, as if her body weighed more than usual.

"I apologise for having to bring you in here, Miss Caesar," the detective said. "I'll be as brief as possible. We just have a few questions. Formalities."

"I understand." She smiled bravely.

"Where were you at ten thirty this evening?"

"I'd gone back to my rooms at Uffington after the meal. There was some lab work which I needed to type up."

"Lab work?"

"I'm taking biochemistry. It's a busy subject right now, so much is opening up to us. It won't be long now before we understand the genetic molecule; that's the heart of life itself. Oh. I'm sorry. I'm rambling. It just takes my thought away from..."

This time I was the one who chivalrously offered a glass of water. She took it gratefully, a small flustered smile touching her lips. "Thank you. I suppose I must have got to Uffers just after ten. The lodgekeepers should be able to tell you the exact time. They sign us in at night."

"Of course. Now what about Justin? You were closest to him, did you know if he was embroiled in any kind of antagonism with someone? Some wild incident? A grudge that wouldn't go away?"

"If you'd ever met Justin you wouldn't have to ask that. But no...he hadn't annoyed anyone. He wasn't the type; he was quiet and loved his subject. Not that we were hermits. We went out to parties, and he played a few games for the college, but not at any level which counted. But we were going to make up for all that time apart after..." She tugged a handkerchief out of her sleeve and pressed it against her face. Tears leaked out of tightly closed eyes.

"I believe that's sufficient information for now," Neill Heller Caesar said, fixing the detective with a pointed gaze.

Gareth Alan Pitchford nodded his acceptance, clearly glad of the excuse to end the questioning. Neill Heller Caesar put his arm round Bethany's trembling shoulders, and helped guide her from the interview room.

"Not much to go on," the detective muttered gloomily once she was outside. "I'd welcome any suggestions." He looked straight at Francis, who was staring at the closed door.

"Have patience. We simply don't have enough information yet. Though I admit to being mystified as to any possible motive there could be for ending this young man's life in such a terrifying way. We do so desperately need to uncover what it was that Justin encountered which led to this."

"I have a good team," the detective said, suddenly bullish. "You can depend on our investigation to uncover the truth."

"I don't doubt it," Francis said with a conciliatory smile. "I think my colleague and I have seen enough for tonight. Why don't we reconvene tomorrow—or rather later this morning, to review the case so far. The remaining interviews should be over by then, and forensic ought have finished with Justin's room."

"As you wish," the detective said.

Francis said nothing further until we were safely strapped up in his car and driving away from the station. "So, my boy, first impressions? I often find them strangely accurate. Human instinct is a powerful tool."

"The obvious one is Alexander," I said. "Which in itself would tend to exclude him. It's too obvious. Other than that, I'm not sure. None of them has any apparent motive."

"An interesting comment in itself."

"How so?"

"You—or your subconscious—hasn't included anyone else on your suspect list."

"It must be someone he knows," I said, a shade defensively. "If not his immediate coterie, then someone else who was close. We can start to expand the list tomorrow."

"I'm sure we will," Francis said.

It seemed to me that his mind was away on some other great project or problem. He sounded so disinterested.

MURDER. IT WAS THE banner scored big and bold across all the street corner newspaper placards, most often garnished with adjectives such as *foul*, *brutal*, and *insane*. The vendors shouted the word in endless repetition, their scarves hanging loosely from their necks as if to give their throats the freedom necessary for such intemperate volume. They waved their lurid journals in the air like some flag of disaster to catch the attention of the hapless pedestrians.

Francis scowled at them all as we drove back to the police station just before lunchtime. The road seemed busier than usual, with horse-drawn carriages and carts jostling for space with cars. Since the law banning combustion engines, electric vehicles were growing larger with each new model; the newest ones were easily recognisable, with six wheels supporting long bonnets that contained ranks of heavy batteries.

"Those newspapers are utter beasts," he muttered. "Did you hear, we've had to move Justin's parents from their home so they might grieve in peace? Some reporter tried to pretend he was a relative so he could get inside for an interview. Must be a Short. What is the world degenerating into?"

When we arrived at the station it was besieged with reporters. Flashbulbs hissed and fizzled at everyone who hurried in or out of the building. Somehow Francis's angry dignity managed to clear a path through the rabble. Not that we escaped unphotographed, or unquestioned. The impertinence of some was disgraceful, shouting questions and comments at me as if I were some circus animal fit only to be provoked. I wished we could have taken our own photographs in turn, collecting their names to have them hauled before their senior editors for censure.

It was only after I got inside that I realised our family must have interests in several of the news agencies involved. Commerce had become the driving force here, overriding simple manners and decency.

We were shown directly to Gareth Alan Pitchford's office. He had the venetian blinds drawn, restricting the sunlight and, more importantly, the reporters's view inside. Neill Heller Caesar was already there. He wore the same smart suit and shirt that he'd had on for the interviews. I wondered if he'd been here the whole time, and if we'd made a tactical error by allowing him such freedom. I judged Francis was making the same calculation.

The detective bade us sit, and had one of his secretaries bring round a tray with fresh coffee.

"You saw the press pack outside," he said glumly. "I've had to assign officers to escort Justin's friends."

"I think we had better have a word," Francis said to Neill Heller Caesar. "The editors can be relied upon to exert some restraint."

Neill Heller Caesar's smile lacked optimism. "Let us hope so."

"What progress?" I enquired of the detective.

His mood sank further. "A long list of negatives, I'm afraid. I believe it's called the elimination process. Unfortunately, we're eliminating down to just about nothing. My team is currently piecing together the movements of all the students at Dunbar preceding the murder, but it's not a promising avenue of approach. There always seems to be several people in the corridor outside Mr Raleigh's room. If anyone had come out, they would have been seen. The murderer most likely did use the window as an exit. Forensic is going over the wisteria creeper outside, but they don't believe it to be very promising."

"What about footprints in the snow directly underneath the window?"

"The students have been larking about in the quad for days. They even had a small football game during that afternoon, until the lodgekeepers broke it up. The whole area has been well trampled down."

"What about someone going into the room?" Francis asked. "Did the students see that?"

"Even more peculiar," the detective admitted. "We have no witness of anyone other than Mr Raleigh going in."

"He was definitely seen going in, then?" I asked.

"Oh yes. He chatted to a few people in the college on his way up to his room. As far as we can determine, he went inside at about ten past ten. That was the last anyone saw him alive."

"Did he say anything significant to any of those people he talked to? Was he expecting a guest?"

"No. It was just a few simple greetings to his college mates, nothing more. Presumably the murderer was waiting for him."

"Justin would have kept those windows closed yesterday," I said. "It was freezing all day. And if the latch was down, they'd be very difficult to open from the outside, especially by anyone clinging to the creeper. I'm sure a professional criminal could have done it, but not many others."

"I concur," Francis said. "It all points to someone he knew. And knew well enough to open a window for them to get in."

"That's a very wild assumption," Neill Heller Caesar said. "Someone could simply have gone to his room hours earlier and waited for him. There would have been several opportunities during the day when there was nobody in that corridor outside. I for one refuse to believe it was in use for every second of every minute during the entire afternoon and evening."

"The method of entry isn't too relevant at this time," the detective said. "We still have absolutely no motive for the crime."

I resisted giving Francis a glance. I have to say I considered the method of entry to be extremely relevant. A professional break-in opened up all sorts of avenues. As did Justin opening the window for a friend.

"Very well," Francis said levelly. "What is your next step?"

"Validating the alibis of his closest friends. Once I'm satisfied that they are all telling the truth, then we'll get them back in for more extensive interviews. They knew him best, and one of them may know something without realising it. We need to review Mr Raleigh's past week, then month. Six months if that's what it takes. The motive will be there somewhere. Once we have that, we have the murderer. How they got in and out ceases to be an issue."

"I thought all the alibis were secure, apart from Maloney's," Neill Heller Caesar said.

"Maloney's can probably be confirmed by his professor," the detective said. "One of my senior detectives is going out to the chemistry laboratory right away. Which leaves Antony Caesar Pitt with the alibi most difficult to confirm. I'm going to the Westhay Club myself to see if it can be corroborated."

"I'd like to come with you," I said.

"Of course."

"I'll go to the chemistry laboratory, if you don't mind," Neill Heller Caesar said.

Touché, I thought. We swapped the briefest of grins.

UNLESS YOU KNEW EXACTLY where to go, you'd never be able to locate the Westhay. Norfolk Street was an older part of Oxford, with buildings no more than three or four storeys. Its streetlights were still gas, rather than the sharp electric bulbs prevalent through most of the city. The shops and businesses catered for the lower end of the market, while most of the houses had been split into multiple apartments, shared by students from minor families, and young manual workers. I could see that it would be redeveloped within fifty years. The area's relative lack of wealth combined with the ever-rising urban density pressure made that outcome inevitable.

The Westhay's entrance was a wooden door set between a bicycle shop and a bakery. A small plaque on the wall was the only indication it existed.

Gareth Alan Pitchford knocked loudly and persistently until a man pulled back a number of bolts and thrust an unshaven face round the side. It turned out he was the manager. His belligerence was washed away by the detective's badge, and we were reluctantly allowed inside.

The club itself was upstairs, a single large room with bare floorboards, its size decrying a grander purpose in days long gone. A line of high windows had their shutters thrown back, allowing broad beams of low winter sunlight to shine in through the grimy, cracked glass. Furniture consisted of sturdy wooden chairs and tables, devoid of embellishments like cushioning. The bar ran the length of one wall, with beer bottles stacked six deep on the mirrored shelving behind. A plethora of gaudy labels advertised brands which I'd never heard of before. In front of the bar, an old woman with a tight bun of iron-grey hair was sweeping the floor without visible enthusiasm. She gave us the most fleeting of glances when we came in, not even slowing her strokes.

The detective and the manager began a loud argument about the card game of the previous evening, whether it ever existed and who was taking part. Gareth Alan Pitchford was pressing hard for names, issuing threats of the city licensing board, and immediate arrest for the suspected withholding of information, in order to gain a degree of compliance.

I looked at the cleaning woman again, recalling one of my lectures at the investigatory course: a line about discovering all you need to know about people from what you find in their rubbish. She brushed the pile of dust she'd accrued into a tin pan, and walked out through a door at the back of the bar. I followed her, just in time to see her tip the pan into a large corrugated metal bin. She banged the lid down on top.

"Is that where all the litter goes?" I asked.

She gave me a surprised nod.

"When was it emptied last?"

"Two days ago," she grunted, clearly thinking I was mad.

I opened my attaché case, and pulled on some gloves. Fortunately the bin was only a quarter full. I rummaged round through the filthy debris it contained. It took me a while sifting through, but in among the cellophane wrappers, crumpled paper, mashed cigarette ends, shards of broken glass, soggy beer mats, and other repellent items, I found a well-chewed cigar butt. I sniffed tentatively at it. Not that I'm an expert, but to me it smelled very similar to the one which Antony Caesar Pitt had lit in the interview room. I dabbed at it with a forefinger. The mangled brown leaves were still damp.

I dropped the cigar into one of my plastic bags, and stripped my gloves off. When I returned to the club's main room, Gareth Alan Pitchford was writing names into his notebook whilst the manager wore the countenance of a badly frightened man.

"We have them," the detective said in satisfaction. He snapped his notebook shut.

WATCHING TREES GROW

I TOOK A TRAIN down to Southampton the following day. A car was waiting for me at the station. The drive out to the Raleigh family institute took about forty minutes.

Southampton is our city, in the same way Rome belongs to the Caesars, or London to the Percys. It might not sprawl on such grand scales, or boast a nucleus of Second Era architecture, but it's well-ordered and impressive in its own right. With our family wealth coming from a long tradition of seafaring and merchanteering, we have built it into the second largest commercial port in England. I could see large ships nuzzled up against the docks, their stacks churning out streamers of coal smoke as the cranes moved ponderously beside them, loading and unloading cargo. More ships were anchored offshore, awaiting cargo or refit. It had only been two years since I was last in Southampton, yet the number of big ocean-going passenger ships had visibly declined since then. Fewer settlers were being ferried over to the Americas, and even those members of families with established lands were being discouraged. I'd heard talk at the highest family councils that the overseas branches of the families were contemplating motions for greater autonomy. Their population was rising faster than Europe's, a basis to their claim for different considerations. I found it hard to believe they'd want to abandon their roots. But that was the kind of negotiation gestating behind the future's horizon, one that would doubtless draw me in if I ever attained the levels I sought.

The Raleigh institute was situated several miles beyond the city boundaries, hugging the floor of a wide rolling valley. It's the family's oldest estate in England, established right at the start of the Second Era. We were among the first families out on the edge of the Empire's hinterlands to practise the Sport of Emperors. The enormous prosperity and influence we have today can all be attributed to that early accommodation.

The institute valley is grassy parkland scattered with trees, extending right up over the top of the valley walls. At its heart are more than two dozen beautiful ancient stately manor houses encircling a long lake, their formal gardens merging together in a quilt of subtle greens. Even in March they retained a considerable elegance, their designers laying out tree and shrub varieties in order that swathes of colour straddled the land whatever the time of year.

Some of the manors have wings dating back over nine hundred years, though the intervening time has seen them accrue new structures at a bewildering rate until some have become almost like small villages huddled under a single multifaceted roof. Legend has it that when the last of the original manors was completed, at least twelve generations of Raleighs lived together in the valley. Some of the buildings are still lived in today. For indeed I grew up in one; but most have been converted to cater for the demands of the modern age, with administration and commerce becoming the newest and greediest residents. Stables and barns contain compartmentalised offices populated by secretaries, clerks, and managers. Libraries have undergone a transformation from literacy to numeracy, their leather-bound tomes of philosophy and history replaced by ledgers and records. Studies and drawing rooms have become conference rooms, while more than one chapel has become a council debating chamber. Awkley Manor itself, built in the early fourteen hundreds, has been converted into a single giant medical clinic, where the finest equipment which science and money can procure tends to the senior elders.

The car took me to the carved marble portico of Hewish Manor, which now hosted the family's industrial science research faculty. I walked up the worn stone steps, halting at the top to take a look round. The lawns ahead of me swept down to the lake, where they were fringed with tall reeds. Weeping willows stood sentry along the shore, their denuded branches a lacework of brown cracks across the white sky. As always a flock of swans glided over the black waters of the lake. The gardeners had planted a new avenue of oaks to the north of the building, running it from the lake right the way up the valley. It was the first new greenway for over a century. There were some fifty of them in the valley all told, from vigorous century-old palisades, to lines of intermittent aged trees, their corpulent trunks broken and rotting. They intersected each other in a great meandering pattern of random geometry, as if marking the roads of some imaginary city. When I was a child, my cousins and I ran and rode along those arboreal highways all summer long, playing our fantastical games and lingering over huge picnics.

My soft sigh was inevitable. More than anywhere, this was home to me, and not just because of a leisurely childhood. This place rooted us Raleighs.

The forensic department was downstairs in what used to be one of the wine vaults. The arching brick walls and ceiling had been cleaned and painted a uniform white, with utility tube lights running the length of every section. White coated technicians sat quietly at long benches, working away on tests involving an inordinate amount of chemistry lab glassware.

Rebecca Raleigh Stothard, the family's chief forensic scientist, came out of her office to greet me. Well into her second century, and a handsome woman, her chestnut hair was only just starting to lighten towards grey. She'd delivered an extensive series of lectures during my investigatory course, and my attendance had been absolute, not entirely due to what she was saying.

I was given a demure peck on the cheek, then she stepped back, still holding both of my hands, and looked me up and down. "You're like a fine wine, Edward," she said teasingly. "Maturing nicely. One decade soon, I might just risk a taste."

"That much anticipation could prove fatal to a man."

"How's Myriam?"

"Fine."

Her eyes flashed with amusement. "A father again. How devilsome you are. We never had boys like you in my time."

"Please. We're still very much in your time."

I'd forgotten how enjoyable it was to be in her company. She was so much more easy-going than dear old Francis. However, her humour faded after we sat down in her little office.

"We received the last shipment of samples from the Oxford police this morning," she said. "I've allocated our best people to analyse them."

"Thank you."

"Has there been any progress?"

"The police are doing their damnedest, but they've still got very little to go on at this point. That's why I'm hoping your laboratory can come up with something for me, something they missed."

"Don't place all your hopes on us. The Oxford police are good. We only found one additional fact that wasn't in their laboratory report."

"What's that?"

"Carter Osborne Kenyon and Christine Jayne Lockett were imbibing a little more than wine and spirits that evening."

"Oh?"

"They both had traces of cocaine in their blood. We ran the test twice, there's no mistake."

"How much?"

"Not enough for a drug induced killing spree, if that's what you're thinking. They were simply having a decadent end to their evening. I gather she's some sort of artist?"

"Yes."

"Narcotic use is fairly common amongst the more Bohemian sects, and increasing."

"I see. Anything else?"

"Not a thing."

I put my attaché case on my knees, and flicked the locks back. "I may have something for you." I pulled the bag containing the cigar butt from its compartment. "I found this in the Westhay Club, I think it's Antony Caesar Pitt's. Is there any way you can tell me for sure?"

"Pitt's? I thought his alibi had been confirmed?"

"The police interviewed three people, including the manager of the Westhay, who all swear he was in there playing cards with them."

"And you don't believe them?"

"I've been to the Westhay, I've seen the manager and the other players. They're not the most reliable people in the world, and they were under a lot of pressure to confirm whether he was there or not. My problem is that if he was there that evening the police will thank them for their statement and their honesty and let them go. If he wasn't, there could be consequences they'd rather avoid. I know that sounds somewhat paranoid, but he really is the only one of the friends who had anything like a motive. In his case, the proof has to be absolute. I'd be betraying my responsibility if I accepted anything less."

She took the bag from me, and squinted at the remains of the cigar which it contained.

"It was still damp with saliva the following morning," I told her. "If it is his, then I'm prepared to accept he was in that club."

"I'm sorry, Edward, we have no test that can produce those sort of results. I can't even give you a blood type from a saliva sample."

"Damn!"

"Not yet, but one of my people is already confident he can determine if someone has been drinking from a chemical reaction with their breath. It should deter those wretched cab drivers from having one over the eight before they take to the roads if they know the police can prove they were drunk on the spot. Ever seen a carriage accident? It's not nice. I imagine a car crash is even worse."

"I'm being slow this morning. The relevance being?"

"You won't give up. None of us will, because Justin was a Raleigh, and he deserves to rest with the knowledge that we will not forget him, no matter how much things change. And change they surely do. Look at me, born into an age of leisured women, at least those of my breeding and status. Life was supposed to be a succession of grand balls interspersed with trips to the opera and holidays in provincial spa towns. Now I have to go out and earn my keep."

I grinned. "No you don't."

"For Mary's sake, Edward; I had seventeen fine and healthy children before my ovaries were thankfully exhausted in my late nineties. I need something else to do after all that child rearing. And, my dear, I always hated opera. This, however, I enjoy to the full. I think it still shocks mummy that I'm out here on the scientific frontier. But it does give me certain insights. Come with me."

I followed her along the length of the forensic department. The end wall was hidden behind a large free standing chamber made from a dulled metal. A single door was set in the middle, fastened with a heavy latch mechanism. As we drew closer I could hear an electrical engine thrumming incessantly. Other harmonics infiltrated the air, betraying the presence of pumps and gears.

"Our freezer," Rebecca announced with chirpy amusement.

She took a thick fur coat from a peg on the wall outside the chamber, and handed me another.

"You'll need it," she told me. "It's colder than these fridges which the big grocery stores are starting to use. A lot colder."

Rebecca told the truth. A curtain of freezing white fog tumbled out when she opened the door. The interior was given over to dozens of shelves, with every square inch covered in a skin of hard white ice. A variety of jars, bags, and sealed glass dishes were stacked up. I peered at their contents with mild curiosity before hurriedly looking away. Somehow, scientific slivers of human organs are even more repellent that the entirety of flesh.

"What is this?" I asked.

"Our family's insurance policy. Forensic pathology shares this freezer with the medical division. Every biological unknown we've encountered is in here. One day we'll have answers for all of it."

"And one day the Borgias will leave the Vatican," I said automatically.

Rebecca placed the bag on a high shelf, and gave me a confident smile. "You'll be back."

TWO
MANHATTAN CITY AD 1853

IT WAS LATE AFTERNOON as the SST came in to land at Newark aerodrome. The sun was low in the sky, sending out a red gold light to soak the skyscrapers. I pressed my face to the small port, eager for the sight. The overall impression was one of newness, under such a light it appeared as though the buildings had just been erected. They were pristine, flawless.

Then we cruised in over the field's perimeter, and the low commercial buildings along the side of the runway obscured the view. I shuffled my papers into my briefcase as we taxied to the reception building. I'd spent the three hour flight over the Atlantic re-reading all the principal reports and interviews, refreshing my memory of the case. For some reason the knowledge lessened any feeling of comfort. The memories were all too clear now: the cold night, the blood-soaked body. Francis was missing from the investigation now, dead these last five years. It was he, I freely admit, who had given me a degree of comfort in tackling the question of who had killed poor Justin Ascham Raleigh. Always the old *missi dominici* had exuded the air of conviction, the epitome of an irresistible force. It would be his calm persistence who would unmask the murderer, I'd always known and accepted that. Now the task was mine alone.

I emerged from the plane's walkway into the reception lounge. Neill Heller Caesar was waiting to greet me. His physical appearance had changed little, as I suppose had mine. Only our styles were different; the fifties had taken on the air of a colourful radical period that I wasn't altogether happy with. Neill Heller Caesar wore a white suit with flares that covered his shoes. His purple and green cheesecloth shirt had rounded collars a good five inches long. And his thick hair was waved, coming down below his shoulders. Tiny gold-rimmed amber sunglasses were perched on his nose.

He recognised me immediately, and shook my hand. "Welcome to Manhattan," he said.

"Thank you. I wish it was under different circumstances."

He prodded the sunglasses back up his nose. "For you, of course. For myself, I'm quite glad you're here. You've put one of my charges in the clear."

"Yes. And thank you for the co-operation."

"A pleasure."

We rode a limousine over one of the bridges into the city itself. I complimented him on the height of the buildings we were approaching. Manhattan was, after all, a Caesar city.

"Inevitable," he said. "The population in America's northern continent is approaching one and a half billion—and that's just the official figure. The only direction left is up."

We both instinctively looked at the limousine's sunroof.

"Speaking of which: how much longer?" I asked.

He checked his watch. "They begin their descent phase in another five hours."

The limousine pulled up outside the skyscraper which housed the Caesar family legal bureau in Manhattan. Neill Heller Caesar and I rode the lift up to the seventy-first floor. His office was on the corner of the building, its window walls giving an unparalleled view over ocean and city alike. He sat behind his desk, a marble-topped affair of a stature equal to the room as a whole, watching me as I gazed out at the panorama.

"All right," I said. "You win. I'm impressed." The sun was setting, and in reply the city lights were coming on, blazing forth from every structure.

He laughed softly. "Me too, and I've been here fifteen years now. You know they're not even building skyscrapers under a hundred floors any more. Another couple of decades and the only time you'll see the sun from the street will be a minute either side of noon."

"Europe is going the same way. Our demographics are still top weighted, so the population rise is slower. But not by much. Something is going to have to give eventually. The Church will either have to endorse contraception, or the pressure will squeeze us into abandoning our current restrictions." I shuddered. "Can you imagine what a runaway expansion and exploitation society would be like?"

"Unpleasant," he said flatly. "But you'll never get the Borgias out of the Vatican."

"So they say."

Neill Heller Caesar's phone rang. He picked it up and listened for a moment. "Antony is on his way up."

"Great."

He pressed a button on his desk, and a large wall panel slid to one side. It revealed the largest TV screen I'd ever seen. "If you don't mind, I'd like to keep the Prometheus broadcast on," he said. "We'll mute the sound."

"Please do. Is that thing colour?" Our family channel had only just begun to broadcast in the new format. I hadn't yet availed myself with a compatible receiver.

His smile was the same as any boy given a new football to play with. "Certainly is. Twenty eight inch diameter, too—in case you're wondering."

The screen lit up with a slightly fuzzy picture. It showed an external camera view, pointing along the fuselage of the Prometheus, where the silver grey moon hung over it. Even though it was eight years since the first manned spaceflight, I found it hard to believe how much progress the Joint Families Astronautics Agency had made. Less than five hours now, and a man would set foot on the moon!

The office door opened and Antony Caesar Pitt walked in. He had done well for himself over the intervening years, rising steadily up through his family's legal offices. Physically, he'd put on a few pounds, but it hardly showed. The biggest change was a curtain of hair, currently held back in a ponytail. There was a mild frown on his face to illustrate his disapproval at being summoned without explanation. As soon as he saw me the expression changed to puzzlement, then enlightenment.

"I remember you," he said. "You were one of the Raleigh representatives assigned to Justin's murder. Edward, isn't it?"

"That's helpful," I said.

"In what way?"

"You have a good memory. I need that right now."

He gave Neill Heller Caesar a quick glance. "I don't believe this. You're here to ask me questions about Justin again, aren't you?"

"Yes."

"For Mary's sake! It's been twenty one years."

"Yes, twenty one years, and he's still just as dead."

"I appreciate that. I'd like to see someone brought to justice as much as you. But the Oxford police found nothing. Nothing! No motive, no enemy. They spent weeks trawling through every tiny little aspect of his life. And with you applying pressure they were thorough, believe me. I should know, with my gambling debt I was the prime suspect."

"Then you should be happy to hear, you're not any more. Something's changed."

He flopped down into a chair and stared at me. "What could possibly have changed?"

"It's a new forensic technique." I waved a hand at the television set. "Aeroengineering isn't the only scientific discipline to have made progress recently, you know. The families have developed something we're calling genetic fingerprinting. Any cell with your DNA in it can now be positively identified."

"Well, good and fabulous. But what the hell has it got to do with me?"

"It means I personally am now convinced you were at the Westhay that night. You couldn't have murdered Justin."

"The Westhay." He murmured the name with an almost sorrowful respect. "I never went back. Not after that. I've never played cards since, never placed a bet. Hell of a way to get cured." He cocked his head to one side, looking up at me. "So what convinced you?"

"I was there at the club the following morning. I found a cigar butt in the rubbish. Last month we ran a genetic fingerprint test on the saliva residue, and cross referenced it with your blood sample. It was yours. You were there that night."

"Holy Mary! You kept a cigar butt for twenty-one years?"

"Of course. And the blood, as well. It's all stored in a cryogenic vault now along with all the other forensic samples from Justin's room. Who knows what new tests we'll develop in future."

Antony started laughing. There was a nervous edge to it. "I'm in the clear. Shit. So how does this help you? I mean, I'm flattered that you've come all this way to tell me in person, but it doesn't change anything."

"On the contrary. Two very important factors have changed thanks to this. The number of suspects is smaller, and I can now trust what you tell me. Neill here has very kindly agreed that I can interview you again. With your permission, of course."

This time the look Antony flashed at the family representative was pure desperation. "But I don't have anything new to tell you. Everything I knew I told the police. Those interviews went on for *days.*"

"I know. I spent most of last week reading through the transcripts again."

"Then you know there's nothing I can add."

"Our most fundamental problem is that we never managed to establish a motive. I believe it must originate from his personal or professional life. The murder was too proficient to have been the result of chance. You can give me the kind of access I need to Justin's life to go back and examine possible motives."

"I've given you access, all of it."

"Maybe. But everything you say now has more weight attached. I'd like you to help."

"Well sure. That's if you're certain you can trust me now. Do you want to wire me up to a polygraph as well?"

I gave Neill Heller Caesar a quick glance. "That won't be necessary."

Antony caught it. "Oh great. Just bloody wonderful. OK. Fine. Ask me what the hell you want. And for the record, I've always answered honestly."

"Thank you. I'd like to start with the personal aspect. Now, I know you were asked a hundred times if you'd seen or heard anything out of the ordinary. Possibly some way he acted out of character, right?"

"Yes. Of course. There was nothing."

"I'm sure. But what about afterwards, when the interviews were finished, when the pressure had ended. You must have kept on thinking, reviewing all those late night conversations you had over cards and a glass of wine. There must have been something he said, some trivial non sequitur, something you didn't bother going back to the police with."

Antony sank down deeper into his chair, resting a hand over his brow as weariness claimed him. "Nothing," he whispered. "There was nothing he ever said or did that was out of the ordinary. We talked about everything men talk about together, drinking, partying, girls, sex, sport; we told each other what we wanted to do when we left Oxford, all the opportunities our careers opened up for us. Justin was a template for every family student there. He was almost a stereotype, for Mary's sake. He knew what he wanted; his field was just taking off, I mean..." he waved at the TV screen. "Can you get anything more front line? He was going to settle down with Bethany, have ten kids, and gaze at the stars for the rest of his life. We used to joke that by the time he had his three hundredth birthday he'd probably be able to visit them, all those points of light he stared at through a telescope. There was *nothing* unusual about him. You're wasting your time with this, I wish you weren't, I really do. But it's too long ago now, even for us."

"Can't blame me for trying," I said with a smile. "We're not Shorts, for us time is always relevant, events never diminish no matter how far away you move from them."

"I'm not arguing," he said weakly.

"So what about his professional life? His astronomy?"

"He wasn't a professional, he was still a student. Every week there was something that would excite him; then he'd get disappointed, then happy again, then disappointed... That's why he loved it."

"We know that Justin had some kind of project or theory which he was working on. Nobody seemed to know what it was. It was too early to take it to his professor, and we couldn't find any notes relating to it. All we know is that it involved some kind of spectrography. Did he ever let slip a hint of it to you?"

"His latest one?" Antony closed his eyes to assist his recall. "Very little. I think he mentioned once he wanted to review pictures of supernovae. What for, I haven't got the faintest idea. I don't even know for certain if that was the new idea. It could have been research for anything."

"Could be," I agreed. "But it was a piece of information I wasn't aware of before. So we've accomplished something today."

"You call that an accomplishment?"

"Yes. I do."

"I'd love to know what you call building the Channel Tunnel."

My smile was pained. Our family was the major partner in that particular venture. I'd even been involved in the preliminary negotiations. "A nightmare. But we'll get there in the end."

"Just like Justin's murder?"

"Yes."

THREE
GANYMEDE AD 1920

MY JOURNEY OUT TO Jupiter was an astonishing experience. I'd been in space before, of course, visiting various low Earth orbit stations which are operated by the family, and twice to our moonbase. But even by current standards, a voyage to a gas giant was considered special.

I took a scramjet-powered spaceplane from Gibraltar spaceport up to Vespasian in its six hundred mile orbit. There wasn't much of the original asteroid left now, just a ball of metal-rich rock barely half a mile across. Several mineral refineries were attached to it limpet-fashion, their fusion reactor cooling fins resembling black peacock tails. In another couple of years it would be completely mined out, and the refineries would be manoeuvred to the new asteroids being eased into Earth orbit.

A flotilla of industrial and dormitory complexes drifted around Vespasian, each of them sprouting a dozen or more assembly platforms. Every family on Earth was busy constructing more microgravity industrial systems and long-range spacecraft. In addition to the twenty-seven moonbases, there were eight cities on Mars and five asteroid colonies; each venture bringing some unique benefit from the purely scientific to considerable financial and economic reward. Everyone was looking to expand their activities to some fresh part of the solar system, especially in the wake of the Caesar settlement claim.

Some of us, of course, were intent on going further still. I saw the clearest evidence of that as the *Kuranda* spiralled up away from Earth. We passed within eight thousand miles of what the planetbound are calling the Wanderers Cluster. Five asteroids in a fifty thousand mile orbit, slowly being hollowed out and fitted with habitation chambers. From Earth they appeared simply as bright stars performing a strange slow traverse of the sky. From the *Kuranda* (with the aid of an on-board video sensor) I could clearly see the huge construction zones on their surface where the fusion engines were being fabricated. If all went well, they would take two hundred years to reach Proxima Centuri. Half a lifetime cooped up inside artificial caves, but millions of people had applied to venture with them. I remained undecided if that was a reflection of healthy human dynamism, or a more subtle comment on the state of our society. Progress, if measured by the yardstick of mechanisation, medicine, and electronics, seemed to be accelerating at a rate which even I found perturbing. Too many people were being made redundant as new innovations came along, or AIs supplanted them. In the past that never bothered us—after all who wants to spend four hundred years doing the same thing. But back then it was a slow transition, sliding from occupation to occupation as fancy took you. Now such migrations were becoming forced, and the timescale shorter. There were times I even wondered if my own job was becoming irrelevant.

The *Kuranda* took three months to get me to Jupiter, powered by low-temperature ion plasma engines, producing a small but steady thrust the whole way. It was one of the first of its class, a long-duration research and explorer ship designed to take our family scientists out as far as Neptune. Two hundred yards long, including the propellant tanks and fusion reactors.

We raced round Jupiter's pale orange cloudscape, shedding delta-V as captain Harrison Dominy Raleigh aligned us on a course for Ganymede. Eight hours later when we were coasting up away from the gas-giant, I was asked up to the bridge. Up is a relative term on a spaceship which wasn't accelerating, and the bridge is at the centre of the life-support section. There wasn't a lot of instrumentation available to the three duty officers, just some fairly sophisticated consoles with holographic windows and an impressive array of switches. The AI actually ran *Kuranda*, while people simply monitored its performance and that of the primary systems.

Our captain, Harrison Dominy Raleigh, was floating in front of the main sensor console, his right foot velcroed to the decking.

"Do we have a problem?" I asked.

"Not with the ship," he said. "This is strictly your area."

"Oh?" I anchored myself next to him, trying to comprehend the display graphics. It wasn't easy, but then I don't function very well in low gravity situations. Fluids of every kind migrate to my head, which in my case brings on the most awful headaches. My stomach is definitely not designed to digest floating globules of food. And you really would think that after seventy-five years of people travelling through space that someone would manage to design a decent freefall toilet. On the plus side, I'm not too nauseous during the aerial manoeuvres that replace locomotion, and I am receptive to the anti-wasting drugs developed to counter calcium loss in human bones. It's a balance which I can readily accept as worthwhile in order to see Jupiter with my own eyes.

The captain pointed to a number of glowing purple spheres in the display, each one tagged by numerical icons. "The Caesars have orbited over twenty sensor satellites around Ganymede. They provide a full radar coverage out to eighty thousand miles. We're also picking up similar emissions from the other major moons here. No doubt their passive scans extend a great deal further."

"I see. The relevance being?"

"Nobody arrives at any of the moons they've claimed without them knowing about it. I'd say they're being very serious about their settlement rights."

"We never made our voyage a secret. They have our arrival time down to the same decimal place as our own AI."

"Which means the next move is ours. We arrive at Ganymede injection in another twelve hours."

I looked at those purple points again. We were the first non-Caesar spaceship to make the Jupiter trip. The Caesars sent a major mission of eight ships thirteen years ago, which the whole world watched with admiration right up until commander Ricardo Savill Caesar set his foot on Ganymede and announced to his massive television audience that he was claiming not only Ganymede, but Jupiter and all of its satellites for the Caesar family. It was extraordinary, not to say a complete violation of our entire world's rationalist ethos. The legal manoeuvring had been going on ever since, as well as negotiations amongst the most senior level of family representatives in an attempt to get the Caesars to repudiate the claim. It was a standing joke for satirical show comedians, who got a laugh every time about excessive greed and routines about one person one moon. But in all that time, the Caesars had never moved from their position that Jupiter and its natural satellites now belonged to them. What they had never explained in those thirteen years is why they wanted it.

And now here we were. My brief wasn't to challenge or antagonise them, but to establish some precedents. "I want you to open a communication link to their primary settlement," I told the captain. "Use standard orbital flight control protocols, and inform them of our intended injection point. Then ask them if there is any problem with that. Treat it as an absolutely normal everyday occurrence…we're just one more spaceship arriving in orbit. If they ask what we're doing here, we're a scientific mission and I would like to discuss a schedule of geophysical investigations with their Mayor. In person."

Harrison Dominy Raleigh gave me an uncomfortable grimace. "You're sure you wouldn't like to talk to them now?"

"Definitely not. Achieving a successful Ganymede orbit is not something important enough to warrant attention from a family representative."

"Right then." He flipped his headset mike down, and instructed the AI on establishing a communication link.

It wasn't difficult. The Caesars were obviously treading as carefully as we were. Once the *Kuranda* was in orbit, the captain requested spaceport clearance for our ground to orbit shuttle, which was granted without comment.

The ride down was an uneventful ninety minutes, if you were to discount the view from the small, heavily-shielded ports. Jupiter at a quarter crescent hung in the sky above Ganymede. We sank down to a surface of fawn-coloured ice pocked by white impact craters and great *sulci*, clusters of long grooves slicing through the grubby crust, creating broad river-like groupings of corrugations. For some reason I thought the landscape more quiet and dignified than that of Earth's moon. I suppose the icescape's palette of dim pastel colours helped create the impression, but there was definitely an ancient solemnity to this small world.

New Milan was a couple of degrees north of the equator, in an area of flat ice pitted with small newish craters. An undisciplined sprawl of emerald and white lights covering nearly five square miles. In thirteen years the Caesars had built themselves quite a substantial community here. All the buildings were free standing igloos whose base and lower sections were constructed from some pale yellow silicate concrete, while the top third was a transparent dome. As the shuttle descended towards the landing field I began to realise why the lights I could see were predominately green. The smallest igloo was fifty yards in diameter, with the larger ones reaching over two hundred yards; they all had gardens at their centre illuminated by powerful lights underneath the glass.

After we landed, a bus drove me over to the administration centre in one of the large igloos. It was the Mayor, Ricardo Savill Caesar himself, who greeted me as I emerged from the airlock. He was a tall man, with the slightly flaccid flesh of all people who had been in a low-gravity environment for any length of time. He wore a simple grey and turquoise one-piece tunic with a mauve jacket, standard science mission staff uniform. But on him it had become a badge of office, bestowing that extra degree of authority. I could so easily imagine him as the direct descendant of some First Era Centurion commander.

"Welcome," he said warmly. "And congratulations on your flight. From what we've heard, the *Kuranda* is an impressive ship."

"Thank you," I said. "I'd be happy to take you round her later."

"And I'll enjoy accepting that invitation. But first it's my turn. I can't wait to show off what we've done here."

Thus my tour began; I believe there was no part of that igloo into which I didn't venture at some time during the next two hours. From the life support machinery in the lower levels to precarious walkways strung along the carbon reinforcement strands of the transparent dome. I saw it all. Quite deliberately, of course. Ricardo Savill Caesar was proving that they had no secrets, no sinister apparatus under construction. The family had built themselves a self sustaining colony, capable of expanding to meet their growing population. Nothing more. What I was never shown nor told was the reason why.

After waiting as long as politeness required before claiming I had seen enough we wound up in Ricardo Savill Caesar's office. It was on the upper storey of the habitation section, over forty feet above the central arboretum's lawn, yet the tops of the trees were already level with his window. I could recognise several varieties of pine and willow, but the low gravity had distorted their runaway growth, giving them peculiar swollen trunks and fat leaves.

Once I was sitting comfortably on his couch he offered me some coffee from a delicate china pot.

"I have the beans flown up and grind them myself," he said. "They're from the family's estates in the Caribbean. Protein synthesis might have solved our food supply problems, but there are some textures and tastes which elude the formulators."

I took a sip, and pursed my lips in appreciation. "That's good. Very good."

"I'm glad. You're someone I think I'd like to have on my side."

"Oh?"

He sat back and grinned at me. "The other families are unhappy to say the least about our settlement claim on this system. And you are the person they send to test the waters. That's quite a responsibility for any representative. I would have loved to sit in on your briefing sessions and hear what was said about us terrible Caesars."

"Your head would start spinning after the first five hours," I told him, dryly. "Mine certainly did."

"So what is it you'd like your redoubtable ship and crew to do while they're here?"

"It is a genuine scientific mission," I told him. "We'd like to study the bacterial life you've located in the moons here. Politics of settlement aside, it is tremendously important, especially after Mars turned out to be so barren."

"I certainly have no objection to that. Are we going to be shown the data?"

"Of course." I managed to sound suitably shocked. "Actually, I was going to propose several joint expeditions. We did bring three long-duration science station vehicles with us that can be deployed on any of the lunar surfaces."

Ricardo Savill Caesar tented his forefingers, and rested his chin on the point. "What kind of duration do these vehicles have?"

"A couple of weeks without resupply. Basically they're just large caravans we link up to a tractor unit. They're fully mobile."

"And you envisage a dispatching mission to each moon?"

"Yes. We're also going to drop a number of probes into Jupiter to investigate its structural composition."

"Interesting. How far down do you believe they can reach?"

"We want to examine the supercritical fluid level, the surface of it at least."

He raised an eyebrow. "I shall be most impressed if your probe design is good enough to reach that level. The furthest we've ever reached is seven hundred kilometres down."

"Our engineers seem quite confident it can be reached. The family has always given solid state science a high priority."

"A kind of technological machismo."

"I suppose so."

"Well, this is all very exciting. I'm very keen to offer you our fullest co-operation and assistance. My science team has been looking forward to your arrival for months. I don't think they'll be disappointed. Fresh angles are always so rewarding, I find."

I showed him a satisfied nod. This stalemate was the outcome with the highest probability according to our council strategists. We'd established that our family was free to roam where it chose on any of the moons, but not to stay. Which meant the most popular, if somewhat whimsical theory, was unlikely. Several senior family councils had advanced the notion that the Caesars had discovered high-order life out here, and wanted to keep it for themselves. After all, since they found bacteria in the undersurface seas of both Ganymede and Europa, then more complex life was an ultra-remote possibility. Personally, I had always considered that just too far fetched. More curiously, Ricardo Savill Caesar hadn't objected to us probing Jupiter itself. The second most likely theory was that they'd found something of extraordinary value in its atmosphere. Again unlikely. There had been dozens of robot probes sent here in the decades before their flight. Which put me far enough down the list to start considering alien spaceships and survivors of Atlantis. Not an enjoyable prospect for any rational man. But as Ricardo Savill Caesar wasn't giving anything away, my options were reducing. It was an annoying challenge. He knew that I knew the reason for the settlement claim had to be staring right at me. I simply couldn't see it.

I told myself it didn't matter. I never expected to catch it straight away, and we were due to stay at Jupiter for six months. There was plenty of time.

"Then we're all done bar the details," I said. "I'll get my AI to link to your AI. I'm sure they can organise schedules and personnel rosters between them."

He raised his cup in happy salute. "I'm sure they can. I'll authorise a link to the *Kuranda* immediately."

"There is one other thing. A small matter."

"Oh?"

"I'd like to see someone while I'm here. One of your deputies, in fact. It relates to an old investigation of mine. There are one or two points I need to clear up with her."

"Who are we talking about?"

"Bethany Maria Caesar. I gather she's on Io."

"Yes," he said cautiously. "She runs the science team there."

His abrupt shift in attitude was fascinating. It was as though I'd suddenly won a point in our game of words and nuances. If only I could have worked out how I'd done that. All I'd said was her name. "You don't object me talking to her, do you?"

"Not at all. If it isn't confidential, what is this old investigation, exactly?"

"A murder."

"Good Lady Mary. Really?"

"As I say, it's an old one. However, I have a new theory I'd like to run past her."

THE IO SCIENCE OUTPOST was nothing like New Milan. It consisted of two dozen cylindrical compartments resting on concrete cradles sunk deep into the carmine-coloured crust; they were all plugged into each other like some array of antique electronic components. For years they'd suffered from the exhalations of the volcano. Its furious sulphur emission clouds had gently drizzled down, staining their metallic-white casings with a thin film of dirty amber colloid which dribbled round the exterior to drip from the belly. But for all its functionalism, the Caesars had certainly chosen a location with a view. One of the compartments had an observation gallery, aligned so that its curving windows looked directly out at the distant sulphur volcano, which appeared as a dark conical silhouette rising out of the horizon.

I waited for Bethany Maria Caesar at one of the refractory tables in the gallery, staring straight out at the volcano through the gritty, smeared windows, hoping I would get to see an eruption. The only evidence of any seismic activity was the occasional tremor which ran through the compartment, barely enough to create a ripple in my teacup.

"Hello, Edward, it's been a long time."

I would never have recognised her. This woman standing before me bore only the faintest resemblance to that beautiful, distraught girl I'd sat with through innumerable interviews eight decades ago. She looked, for want of a better word, old. Her face was lined with chubby wrinkles that obscured the features I once knew; nor was there any more of that flowing blonde hair—she'd had a crew cut so severe it barely qualified as stubble, and that was greyish. The tunic she wore was loose-fitting, but even that couldn't disguise her stooped posture.

She put both hands on the table and lowered herself into a chair opposite me with a slight wheeze. "Quite a sight, aren't I?"

"What happened?" I asked, appalled. No briefing file had mentioned any sort of accident or chronic illness.

"Low gravity happened, Edward. I can see your face is all puffed up with fluid retention, so you already know a fraction of the suffering possible. Content yourself with that fraction. Low gravity affects some people worse than others, a lot worse. And after thirteen years constant exposure, I'm just about off the scale."

"Dear Mary! I don't know what you Caesars want with Jupiter, but nothing is worth abusing yourself like this. Come home, back to Earth."

Her smile alluded to a wisdom denied me. "This is my home. Jupiter is the frontier of humanity."

"How can you say that? It's killing you."

"Life!" The word was spat out. "Such a treacherous gift."

"A precious gift," I countered.

"Ah yes. Poor old Justin. I was quite surprised when I saw you were the representative the Raleighs were sending. You caused me quite a little trip down memory lane."

"I won't lie to you, you're not my primary reason for being here."

"Ha. The great mystery of our time. What can those wicked Caesars want with Jupiter? Had any luck working it out yet?"

"None at all. But we'll get there in the end."

"I'm sure you will. Devote enough processing power to any problem, and ultimately it will be solved."

"That's more like the Bethany I remember."

"I doubt it. This is experience talking. We have more AIs per head of population up here than anywhere on Earth. Every scrap of research data is analysed and tabulated—our knowledge base is expanding at a rate we can barely keep track of. And we can devote so much of ourselves to understanding it. We don't have to worry so much about our physical requirements. The AIs take care of that for us; they run the food synthesis plants, the cybernetics factories, administration. I consider my life here to be my liberation, Edward. I don't have to concern myself with the mundane any more. I can use my mind full time."

"Then I'm glad for you. You've found something new out here. AI utilisation on Earth is causing no end of problems. They can take over the running of just about all mechanical operations and do it with increased efficiency. Industry and utility provision are discarding more and more human operatives. We're seeing large scale patterns of unemployment evolving. And it brings a host of social unrest with it. There's more petty crime than there ever used to be; psychologists need counselling they have such a heavy work load these days. People are starting to question the true worth of introducing AIs."

"I'm sure there will be temporary problems thrown up by AI integration. You never get smooth transitions of this magnitude. Moving to a leisure-based society is going to be hard for a people who are so set in their ways. The penalty for a long life is the increasing resistance to change. The familiar is too easy and comfortable for it to be discarded quickly. And the families are very familiar with their life as it is. But the change will happen. If we have a purpose it is to think and create; that's our uniqueness. Any non-sentient animal can build a nest and gather food. Now this march through progress has finally started to relieve us of that physical distraction. I mean, that's what we were doing it for in the first place, right? Once you set out to determine how the universe works, then as a species there's no turning back. We're freefalling to the plateau, Edward."

"The plateau?"

"The moment at which science has explained everything, and machines are perfect. After that, human life becomes one long summer afternoon picnic. All we do then is think, dream, and play."

"I can't quite see that myself."

"That's a shame. You must adapt or die, Edward. I took you as someone bright enough to surmount that last hurdle and climb up there to the plateau. Perhaps the Sport of Emperors wasn't the blessing we like to believe, at least, not for everyone. The original Caesars were so certain they were doing the right thing with their gift for all of the Empire. They'd bred stables of gladiators for generations, evolving their speed and strength until they were invincible in the arena. Only age slowed and weakened them. It was such a short leap to breed for longevity, and what a political weapon that was. The one thing everybody always wants. But the life they bred for in the children of the Empire was longer than nature ever intended. And messing with nature however crudely is always dangerous. Humans change their environment. That is our true nature. The cycle of life and death, of constant renewal, is nature's way of adapting us as a species to the freshness we create for ourselves."

"Are you saying I've outlived my usefulness?"

"I don't know, Edward. Can you give up everything you've lived for in order to face the unknown? Or are you going to watch trees grow as the same old seasons wash past you to no effect?"

"That's what you believe you're doing by living out here, is it?"

"I enjoy change. It's the most magnificent challenge."

"You have the luxury of enjoying it."

Her laugh was a fluid-clogged cackle. "Oh Edward, so single minded. You and I are alive, which is more than can be said for Justin. I have to admit, I'm very curious. What can you possibly have to add to the matter at this stage?"

I waved a hand at the curving windows, with their slim reinforcement mesh of carbon strands. That particular carbon allotrope was the reason the glass could be so thin, one of the new miracles we took so much for granted. "Carbon 60."

"How the hell can pentospheres possibly be connected to Justin's murder? We only discovered the stuff ten years ago... Oh. Mary, yes! It was Alexander, wasn't it? He was the one who found it."

"I hope so."

"*Hope?*"

"Carbon 60 is an awesome substance. There are so many theoretical applications, from ultrastrength fibres to superconductivity. It's being incorporated into just about every process and structure we use. And they're still finding new uses on a daily basis."

"So?"

"So I need to know about Justin's great project, the one he was working on when he was killed. Was he studying supernovae for carbon signatures?"

"Heavens." She sat back and gave me an admiring look. "You really don't give up, do you?"

"No."

"We only found out that carbon 60 existed in stellar nebulae after we—or rather Alexander—produced it in a laboratory. What you're saying is that it could have happened the other way round, aren't you? That some astronomer found traces, proof that it physically existed, and chemists worked at synthesising it afterwards."

"It's certainly possible. The existence of carbon 60 has been postulated for a long time; I traced an early reference back to 1815—it was some very speculative paper on theoretical molecular structures. Justin might have had the idea carbon 60 could be produced by stellar events, and found the spectral signature."

"And Alexander, who was a chemist, immediately realised the practical use such a find would have, and killed him for it. Then when a decent interval had past, in this case, ninety years, he miraculously produces the elusive substance in his lab, to the enormous benefit of his family who have lauded him ever since. Who would possibly suspect any connection with a tragic murder all that time ago? And..." She gave a start. "Alexander never had an air tight alibi for that night, plus he was working on carbon at the time. Yes, I can see why you've invested so much effort into this."

"I've never been able to find out what Justin was working on," I said. "Even you said you weren't sure. But considering the state you were in after his murder, you weren't even sure what day it was. And you've had a long time to reflect on everything he ever said to you."

"I'm sorry, Edward, you've had a wasted trip."

"You don't know?" I couldn't keep the bitterness from my voice. It had been a desperately long shot. But it was the first possible lead I'd got in sixty seven years.

"I know exactly what Justin was working on," she said sorrowfully. "I just didn't want to tell anyone at the time."

"Why?" I demanded, suddenly furious. "Information like that was critical to the investigation."

"No it wasn't. Don't you understand anything? I loved him, I really did. And he had a crazy theory. He thought there might be life in space. Bacteria that floated through the void like interstellar dust clouds, propelled by solar wind. That's the spectral signature he was looking for, not carbon 60. He said it was possible all our plagues came from outer space—that was why our immune system always takes time to respond, because each one was new to our planet. He believed all that back in the 1830s. Holy Mary, what a brilliant mind."

"But—"

"Yes I *know*," she snapped at me. "He was right, damnit. He was absolutely right. And I was on the mission which proved it beyond any doubt. We're convinced the bacterial life we found on Ganymede and Europa originated from space—there's evidence for it all over the Jovian system. Do you have any idea how painful that was for me after so many years? It's not an irony, it's a tragedy. And I can't tell anybody he thought of it first, because there's no proof. He'll never get the credit he deserves, and that's my fault."

"So why didn't you tell us at the time?" I asked.

"To protect his memory. I didn't want people laughing at my beautiful lover. He was too precious to me for that. I wouldn't have been able to stand it. And they would have done, the newspapers would have ridiculed him, because it was all too fantastic back then. Invasion of the space flu! I wanted to give him some dignity. He deserved that much."

I sighed in defeat. She was right, I'd put a lot of hope on her confirming my theory. "I don't suppose I can blame you for protecting him. In fact, I'd probably do the same thing."

She rested her hand on mine as another little tremor ran through the gallery. "What will you do now?"

"Me? Complete the *Kuranda* mission, then go home and get on with my life. My changeable life, that is."

Her heavy, wrinkled cheeks lifted in a melancholy smile. "Thank you, Edward. It's nice to know that someone else cared about him."

FOUR
RALEIGH FAMILY INSTITUTE AD 1971

THE LONE OAK TREE was over two hundred years old, its upper half broken long ago, leaving just an imposing stump to support several sturdy boughs. Rich emerald moss was creeping into the wrinkly bark around the base. I settled down in the cusp of a forking root and looked back down the sloping grassland towards the lake. My FAI shrank to a discrete soap bubble beside my head, emission functions on standby, isolating me from the digital babble of family business. It left my own thoughts free to circulate quietly in my head. It was a lovely day, the sun rising above the valley walls, already warm enough to burn off the dew. Buttercups and daisies starred the thick grass, their tiny petals already fully open, receptive. As always, the vista allowed me considerable serenity.

I made a point of taking a walk around the institute grounds every day, unless the weather was truly awful of course. And it could be on occasion. Climate control was one thing we hadn't got round to implementing. I was glad about that—there should be some unpredictability in our lives. I suppose that's why I enjoyed the grounds so much. They were wholly natural. Since I was appointed to the senior family council eight years ago, I'd made damn sure that the only trees planted in the institute valley had been genuine genotypes—same went for the rest of the flora.

A folly, perhaps. But on the rare occasions when anyone questioned me about it, I maintained that it was a valid cultural enclave, and what I was doing was essential preservation. Now that our urban areas were depopulating, everyone wanted to enjoy their own little piece of the rural idyll. Farming had been in a solid decline ever since food synthetics became available at the start of the century. The individual farms which carried on were run by cantankerous old conservationists, or simply families who were determinedly clinging to the old ways. There weren't many such anachronisms—they didn't take up much land area, so it didn't affect the joint council's overall habitation development strategy. As a result, abandoned farmland right across the country was being reinvented as the kind of pastoral woodland that only ever existed in the most romanticised notions of pre-First Era history. Everybody who left the city wanted their own forest, complete with a glade that had a pool fed by a babbling brook, where their mock First Era villa could be sited. Nobody wanted to wait a hundred years for the trees to grow, so reformatted DNA varieties were the *grande* fashion, taking just a couple of years to grow sixty or seventy feet, then slowing into a more natural growth model. It struck me as strange, as if our new biononic technology had infected us with different mental patterns; as society matured we were slowly reverting to a Short mentality. Everything had to be *now*, as if there were no tomorrow rather than the awesome potential future which Bethany Maria Caesar established for us in nineteen sixty three.

My FAI expanded, chiming melodically. I still used the old interface mode, despite the ease of modern direct sensory linkages. It was, I suspected, a quiet personal admission that Bethany Maria Caesar had been right those many years ago back on Io when she claimed that resistance to evolution was derived from age. None of my great-great-great-great-grandchildren had shown any recalcitrance in being fitted with interfaces, nor demonstrated any psychological harm resulting from them. Not that I could hold my own childhood up as any kind of template to the modern world. However, I remained aloof. When you've had to upgrade through as many different types of interfaces and operating programs as I have you remain profoundly sceptical as to how long the latest is going to last before it achieves obsolescence. Best you stay with the one you found most comfortable for a few decades.

It was Rebecca Raleigh Stothard's face who filled the FAI. I might have guessed, there weren't many people my AI would allow to intrude on my private time. Her holographic image grinned at me, conjuring up a host of most pleasurable memories. Rebecca had undergone DNA reset five years ago, reverting her physiological age to her mid-twenties. She'd been an attractive woman when we had our first dalliance a hundred years ago; now she was simply angelic.

"I thought you'd like to be the first to hear," she said. "The Neuromedical Protocol Commission have cleared the procedure, effective from twelve-thirty p.m. Rome mean time today."

"Yes!" the word hissed out from my lips. Given what turbulent times we were living in, it was wholly unjustified for me to feel so elated at such a small piece of news. Yet that didn't prevent me from laughing out loud. "I've finally brought it to an end."

"The Borgias are still in the Vatican," she said primly.

"Show a little confidence. It has to be the pair of them."

"I hope so," she said. There was a note of concern to her voice. "I'd hate to think you were becoming obsessional."

"You know as well as I do the percentage of my time which this case occupies is so small it can't even be measured. This is simply the satisfaction of a job seen through to its end. Besides, I owe it to Francis."

"I know. So what's next?"

"I'll start the ball rolling, and haul her in. Is the system on-line here?"

"Give me three days to complete installation." She winked, and her image vanished. The FAI remained on active status.

The light right across the valley suddenly and silently quadrupled in intensity, turning a vivid violet hue. My iris filters closed, and I looked straight up. A brilliant star was burning in the eastern quadrant of the sky, the backwash of energy from a starship initiating its compression drive. Violet drifted into turquoise which in turn began the shade into emerald. I still think the spectral wash from a compression drive is among the most wondrous sights we have ever created, even if it is an accidental by-product. It wouldn't last, of course. The first generation of faster than light starships were crude affairs, creating their own individual wormhole down which to fly. The families were co-operating on the project to construct exotic matter, which would be able to hold wormholes open permanently. That had to qualify as one of the more favourable signs of recent years—even at the height of the crazed sixties we managed to retain enough sense to see the necessity of such collaboration. Even the Caesars joined with us.

Every time I thought of the negotiations I was involved in to revamp the old Joint Families Astronautics Agency I also remembered my trip to Jupiter, and marvelled at how we were so incapable of seeing the utterly obvious. Size hid their goal from us. But how could we have possibly known we had to think so big?

Bethany Maria Caesar called her murdered lover a visionary, but compared to her he was blind. As soon as she began her work on biononic systems back in eighteen fifty she had realised what would happen should she eventually be successful. The self-replicating biononics she envisaged would be the pinnacle of molecular engineering machinery, organelle-sized modules that could assemble single atoms into whatever structure an AI had designed and, equally important, disassemble. Cluster enough of them together like some patch of black lichen, and they would eat their way through any ore, extracting the atoms you required for whatever project you had in mind. They could then weave those atoms into anything from quantum wire and pentospheres to iron girders and bricks. That included food, clothes, houses, starships... Quite literally, anything you could think of and manage to describe to your AI.

The human race stopped working for a living. Just as she said. Or prophesied, depending on your opinion of her.

The human race had stopped dying, too. Specific versions of biononic modules could travel through the human body, repairing damaged cells. They could also reset DNA.

Amongst all the upheaval, it was our view and attitude towards commodities which underwent the most radical of all our revisions. From valuing all sorts of gems and precious metals and rare chemicals, we had switched to valuing just one thing: matter. Any matter. It became our currency and our obsession. It didn't matter what atom you owned, even if it was only hydrogen—especially hydrogen if you were a Caesar. Fusion could transform it into a heavier element, one which a biononic module could exploit. Every living person in the solar system had the potential to create whatever they wanted, limited only by personal imagination and the public availability of matter.

And the Caesars had the greatest stockpile of unused matter in the solar system: Jupiter. That's how far ahead they were thinking once Bethany spurred them on. The population pressures we'd been facing were nothing compared with what was about to be unleashed. A race of semi-immortals with the potential to increase their numbers at a near exponential rate simply by using the old-fashioned natural method of reproduction—never mind artificial wombs and cloning techniques.

To think, when I was young, I used to worry that our early petrol engine cars would use up all the oil reserves. Within weeks of Bethany's biononic modules coming on-line family spaceships charged off across the solar system to lay claim to any and every chunk of matter a telescope had ever detected. The most disgraceful, shameful year of post Second Era history. A year of madness and greed, when all our rationality seemed to crumble before the forces of avarice. The Crisis Conference of '65 managed to calm things down a little. Thankfully, every family rejected the Rothchild claim on the sun. And the rest of the solar system was apportioned almost equally. We Raleighs came out of it with Titan as well as a joint claim—with 15 other families—on Saturn. But the Caesars still had Jupiter, consolidating their position as the foremost human family. And the FTL starship project was born, the agreement most accredited with easing the tension.

The function of family councils changed to that of resource allocators, enabling us to enforce the original legal framework that underpinned civilisation. Controlling the distribution of raw matter was economics stripped down to its crudest level. But it worked, after a fashion, allowing us to retain order and balance. Given the circumstances, it was a better outcome than I would have predicted.

The last of the compression drive's scarlet light drained away from the sky, taking with it the strange double shadows cast by the oak. I began instructing the FAI to contact a senior representative of the Lockett family.

◆•◆

CHRISTINE JAYNE LOCKETT WAS a stark reminder that I really ought to get myself reset. Men always suffer from the same casual illusion that we simply became more handsome as we matured, and were increasingly desirable as a result. What tosh.

When she walked into my office in the Meridor Manor all I could see was the bitterness leaking from her face. It spoiled her features, a near-permanent scowl highlighting the wrinkles accumulating around her eyes and across her cheeks. Her hair was still long, but not cared for with any great enthusiasm. And the clothes she wore were at least a century out of date; they looked hand made, and badly at that. Paint flecked her hands, lying thick under short, cracked nails.

The small file of personal data which my AI had collected for me told of how she now lived out in the countryside in a naturalist community. They grew their own food, made their own utensils, smoked their hallucinogenics, and generally avoided contact with the rest of their family. No biononics were allowed across the threshold of their compound, although they did have a net interface to call for medical help if any of their number had an accident.

She stalked over to my desk and thrust her face up against mine. "Oppressive bastard! Who the hell do you think you are? How dare you have me arrested and forced away from my home like this. I've done nothing wrong." It was almost a scream.

The Lockett family representative who was accompanying her gave me a tired grimace. Apparently Christine Jayne Lockett had refused point blank to use an airpod, insisting she travelled by groundcar. It had taken them eight hours to drive to the institute from northern England.

"Oh yes you have."

My voice was so cold she recoiled.

"You and Carter Osborne Kenyon are the only people left on my suspect list," I said. "And now I'm finally going to discover the truth."

"But Carter was with me for the whole evening."

I directed a mirthless smile at her. "Yes."

It took a moment for the implication to sink in. Her mouth widened in astonishment. "Holy Mary, you think we did it together, don't you? You think we killed that poor, poor boy."

"The rest of the alibis all check out. You two provided each other's alibi. It's the only weak link left."

"You utter shit!" She sat down heavily in my visitor's chair, staring at me with malice and disbelief. "So you wait all this time until you're some super duper big shot, and exploit your position to pressure my family into handing me over to you, all so you can erase a blemish on your record." Her gaze switched to her family representative. "Gutless coward!" she snarled at him. "The Locketts aren't this feeble that we have to kiss Raleigh arse when they tell us. You're supposed to protect me from this kind of victimisation. I've got strong links to the elder council, you know. Give me a bloody telephone, I'm going to hang you bastards out to dry."

"Your family council agreed to my interviewing you," I said.

"Then I'm taking this to the Roman Congress itself. I have rights! You can't throw me in prison because you've failed to pin this on anyone else. Why didn't you bring Carter here, eh? I'll bet the Kenyons wouldn't stand for being shoved around by the likes of you."

"Firstly, Carter is on the *Aquaries*, they're out exploring stars twenty light years away, and won't be back for another year. Secondly, you're not under arrest, you're here to be interviewed. Thirdly, if what I suspect is true, Carter will be arrested the moment he docks at New Vespasian."

"Interview me? Mary, how dumb is this? I Did Not Murder Justin. Which part of that don't you understand? Because that's all I'm saying."

"It's not that simple any more, not these days."

My FAI floated over to her, and expanded to display a sheet of text. She waved dismissively at it. "I don't use them. What does it say?"

"It's a ruling from the Neuromedical Protocol Commission, clearing a new design of biononic for human application. This particular module takes direct sensory integration a stage further, by stimulating selected synapses to invoke a deep access response."

"We all stopped speaking Latin at the end of the First Era."

"All right, Christine, it's really very simple. We can read your memories. I'm going to send you down to our laboratory, wire you up to a great big machine, and watch exactly what happened that night on a high-resolution, home-theatre-sized colour screen. And there's not a thing you can do to stop me. Any further questions?"

"Bloody hell! Why, Edward? What do you believe was our motive?"

"I have no idea, although this procedure will enable me to trace it through associative location. All I've got left to go on now is opportunity. You and Carter had that."

Her stubborn scowl vanished. She sat there completely blank-faced for a couple of seconds, then gave me a level smile. "If you believe it, then go right ahead."

On a conscious level I kept telling myself she was bluffing, that it was one last brave gesture of defiance. Unfortunately, my subconscious was not so certain.

The family's forensic department had come up in the world over the last century. No longer skulking in the basement of Hewish Manor, it now occupied half of the third floor. Laboratories were crypts of white gloss surfaces, populated by AI pillars with transparent sensor domes on top. Technicians and robots moved around between the units, examining and discussing the results. The clinic room which we had been allocated had a single bed in the middle, with four black boxy cabinets around it.

Rebecca greeted us politely and ushered Christine to the bed. Strictly speaking, Rebecca was a clinical neurologist these days rather than a forensic doctor, but given how new the application was she'd agreed to run the procedure for me.

As with all biononic systems, there's never anything to actually see. Rebecca adjusted a dispenser mechanism against the nape of Christine's neck, and introduced the swarm of modules. The governing AI guided their trajectory through the brain tissue, controlling and regulating the intricate web they wove within her synaptic clefts. It took over an hour to interpret and format the information they were receiving, and map out the activation pathways within her cerebrum.

I watched the primary stages with a growing sense of trepidation. Justin's murder was one of the oldest active legal files the Raleighs had. The weight of so many years was pressing down on this moment, seeking resolution. If we couldn't solve this now, with all our fantastic technological abilities at my disposal, then I had failed him, one of our own.

Rebecca eventually ordered me to sit down. She didn't actually say "be patient" but her look was enough.

An FAI expanded in the air across one end of the clinic room, forming into a translucent sheet flecked with a moiré storm of interference. Colour specks flowed together. It showed a hazy image of an antiquated restaurant viewed at eye level. On the couch Christine moaned softly, her eyes closed, as the memory replayed itself inside her skull, a window into history.

"We're there," Rebecca said. She issued a stream of instructions to the AI.

That March night in eighteen-thirty-two played out in front of me, flickering and jerking like a home movie recorded on an antique strip of film. Christine sat at a table with her friends in the middle of the Orange Grove. Young, beautiful, and full of zest, their smiles and laughter making me ache for my own youth. They told each other stories and jokes, complained about tutors, gossiped about students and university staff, argued family politics. After the waiter brought their main course they went into a giggling huddle to decide if they should complain about the vegetables. More wine was ordered. They became louder.

It was snowing when they collected their coats and left. Tiny flecks of ice adding to the mush of the pavement. They stood as a group outside the restaurant, saying their goodbyes, Christine kissing everybody. Then with Carter's arm around her shoulder, the pair of them made their way through Oxford's freezing streets to the block where she had her artist's garret.

There was the baby-sitter to pay and show out. Then the two of them were alone. They stumbled into her studio, and kissed for a long time, surrounded by Christine's outré paintings. There wasn't much to see of that time, just smears of Carter's face in badly blurred close up. Then she went over to an old chest of drawers, and pulled a stash of cocaine out from an old jewellery box. Carter was already undressing when she turned back to him.

They snorted the drugs, and fondled and groped at each other in an ineffectual manor for what seemed an age. The phone's whistling put an end to it. Christine staggered over to answer it, then handed it to Carter. She watched with a bleary focus as his face showed first annoyance then puzzlement and finally shock. He slammed the handset down and scooped up his clothes. A clock on the studio wall said twenty six minutes to twelve.

I couldn't move from the clinic seat. I sat there with my head in my hands, not believing what I'd just seen. It had to be faked. The Locketts had developed false memory implantation techniques. They'd corrupted our institute AIs. Christine had repeated the alibi to herself for so long it had become stronger than reality. Aliens travelled back in time to alter the past.

"Edward."

When I looked up, Christine Jayne Lockett was staring down at me. There was no anger in her expression. If anything, she was pitying me.

"I wasn't joking when I said I knew people on our elder council," she said. "And let me tell you, you arrogant bastard, if this

...this *mental rape* had been in connection with any other case, I would have kicked up such a stink that your whole family would disown you. The only reason I won't is because I loved Justin. He was my friend, and I'll never forget him for bringing a thread of happiness into my life. I wanted his murderer caught back then, and I want it just as bad now."

"Thank you," I whispered feebly.

"Are you going to give up?"

My smile was one of total self pity. "We're reaching what Bethany called the plateau, the end of scientific progress. I've used every method we know of to find the murderer. Every one of them has failed me. The only thing left now that could solve it is time travel, and I'm afraid our physicists are all pretty much agreed that's just a fantasy."

"Time travel," she said contemptuously. "You just can't see beyond your fabulous technology, can you? Your reliance is sickening. And what use is it when it comes down to the things that are genuinely important?"

"Nobody starves, nobody dies," I snapped at her, abruptly infuriated with her poverty-makes-me-morally-superior attitude. "I notice your happy stone age colony isn't averse to using our medical resources any time something nasty happens."

"Yes, we fall back on technological medicine. We're neither ignorant, nor stupid. We believe technology as sophisticated as ours should be used as a safety net for our lives, not as an integral part, or ruler, as you choose. The simple way we live allows us to return to nature without having to endure the struggle and squalor of the actual stone age. For all things there is a balance, and you have got it badly wrong. Your society is exploiting the universe, not living in harmony with it. The way we live allows our minds to prosper, not our greed."

"While the way we lives allows dreams to become reality. We are a race without limits."

"Without physical limits. What use is that, Edward? What is the ultimate reason to give everyone the power of a god? Look at you, what you're doing—you hoard entire planets in readiness for the day when you can dismantle them and fabricate something in their place. What? What can possibly need building on such a scale? Explore the universe by all means, I'm sure there are miracles and marvels out there just as great as the one we've created for ourselves. But at the end of the day, you should come home to your family and your friends. That's what's truly important."

"I'm glad you've found a way to live with what we've achieved. But you're in a minority. The rest of us want to grab the opportunity this time has gifted us with."

"You'll learn," she said. "After all, you've got eternity."

FIVE
EARTH ORBIT AD 2000

MY FLYER RIPPED UP through the ionosphere like a fish leaving water. The gravatonic and magnetic flux lines which knotted around the little craft tugged a braided haze of auroral streamers out behind us, looking for all the world like some ancient chemical rocket exhaust. Once clear of the atmosphere's bulk, I increased the acceleration to twenty gees, and the slender scintillating strand was stretched to breaking point. Wispy photonic serpents writhed back down towards the planet as we burst free.

I extended my perceptual range, tracking the multitude of flyers falling in and out of the atmosphere all around me. They blossomed like silver comets across my consciousness, dense currents of them arching up from the Earth in a series of flowing hoops with every apex reaching precisely six hundred miles above the equator. The portal Necklace itself, which occupied that orbit, was visualised by nodes of cool jade light sitting atop the hoops. Each of them was nested at the centre of a subtle spatial distortion, lensing the light outwards in curving ephemeral petals.

The flyer soared round in a flat curve, merging with the traffic stream that was heading for the Tangsham portal a thousand miles ahead of me. Africa's eastern coastline drifted past below, its visual clarity taking on a dreamlike quality, perfectly resolved yet impossibly distant. I watched it dwindle behind the flyer as all the wretched old emotions rose to haunt me again. Although I'd never quite had the courage to deactivate the Justin Ascham Raleigh file in the wake of the debacle which was Christine's memory retrieval, I'd certainly abandoned it in my own mind. I couldn't even remember giving my cybershadow the order to tag all the old suspects and watch for any status change within the global dataspace.

Yet when the information slipped into my mind as I awoke that morning I knew I could never ignore it. Whatever would Francis have said?

I kept the flyer's forward perception primary as we approached the portal. The circle of exotic matter had a breadth of nine hundred yards, the rim of a chasm that could be seen only from one direction. Its psudofabric walls glowed green where they intersected the boundaries of normal space-time, forming a tunnel that stretched off into middle-distance. Two lanes of flyers sped along its interior in opposite directions, carrying people to their new world and their hoped-for happiness.

I wished them well, for the next portal led to Nibeza, one of the Vatican-endorsed societies, with complex proscriptions built into its biononics. Essentially they were limited to medical functions and providing raw materials for industry, everything else had to be built the hard way. A society forever frozen on the cusp of the nineteen sixties, where people are kept busy doing their old jobs.

Fully half of the new worlds were variants on the same theme, the only difference being in the level of limitations imposed on their biononics. There were even some deactivated portals now; those that had been used to establish the Restart worlds. There were no bionononics on such planets, nor even the memory of them. The new inhabitants had their memories wiped, awakening on arrival to the belief they had travelled there in hibernation sleep on an old slower-than-light colony ship that left Earth in the nineteen forties. They remained free to carry on their lives as though the intervening years had never happened.

I believe it was our greatest defeat that so many of us were unable to adjust naturally to our new circumstances, where every thought is a treasure to be incubated. It was a failure of will, of self-confidence, which prevented so many from taking that next psychological step. The adjustment necessary was nothing like the re-education courses which used to mark our race's waves of scientific progress—an adaptation which could be achieved by simply going back to school and learning new skills. To thrive today you had to change your attitude and look at life from a wholly new perspective. How sad that for all its triumphs, the superb society we had constructed and systematically laboured to improve for two thousand years was unable to provide that inspiration for everyone at the end.

But as I'd been told so many times, we now had the time to learn, and this new phase of our existence had only just begun. On the Earth below, nearly a third of the older adults spent their time daysleeping. Instead of the falsehood of enforced technological limitation on colony worlds, they immersed themselves in perfectly activated memories of the old days, trading such recollections amongst themselves for those blissful times spent in a simpler world. The vast majority, so they said, relished the days of childhood or first romances set in the age of horse drawn carriages and sailing ships.

Maybe one day they would tire of their borrowed times and wake from their unreality to look around anew at what we have achieved. For out there on the other worlds, the ones defying any restriction, there was much to be proud of. Fiume, where the gas giants were being dismantled to build a vast shell around the star, with an inner surface capable of supporting life. Milligan, whose colonists were experimenting with truly giant wormholes which they hoped could reach other galaxies. Oranses, home to the original sinners, condemned by the Vatican for their project of introducing communal sentience to every living thing on their planet, every worm, insect, and stalk of grass, thus creating Gaia in all her majesty. All this glorious playground was our heritage, a gift from the youth of today to their sulking, inward-looking parents.

My flyer soared out of the traffic stream just before we passed over the rim of Tangsham portal. I directed it round the toroid of exotic matter to the station on the other side. The molecular curtain over the hanger complex entrance parted to let us through, and we alighted on one of the reception platforms. Charles Winter Hutchenson, the station chief, came out to meet me. The Hutchensons are one of our partners in Tangsham, a settlement which is endeavouring to transform people into starvoyagers, a species of immense biomechanical constructs that will spend eternity exploring space. Placing a human mind into the core of such a vessel is simple enough, but its psychology must undergo considerable adaptation to be comfortable with such a body. Yet as I saw on my approach to the portal, there was no shortage of people wishing to join the quest. The solid planets in the Tangsham star system were ringed with construction stations, fed by rivers of matter extracted from asteroids and gas giants. Energy converter nodules had been emplaced deep within the star itself to power such colossal industrial endeavour. It was a place of hard science; there was little of nature's beauty to be found there.

"Pleasure to welcome you on board," Charles Winter Hutchenson said warmly. "I didn't know elder representatives concerned themselves with incidents like this."

"I have several motives," I confessed. "I met Carter Osborne Kenyon a long time ago. Attending to him now is the least I can do. And he is one of the senior nuclear engineers on the project; he's entitled to the best service we can provide. Is he back yet?"

"Yes. He arrived about an hour ago. I halted the trans-shipment as you asked."

"Fine. My cybershadow will take care of the official casework for us. But I'd like to assess the requirements in person first."

"Okay. This way." He led me over to a cathedral-sized cargo hall where the stasis chamber was being kept. It was a translucent grey cylinder suspended between two black glass slabs. The outline of a prone human figure was just visible inside.

My cybershadow meshed me with the chamber's control AI, and I instructed it to give me a status review. Carter Osborne Kenyon wasn't in a good condition. There had been an accident on one of Tangsham's construction stations; even with our technological prowess, machinery isn't flawless. Some power relays had surged, plasma temperature had doubled, there had been a blow-out. Metal was vaporised as the errant plasma jet cut its way through several sheets of decking. Loose panels had swung about, one of them catching Carter a severe blow. The left side of his body had been badly damaged. Worse than that, the edge of the metal had cracked his skull open, pulping the brain tissue inside. It would have been fatal in an earlier age. He was certainly clinically dead before he hit the ground. But the emergency systems had responded efficiently. His body had immediately been sealed in stasis, and microdrones had swept the area, gathering up every cell that had splashed across the floor and nearby walls. The cells were subsequently put in stasis with him.

We had all the component parts, they just had to be reassembled properly. His genome would be read, and each damaged cell repaired, identified, then replaced in its correct location. It could be done on Tangsham, but they would have to commit considerable resources to it. While Earth, with its vast elderly population, retained the greatest level of medical expertise among all of the settled worlds, and subsequently devoted the highest percentage of resources to the field. That concentration of knowledge also meant our software and techniques remained far ahead of everyone else. Carter's best chance for a full reanimation and recovery were with us.

"The damage is within our accepted revival limits," I told Charles Winter Hutchenson. "I'll authorise the procedure and take him back with me to the institute clinic."

The station chief seemed glad that the disruption to his routine was being dealt with so propitiously. He instructed the cargo hall's gravity field to refocus, and the stasis chamber bobbed up into the air, then slid away to my flyer's hold.

I left the portal, and guided the flyer directly to the Raleigh institute. It wasn't just the physical cell structure of Carter's brain which the medical technicians would repair, his memories too would have to be re-established. That was the part of him I was most interested in salvaging. It was as close to time travel as I would ever get.

With the sensorium integration routines developed for the day-sleepers I would be able to drop right into his world. I would be there, observing, listening, and tasting, right from the very first time he met Justin Ascham Raleigh during that initial freshers week until the night of the murder. And unlike him, I wouldn't view those moments through sentiment—I'd be scouring every second for anomalies, hints of out of character behaviour, the misplaced nuance of a single word.

There was three and a half solid years to reconnoitre. I wasn't just examining the time they were in each other's presence. Anything that was said and done during that time could prove crucially relevant. Even his dreams might provide a clue.

It would take a while. There were so many resources I had to supervise and negotiate over, I couldn't schedule much current time to the case; maybe an hour a week. But I'd waited this long now. Time was no longer a relevant factor.

SIX

ETA CARINAE AD 2038

THE DEEPFLIGHT SHIP EASED out of the wormhole portal and twisted smoothly to align itself on the habitat disk. Two light years away, Eta Carinae had inflated across half of the universe.

Its blue-white ejecta lobes were webbed with sharp scarlet lines as the outer plasma envelope slowly radiated away their incredible original temperature. The entire edifice was engulfed in a glowing crimson corona that bristled with spiky gas jets slowly dissipating out towards the stars. Fronds of dark cold dust eddied around it at a greater distance, the remnants of earlier explosive activity.

Eta Carinae is one of the most massive, and therefore unstable, stars in the galaxy. It is also the most dauntingly elegant. I could appreciate why the transcendients had chosen to base themselves here, ten thousand light-years away from Earth. Despite its glory, an ever-present reminder of matter's terrible fragility. Such a monster could never last for more than a few million years. Its triumphant end will come as a detonation that will probably be seen from galactic superclusters halfway towards the edge of infinity.

How Justin Ascham Raleigh would have loved this.

The habitat appeared in our forward sensors. A simple white circle against the swirling red fogs of the hulking sky. Two hundred miles across, it was alone in interstellar space apart from its companion portal. One side flung out towers and spires, alive with sparkling lights. The other was apparently open to space, its surface undulating gently with grassy vales and meandering streams. Forests created random patches of darker green that swarmed over the low hills.

"We have landing clearance," Neill Heller Caesar said.

"Have they changed the governing protocols?" I asked. I wasn't unduly nervous, but I did want this case to go to its absolute completion.

He paused, consulting his cybershadow. "No. The biononic connate acknowledges our authority."

The deepflight ship slid through the habitat's atmospheric boundary without a ripple. We flew along an extensive valley, and alighted at its far end, just before the central stream broke up into a network of silver runnels that emptied into a deep lake. There was a small white villa perched on the slope above the stream, its roof transparent to allow the inhabitants an uninterrupted view of Eta Carinae.

I followed Neill Heller Caesar across the spongy grass, impressed by how clean and natural the air smelt. A figure appeared in the villa's doorway and watched us approach.

It was so inevitable, I considered, that this person should be here of all the places in the universe we had reached. The transcendent project was attempting to imprint a human mind on the fabric of space-time itself. If they succeeded we would become as true angels, creatures of pure thought, distracted by nothing. It was the final liberation to which Bethany Maria Caesar had always aspired.

She smiled knowingly at me as I came through the gate in the white picket fence surrounding her garden. Once again, the elegant twenty-year-old beauty I'd seen in Justin's rooms at Dunbar college. I could scarcely remember the wizened figure who'd talked to me on Io.

"Edward Bucahanan Raleigh." She inclined her head in a slight bow. "So you never gave up."

"No."

"I appreciate the pursuit of a goal, especially over such a length of time. It's an admirable quality."

"Thank you. Are you going to deny it was you?"

She shook her head. "I would never insult you like that. But I would like to know how you found out."

"It was nothing you could have protected yourself from. You see, you smiled."

"I smiled?"

"Yes. When my back was turned. I've spent the last thirty years reviewing Carter's memories of his time at Oxford; accessing a little chunk of them almost every day. I'd gone over everything, absolutely everything, every event I considered remotely relevant was played again and again until I was in danger of becoming more like him than he ever was himself. It all amounted to nothing. Then I played his memories right to the bitter end. That night when Francis and I arrived at Justin's rooms, I asked detective Pitchford to take blood samples from all of you. He was rather annoyed about it, some junior know-it-all telling him how to do his job. Quite rightly, too. And that was when you smiled. I couldn't see it, but Carter did. I think he must have put it down to you being amused by Pitchford's reaction. But I've seen you smile like that on one other occasion. It was when we were on Io and I asked you to come back to Earth because of the way low gravity was harming you. I asked you because I didn't understand then what the Caesars wanted with Jupiter. You did. You'd worked out in advance what would happen when biononics reached their full potential and how it could be used to your advantage. You were quite right too, that particular orthodox branch of your family has already consumed Ganymede to build their habitats, and they show no sign of slowing their expansion."

"So I smiled at you."

"Yes. Both times you were outsmarting me. Which made me wonder about the blood sample. I had your sample taken out of stasis and analysed again. The irony was, we actually had the relevant test back in eighteen thirty. We just never ran it."

"You found I had excessive progestin in my blood. And I smiled because your request confirmed the investigation would go the way I'd extrapolated. I knew I'd be asked for a sample by the police, but it was a risk I was prepared to take, because the odds of anyone making a connection from that to the murder were almost non-existent."

"The most we'd be likely to ask was how you got hold of an illegal contraception. But then you were a biochemist, you were probably able to make it in the lab."

"It wasn't easy. I had to be very careful about equipment usage. The church really stigmatises contraception, even now."

"Like you say, using it still wasn't a reason to murder someone. Not by itself. Then I wondered why you were taking contraception. Nearly a third of the girls at university became pregnant. They weren't stigmatised. But then they're free to come back in fifty or seventy years after they've finished having children, and pick up where they left off. Not you though. I believed you were suffering from low-gravity deterioration on Io because I had no reason to think differently."

"Of course you didn't," she said disdainfully. "Everybody thinks the Sport of Emperors just bred the families for long life. But the Caesars were much cannier and crueller than that. There are branches of the family bred to reinforce other traits."

"Like intelligence. They concentrated on making you smart at the expense of longevity."

"Very astute of you, Edward. Yes, I'm a Short. Without bio-nonic DNA reset I wouldn't have lived past a hundred and twenty."

"You couldn't afford time off from university to have children. It would have taken up half of your life, and you could already see where the emerging sciences were leading. That century was the greatest age of discovery and change we've ever had. It would never be repeated. And you might have been left behind before biononics reached fruition. No problem for us, but in your case being left behind might mean death."

"He didn't care," she said. Her eyes were closed, her voice a pained whisper. "He loved me. He wanted us to be together forever and raise twenty children."

"Then he found out you weren't going to have children with him."

"Yes. I loved him, too, with all my heart. We could have had all this future together, if he'd just made an allowance for what I was. But he wouldn't compromise, he wouldn't listen. Then he threatened to tell my college if I didn't stop taking the progestin. I couldn't believe he would betray me like that. I would have been a disgrace. The college would have sent me away. I didn't know how much value the Caesars would place on me, not back in those days, before I'd proved myself. I didn't know if they'd cover for me. I was twenty one and desperate."

"So you killed him."

"I sneaked up to his room that night to ask him one last time. Even then he wouldn't listen. I actually had a knife in my hand, and he still said no. He was such a traditionalist, a regular bloke, loyal to his family and the world's ideology. So, yes, I killed him. If I hadn't, today wouldn't exist."

I looked up at the delicate strata of red light washing across the sky. What a strange place for this to finally be over. I wondered what Francis would make of it all. The old man would probably have a glass of particularly fine claret, then get on with the next case. Life was so simple when he was alive.

"It would," I said. "If not you, then someone else would have reached the breakthrough point. You said it yourself, we were freefalling to the plateau."

"All this does put us in an extremely awkward position," Neill Heller Caesar said. "You are the inventor of biononics, the mother of today's society. But we can hardly allow a murderer to go around unpunished, now can we."

"I'll leave," she said. "Go into exile for a thousand years or whatever. That way nobody will be embarrassed, and the family won't lose any political respect."

"That's what you want," I said. "I cannot agree to that. The whole reason that we have family command protocols built in to biononics is to ensure that there can be no radical breakaways. Nobody is able to set up by themselves and inflict harm on the rest of us. Humanity even in its current state has to be able to police itself, though the occasions where such actions are needed are thankfully rare. You taking off by yourself, and probably transcending into a pure energy form is hardly an act of penance. You killed a member of my family so that you could have that opportunity. Therefore, it must be denied you." My cybershadow reported that she issued a flurry of instructions to the local biononic connate. It didn't acknowledge. Neill Heller Caesar had kept his word. And I marvelled at the irony in that. Justice served by an act of trust, enacted by a personality forged in a time where honesty and integrity were the highest values to which anyone could aspire. Maybe the likes of he and I did have something valid to contribute to everything today's youngsters were busy building.

Bethany Maria Caesar stiffened as she realised there was to be no escape this time. No window with a convenient creeper down which to climb. "Very well," she said. "What do you think my punishment should be? Am I to hang from the gallows until I'm dead."

"Don't be so melodramatic," Neill Heller Caesar told her. "Edward and I have come to an agreement which allows us to resolve this satisfactorily."

"Of course you have," she muttered.

"You took Justin's life away from him," I said. "We can produce a physical clone of him from the samples we kept. But that still won't be *him*. His personality, his uniqueness is lost to us forever. When you're dealing with a potentially immortal being there could be no crime worse. You have wasted his life and the potential it offered; in return you will be sentenced to exactly that same punishment. The difference is, you will be aware of it."

Was that too cruel of me? Possibly. But then consider this: I once knew a man who knew a man who had seen the Empire's legionaries enforcing Rome's rule at the tip of a sword. None of us is as far removed from barbarism as we like to think.

SEVEN
LIFE TIME

BETHANY MARIA CAESAR WAS taken from the Eta Carinae habitat on our deepflight ship. We disembarked her on a similar habitat in Jupiter orbit which the Caesars had resource funded. She is its sole inhabitant. None of its biononics will respond to her instructions. The medical modules in her body will continue to reset her DNA. She will never age nor succumb to disease. In order to eat, she must catch or grow her own food. Her clothes have to be sewn or knitted by herself. Her house must be built from local materials, which are subject to entropy hastened by climate, requiring considerable maintenance. Such physical activities occupy a great deal of her time. If she wishes to continue living she must deny herself the luxury of devoting her superb mind to pure and abstract thoughts. However, she is able to see the new and wondrous shapes which slide fluidly past her region of space, and know her loss.

Her case is one of the oldest to remain active within our family thoughtcluster. One day, when I've matured and mellowed, and the Borgias have left the Vatican, I may access it again.

FOOTVOTE

◆◆◆

I Bradley Ethan Murray pledge that starting from this day the First of January 2010, and extending for a period of two years, I will hold open a wormhole to the planet New Suffolk in order that all decent people from this United Kingdom can freely travel through to build themselves a new life on a fresh world. I do this in the sad knowledge that our old country's leaders and institutions have failed us completely.

Those who seek release from the oppression and terminal malaise which now afflict the United Kingdom are welcome to do so under the following strictures.

WITH CITIZENSHIP COMES RESPONSIBILITY.

The monoculture of New Suffolk will be derived from current English ethnicity.

Government will be a democratic republic.

It is the job of Government to provide the following statutory services to the citizenship to be paid for through taxation.

1) The enforcement of Law and Order consisting of a police force and independent judiciary. All citizens have the right to trial by jury for major crimes.

2) A socialized health service delivered equally to all. No private hospitals or medical clinics will be permitted, with the exception of 'vanity' medicine.

3) Universal education, to be provided from primary to higher levels. No private schools are permitted. Parents of primary and secondary school pupils are to be given a majority stake in governorship of the school, including its finances. All citizens have the right to be educated to their highest capability.

4) Provision and maintenance of a basic civil infrastructure, including road, rail, and domestic utilities.

5) It is not the job of Government to interfere with and over-regulate the life of the individual citizen. Providing they do no harm to others or the state, citizens are free to do and say whatever they wish.

Citizens do not have the right to own or use weapons.

JANNETTE

IT WAS THE DAY Gordon Brown was due to appear before the Iraq Enquiry again. He'd been called back because of discrepancies in his previous evidence. Opposition politicians (those we still had left) interviewed on Radio Four's *Today* programme were full of eager anticipation, taunting their opponent to come out and face allegations about military funding deficits full on, confident he would screw up. Over in Brussels, the EU Commission was drawing up plans to send in teams of German and French engineers to take over critical shutdown procedures in UK nuclear reactors from our rapidly declining numbers of power station technicians. While in Russia, NovGaz was talking about payment in advance for supplying us with gas this winter. And I'd forgotten to buy Frosties for Steve.

"Not muesli again!" he spat with the true contempt which only seven-year-olds can muster. If only the Civil Service union leadership had that kind of determination when facing the latest round of abysmal Treasury budget cuts to compensate for the 'migration situation'.

"It's good for you," I said without engaging my brain. After seven years you'd think I'd know not to make that kind of tactical error with my own son.

"Mum! It's just dried pigeon crap," he jeered as I stopped pouring it into the bowl. Olivia, his little sister, started to giggle at the use of the NN word. At least she was spooning up her organic yogurt without a fuss. "Not nice, not nice," she chanted.

"What do you want then?" I asked.

"McDonalds. Big Cheesy One."

"No!" I know he only says it to annoy me, but the reflex is too strong to resist. And I'm the Bad Mother yet again. Maybe I shouldn't preach so hard. But then that's Colin speaking.

"How about toast?" I pleaded as a compromise.

"Okay."

I couldn't believe it was that easy. But he sat down at the table and waited with a smug look on his face while I put the granary bread in the toaster. God he does so look like Colin these days. Is that why he's becoming more impossible?

"What's the *prim*?" Olivia asked.

Today had moved on from sniping at the Prime Minister to cover the demonstration at Stanstead.

"Public Responsibility Movement," I said. "Now please finish your breakfast. Daddy will be here soon." *He'd better be.*

I put the toast down in front of Steve, and he squirted too much liquid honey over it. I didn't chide. Both of them were suddenly silent and eating quickly, as if that would speed their father's arrival.

I opened the flat's back door in an attempt to let in some cooler air. Summer was so damn hot and dry this year. Here in Islington the breeze coursed along the baking streets like gusts of desert air. Desert air that had blown across a sewage plant.

"Poooeee," Steve said, holding his nose as he munched down more toast. I had to admit the smell which drifted in wasn't good.

Olivia crumpled her face up in real dismay. "That's horrid, mum. What is it?"

"Someone hasn't tied up their bin bags properly." Which was true enough. The pile of bags in the corner of De Beauvoir Square was getting ridiculously big. As more bags were flung on top, so the ones at the bottom split open. The SkyNews and News24 programmes always showed them with comparison footage of the '79 Winter of Discontent.

"When are they going to clear it?" Steve asked.

"Once a fortnight." Which was optimistic. Mass news media said that nearly ten per cent of the Army had deserted; the remaining political bloggers were putting the figure a lot higher. What was left of our armed forces was now having to provide civic utility assistance squads along with fire service cover, prison guard duties, engineering support to power stations. And a good percentage of the RAF was involved with the rollback from Afghanistan, getting the remaining ground troops out—much to the Americans' disgust. We'd be lucky if the pile was cleared every month. I'd seen a rat the size of a cat run across the square the other day. I always though rodents that big were just urban legend.

"Why can't they take rubbish away like they used to?" Olivia asked.

"Not enough people to do that any more, darling."

"There's hundreds of people standing round the streets all day," she pointed out. "It's scary. I don't like the park anymore."

She was right in a way. It wasn't the lack of people, of course, it was money to pay them to work. The way Sterling was collapsing while the rest of the world climbed out of the recession was chilling. What would happen when the true tax revenue figures for the last six months came in was anyone's guess. Officially, tax received by the Treasury had only fallen by ten per cent since that little *shit* Murray opened his racist, fascist, arseholing wormhole. Nobody believed that. But naturally, the first thing the Treasury had reduced was local government funding, with Brown standing up in Westminster and telling the councils to *cut back on wastage*. What was left of the opposition parties had rocked with laughter when he said it. Who could blame them? That phrase has been a Central Government mantra for fifty years whoever is in power. It never happens, of course. This time, however, things are different for all the wrong reasons.

As a way to finally get the UK to sign on for the Euro, the pound in Zimbabwe-style freefall couldn't be beaten. We desperately needed a currency that wasn't so susceptible to our traitors. Except that suddenly, France and Germany were blocking us from joining, saying that Greece and the Mediterranean countries need to regain their pre-recession economic stability levels first. Bastards.

For once Colin actually turned up on time. He did his silly little ring tune on the front door, and both kids shot off from the table screeching hellos. Do they do that when I turn up to his place to collect them? I think not.

He came in to the kitchen wearing a smart new sweatshirt and clean jeans; his curly brown hair neatly trimmed. I hate that old saying that men just get more handsome as they get older. But they do seem to preserve themselves well after thirty. Colin hadn't put on a pound in the last two years. Well, not since he started jogging and visiting the gym on a regular basis again. I suppose that teenage bimbo he's shacked up with doesn't appreciate a sagging beer gut. Damn: why do I always sound like a stereotype bitch?

Colin scooped Olivia up under one arm and swung her around. "Hiya," he called out to me. "Seen my daughter anywhere?"

She was shrieking: "Daddy, daddy!" as she was twirled about.

"Don't do that," I mumbled. "She's just eaten."

"Okey dokey," he dropped her to the floor and collected a happy kiss from her.

"Come on then," he clapped his hands, hustling them along. "Get ready. I'm leaving in five...four...three..."

They both ran downstairs to collect their bags.

"How are you doing?" he asked.

"Never better." I gave the kitchen table and its mess a weary look, the work surfaces were covered in junk, too, and the sink was a cliché of unwashed pans. "How about you, still servicing the rich?"

His expression hardened, that way it always did when he had to speak slowly and carefully to explain the bleeding obvious to me. "I have to work at the BUPA hospital now as well as my NHS practice. It's the only way I can earn enough money after your lawyer took me to the cleaners in that sexist divorce court of yours."

I almost opened my jaw in surprise—I was the one that always made the needling comments. He was Mr Reasonable through everything. "Oh fine, sure," I said. "I thought it would be my fault."

He gave one of those smug little victory smiles. They used to annoy the hell out of me as well.

"What time do you want them back tomorrow?" he asked.

"Um, in the afternoon. Before six?"

"Okey dokey. No problem."

"Thanks. Are you taking them anywhere special?"

"The reviews for *Splat the Cat* have been good. I'll take them to that this evening if there isn't another power cut."

"As long as you don't take them for burgers."

He rolled his eyes.

I glanced out through the window, seeing his new Navy-blue BMW 4x4 parked on the pavement outside. The stupid thing was the size of an Army tank. I couldn't see anyone sitting in the passenger seat. "Is she coming with you today?"

"Who's that, then?"

"Zoe."

"Ah, you remembered her name."

"I think I read it on her school report."

"As a matter of fact, yes, she is coming with us. She took the day off to help out. The kids do like her you know. And if you ever find yourself someone, I won't kick up about them going out with him."

Oh well done Colin, another point scored off your shrew of an ex, especially with that emphasis on 'ever'. Aren't you the clever one.

The kids charged back into the kitchen, hauling their overnight bags along the floor. "Ready!"

"Have a lovely time," I said, *ever* gracious.

Colin's smile faltered. He hesitated, then leant forward and kissed me on the cheek. Nothing special, not a peace offering, just some platonic gesture I didn't understand. "See you," he said.

I was too surprised to answer. Then the door slammed shut. The kids were gone. The flat was silent.

I had fifteen minutes to make the bus. I was going on a protest for the first time in years. Making my voice heard, and my feelings known. Doing exactly what Colin despised and ridiculed. God, it felt wonderful.

◆•◆

33) There will be no prisons. Convicted criminals will spend their sentence in isolated penal colonies, working for the public good.

34) New Suffolk will use the Imperial system of measurement for length, weight, and volume.

35) Police are required to uphold the law and curtail anti-social behaviour. Police will not waste their time criminalizing trivial offences.

36) Citizens are not entitled to unlimited legal funding. Citizens facing prosecution are entitled to have their defence fees paid for by public funding at total of three times during their lifetime. They may select which cases.

37) The intake of alcohol, nicotine, and other mild narcotics is permitted. Citizens found endangering others when intoxicated, e.g. driving under the influence, will face a minimum sentence of four years in a penal colony.

38) New Suffolk laws will not be structured to support or encourage any type of compensation culture.

39) Any lawyer who has brought three failed cases of litigation judged to be frivolous is automatically sentenced to a minimum five years in a penal colony.

COLIN

THE FINANCE AGENCY'S SOLICITOR was waiting on the doorstep, talking to Zoe, when I drove up in front of the house. I'd met him twice before; he was from Belgium, arrived here a month after the wormhole opened.

"Who's that?" Steve asked as I started to manoeuvre the BMW up the gravel, backing it up to the horsebox.

"Bloke from the bank," I told him. "I've just got a few papers to sort out, then we're off." At least the agency didn't stick a For Sale sign up outside the house. That tended to earn you a brick—or worse—through the window these days.

Zoe smiled and waved as I stopped just short of the horsebox. "Wait in the car for me," I told the kids. I didn't want them to see the empty house. Last night we'd used sleeping bags on the bare carpet. Zipped together. Very romantic.

The solicitor shook my hand and produced a file of documents for me to sign. He glanced at the kids, who were pressed up against the BMW's window, but didn't comment. I guess he'd seen it many times before.

Zoe opened the garage door, and picked up the first of the boxes stacked on the concrete floor. She carried it over to the rear of the BMW, and put it in the boot.

The solicitor wanted five signatures from me, and that was it—the house belonged to the agency. A four-bedroom house with garage and a decent size garden in Enfield along with all the contents, sold for £320,000. Maybe two thirds of what I could have got last year. But that gave me enough to pay off the mortgage, and leave me with £30,000 in equity, which the agency had advanced me. That's what they specialize in, one of many such businesses to spring up since January. A Franco-Dutch company who sell little bits of England to people who aren't going to be accepted on the other side of the wormhole. Heaven knows there are enough takers from overseas, mainly India and North Africa, though for the life of me I can't work out why they'd come here now.

I'd bought the BMW on finance from the garage. My pension portfolio had been sold to another specialist agency based in Luxembourg—God bless our sneaky EU partners—giving me

£25,000. That just left the credit cards. I'd applied for another two; more than that and the monitor programs would spot the new loan pattern. But they'd given me an extra £15,000 to spend over the last month.

It had all gone into a community partnership I signed up for at www.newsuffolklife.co.uk. Most of the stuff was being shipped out in a convoy, with all the personal items we'd need crammed into the horsebox. The website recommended using them, they could take a lot more weight than a caravan.

The solicitor shook my hand and said: "Good luck, monsieur." I handed him the keys, and that was it.

Zoe had jammed the last box in the back of the BMW. There were just four suitcases left. I picked up two of them. She was giving the house a forlorn look.

"We're doing the right thing," I told her.

"I know." She produced a brave smile. "I just didn't expect it to be like this. Murray surprised all of us, didn't he?"

"Yeah. You know I grew up with a whole bunch of sci-fi shows and films; it's amazing how their vocabulary and images integrated with modern culture. They all had bloody great ships flying through space; captains sitting in their command chair and making life and death decisions, shooting lasers and missiles at bug eyed monsters. Everybody knew that was how it would happen for real. Then Murray found a way to open his wormhole, and the little sod won't tell anyone how he does it. Not that I blame him. He's quite right, we'd only misuse the technology. We always do. It's just that…this isn't the noble crossing of the void I expected. It feels almost like a betrayal of my beliefs."

Zoe looked embarrassed. She's nothing like Jannette makes out: some piece of barely-legal nurse totty I pulled because she's blinded by the title of Dr in front of my name. In fact, she's training to be a midwife, which takes just as much dedication and intelligence as a doctor. I'm bloody lucky she even looks at a life-wreckage like me. The fact that she'll take me on with a couple of kids in tow makes her extraordinary.

"I meant the way this finally split the country," she said quietly. "Everyone always talked about the North South divide, and the class war, and the distance between rich and poor. But it was just ideology, politicians lobbing spinning sound bites at each other. Murray went and made it physical."

I put my arms round her. "He gave us the chance politicians always promise and never provide. God, can you believe I actually voted for Blair. Twice!"

She grinned evilly. "Wish you'd voted Tory?"

"Stop putting words in my mouth." I gave her a quick kiss, then we shoved the suitcases in on top of the boxes. "Mind you, I still can't believe Gordon Brown won the election."

"The bloggers said Murray allowed Conservative voters from marginal constituencies to travel through first."

"That's such a typical internet bollocks conspiracy theory. Only thirty-eight percent of the population bothered to vote, and they're all the ones who know they're not going through. The rest of us didn't bother, why would we? That's how Brown won the election. Murray doesn't know who votes for which party. All he built was a wormhole, not this bloody surveillance state we wound up being oppressed by. And anyway, Murray doesn't personally organize the exodus. We have to do that ourselves; take responsibility just like the First Article says."

"Gosh, scratch a doctor and he bleeds politics."

"After working for NHS management for fifteen years, what else am I ever likely to whinge about?"

She laughed, which was a lovely sight. By contrast, Steve and Olivia looked unusually solemn when we got into the 4x4. Zoe gave them a welcoming smile. "Hi guys."

"Where are we going, daddy?" Olivia asked.

"I'm going to take you to see something. Something I hope you'll like."

"What?"

"Can't explain. You have to see it."

"What's in the horsebox?" Steve asked. "You don't like horses."

"Tent," I said. "Big tent, actually. Food. Solar panels. Four widescreen laptops. Two i-pads."

"Cool! What kind of apps have you got?"

"As many as I could download last week."

"Yeah! Can I use one?"

"Maybe."

"What else?" Olivia asked, excited.

"Some toys. Lots of new clothes. Books."

"What's it all for?" Steve asked.

"You'll see." I put my hand on the ignition key, and gave Zoe an apprehensive glance. This was such a huge step to be taking, and there didn't seem to be any defining moment, just a long sequence of covert events that had deftly led to this point in time. I didn't feel any guilt about bringing the kids with us; in fact I'd be remiss as a father if I didn't, there was never going to be an opportunity like this again. I'm not stupid and naive enough to believe New Suffolk is going to be paradise, but it has the *potential* to be something better than this world. We're not going to evolve or progress here, not with so much history and inertia shackling us to the past, and the worst politicians of any era running things across the globe.

As for Jannette... Well, I'm afraid, as far as I'm concerned she hasn't been a proper mother to the kids for years now.

"Let's go," Zoe said. "We chose a long time ago."

So I turned the ignition, and pulled out of the drive, the overloaded horsebox rattling along behind.

"What's that ring?" Steve asked suddenly.

That's my boy: sharp and observant.

"This?" Zoe held her finger up.

"It's an engagement ring!" Olivia squeaked. "Are you getting married?"

"Yes," I said. It was the first thing we wanted to do on the other side.

"Does mum know?" Steve asked.

"No."

62) In order to prevent the mistakes of the old country being repeated on New Suffolk, no organized religions will be permitted. All citizens must acknowledge that the universe is a natural phenomenon.

63) In order to prevent the mistakes of the old country being repeated on New Suffolk, members of extremist political parties and undesirable organizations are banned from passing through the wormhole, as well as criminals and others I deem injurious to the public good.

Examples of prohibited groups and professions include (but are not limited to) the following:

a) Labour Party.

b) Conservative Party.

c) Liberal Democrat Party.

d) Communist Party.

e) British Nationalist Party.

f) Socialist Alliance.

g) Tabloid journalists.

h) European Union bureaucrats.

i) Trade union officials.

j) Corporate lawyers.

k) Political lobbyists.

l) Traffic wardens.

JANNETTE

ABBEY WAS WAITING FOR me at Liverpool Street station. It was a miracle I ever found her. The concourse was overrun by backpackers. I'm sure there wasn't one of them over twenty-five, or maybe that's just the way it is when you're looking at young people from the wrong side of thirty-five. And I certainly hadn't seen that much denim in one place since I went to the Reading Festival in the early nineties. Their backpacks were *huge*, I didn't even know they manufactured them that size.

I gawped in astonishment as the youngsters jostled around me. Nearly all of them were couples. And everybody had a Union Jack patch sewn on their clothes or backpack. I don't think one in ten was speaking English; and under half of them were white. *Ha, how do you like that, Murray? One of your big rules was that everyone had to speak English—and we all know what that implies.*

Abbey yelled a greeting, and walked towards me, pushing her way aggressively forwards. She's not a small woman, her progress was causing quite a disturbance amid all the smiley happy people. Her expression was locked into contempt as they flashed hurt looks her way. It softened when she hugged me. "Hi comrade darling, our train's on platform three."

I followed meekly behind as she ploughed onwards. The badges on her ancient jacket were clinking away; one for every cause she'd ever supported or march she'd been on. The rusty Pearly Queen of the protest nation.

Half the station seemed to want to get on our train. Abbey forced her way into a carriage, queuing being a bourgeois concept to her. We found a couple of empty seats with reserved tickets, which she pulled out and threw on the floor.

"I don't know where this lot all think they're going," she announced in a too-loud voice as we settled in. "Murray doesn't approve of poor foreign trash. There's no way he's going to let Europe's potheads live in stoner bliss on his liars-paradise planet. They'll get bounced right off his hole for middle-class worms."

"His restrictions are self-perpetuating," I said. "He doesn't actually have lists of all the people he doesn't like. And even if he did there's no way of checking everyone who goes through. It's pure psychology. Tell Tory tax-dodgers that no big bad pinkos will be allowed, and they'll flock there in their hundreds. While the rest of us see who is actually going and we steer the hell clear. Who wants to live in their world?"

"Ha! I bet the security services sold him our names in return for a nice retirement cottage on the other side."

You can't argue with Abbey when she's in this mood, which admittedly is most of the time.

She pulled a large hip flask out of her jacket and took a slug. "Want some?"

I looked at the battered old flask, ready to refuse. Then I remembered I didn't have the kids tonight. I wasn't stupid enough to take a slug as big as Abbey's. Thankfully. "Jesus, what the hell is that?"

"Proper Russian vodka, comrade," she smiled, and took another. "Nathan went through last week," she said sourly.

"Nathan? Your brother Nathan?"

"Only by DNA, and I'm not even certain of that after this. Little prick. He took Mary and the kids with him."

"Why?"

"Why do any of them go? The economy, sticking with their fellow traitors, blackouts, Global Warming, pay cuts, taxing the poor, NHS collapsing. Or in other words, the real world that everyone actually has to live in and try to make work, that's what he's running away from. He thinks he's going to be living in some kind of tropical tax haven with fairies doing all the hard work, the dumb shit."

"I'm sorry. What did your mum say? She must be devastated."

Abbey growled, and took another slug. "She says she's glad he's gone; that he and the grandkids deserve a fresh start *somewhere nice*. Can you believe that? Selfish cow, she's gone senile if you ask me. And who's going to be looking after her, hey? Did Nathan ever think of that? Oh no, he just sold out, took off and expected me to pick up the pieces, just like everyone else left behind."

"I know, Steve's school is talking about classes of sixty for next term. The remaining Governors have been having emergency meetings all summer, so I know how many staff have left."

I hesitated. "It surprised me, I thought they were more dedicated than that."

"They would be if they were paid properly."

"The Principal has to recruit another fifteen teachers before term starts, or they won't be able to open at all."

"Fifteen? He wouldn't have managed that many in a normal year."

"He said he's quite confident. There's all sorts of new placement agencies starting up to source overseas professionals for the UK. A lot of people are coming in to fill the gaps. Life's going to go on pretty much the same as before once the exodus is over." That last was a straight quote from Gordon Brown last week. *Damn, I so much want to believe it.*

"Great," Abbey grunted. "Just what we're fighting for."

Our train started to pull out of the station. The backpackers were squashed down the length of the aisle, nobody could move anywhere. There was a big cheer when the PA announced the stop at Bishop's Stortford.

Abbey took another swing, and muttered: "Wankers."

"Don't worry," I said. "If we ever get our own wormhole to a new world, we wouldn't let any of this lot through."

"That's the whole fucking point, isn't it?" Abbey snarled. Her anger was directed at me now, which was kind of scary. She gulped back another mouthful of vodka. "We wouldn't want to have a new world even if we could open a wormhole. It's a stupid waste of talent and wealth that could be used to help people here and now. We have to solve the problems we've got on this world first, starting with the biggest problem there is, that traitor Murray and his rathole. Colonization is Imperialism, and the bastard knows it. We've got to teach people to have social responsibility instead." She jabbed an unsteady finger at a badge on her lapel. It was one showing an Icelandic whaler being broken in two by a Soviet-style hammer; but above it was a shiny new Public Responsibility Movement badge. "That's what today is all about. Murray isn't building him and his kind a new world, what he's doing is ruining ours. You can't just do that, just open a doorway to somewhere else because you feel like it, it's fucking outrageous. When did we ever get to make that democratic decision, eh? He never consulted, never warned us. They've got to be stopped."

"You can't stop people leaving," I said. "That's Stalinist. What we're not ready for is this panic exodus that the wormhole has made possible. Emigration to North America in the nineteenth century was slow, it lasted for decades. There was time to adapt. This is too fast. Two years, that's all he's giving us. No wonder the country can't cope with the loss as it happens. But it'll settle down in the long term."

"We can stop them," Abbey said forcefully. "There's enough people taking part in the movement today to block the roads and turn back all those middle-class tax avoiding scum. Murray didn't think it through; half of the police have pissed off through his rathole. Whose going to protect the responsibility-deniers now? People power is going to come back with a vengeance today. This is when the working class finds its voice again. And it's going to say: no more. You see."

n) Local Authority Executives.
o) All quango members.
p) Stockbrokers.
q) Weapons designers and manufacturers.
r) Arts Council executives.
s) Pension fund managers.
t) Cast and production staff of all TV soaps.
u) All sex crime offenders.
v) Child behavioural experts.
w) Call centre owners and managers.

COLIN

AS EVER, THE M 11 was horrendous, a solid queue of bad-tempered traffic. It took us nearly two hours to creep from the M25 to the Stanstead junction. Actually, not as ever: I was smiling most of the way. It didn't bother me anymore. I just kept thinking this was the last time I ever had to drive down one of this country's abysmal, potholed, clogged, anachronistic nineteen-sixties roads. Never again was I going to come home ranting about why can't we have Autobahns, or eight lane freeways like they've got in America. From now on my moaning was going to be reserved for sixteen-legged alien dinosaurs tramping over the vegetable garden.

The estate car in front had a bumper sticker with a cartoon angry Gordon Brown using a phone to hammer on the side of the wormhole. *Tax for the memory* was printed underneath. We'd been seeing more and more pro-exodus stickers as we crawled our way North. I reckoned that all the vehicles sharing the off road with us were heading to New Suffolk. After all those months of furtive preparation it was kind of comforting finally being amongst your own kind.

"It's the wormhole, isn't it?" Steve asked cautiously. "That's where we're going."

"Yeah," I said. "We're going to take a look at what's there."

"Are we going *through*?" Olivia asked, all wide eyes and nervous enthusiasm.

"I think so. Don't you? Now we've come all this way, it'll be fun." I saw the sign for assembly park F2, and started indicating.

"But they're bad people on the other side," Steve said. "Mum said. They're all Tory traitors."

"Has she been there herself?"

"No way!"

"Then she doesn't really know what it's like on the other side, does she?"

The kids looked at each other. "Suppose not," Steve said.

"Just because you don't agree with someone, doesn't make them bad. We'll take a look round for ourselves and find out what's true and what's not. That's fair isn't it?"

"When are we coming back?" Steve asked.

"Don't know. That depends how nice it is on the new planet. We might want to stay a while."

Zoe was giving me a disapproving look. I shrugged at her. She didn't understand, you've got to acclimatize kids slowly to anything this big and new.

"Is mummy coming?" Olivia asked.

"If she wants to, she can come with us. Of course she can," I said.

Zoe let out a little hiss of exasperation.

"Will I have to go to school?" Steve asked.

"Everybody goes to school no matter what planet they're on," Zoe said.

"Bummer."

"Not nice," Zoe squealed happily.

I found the entrance to park F2 and pulled in off the road. It was a broad open field hired out to newsuffolklife.co by the farmer. Hundreds of vehicles had spent all summer driving over it, reducing the grass to shredded wisps of straw pressed down into the dry iron-hard soil. Today, twenty-odd lorries were parked up at the far end, including three refrigerated containers, and a couple of fuel tankers. Over seventy cars, people carriers, transit vans, and 4x4's were clustered around the lorries; most of them contained families, with kids and parents out stretching their legs before the final haul. The fields on either side replicated similar scenes. In fact all the countryside around the wormhole was the same. It made me feel a lot more confident.

I drew up beside a marshal, who was standing just inside the gate, and showed him our card. He looked at it and grinned as he ticked us off his clipboard. "You're the doc, huh?"

"That's me."

"Fine. There's about a dozen more cars to come and we're all set. I'm Barry, your community convoy liaison, so I'll be travelling with you all the way to your new home. Any problems, come and see me."

"Sure."

"You want to check over the medical equipment you'll be taking, make sure it's all there? Your new neighbours have been going through the rest of the stuff."

I drove over to the other cars and we all climbed out. Several men were up in the lorries, looking round the crates and pallets that were inside. Given how much we'd spent between us, I was glad to see how thorough they were being checking off the inventory. In theory the equipment and supplies on the lorries was enough to turn us into a self sufficient community over the next year.

"This shouldn't take long," I told Zoe. "We need to be certain. In the land of the new arrivals, the owner of the machine tool is king."

"We'll go meet people," she said.

I met a few of them myself as I tracked down the five crates of medical supplies and equipment. They seemed all right—decent types. A little over-eager in their greetings, as I suppose I was. But then we were going to spend an awful long time together. The rest of our lives, if everything went smoothly.

Half an hour later the last members of the group had arrived, we were satisfied everything we'd bought through newsuffolklife.co was with us, and the marshals were getting the convoy organized for the last segment on Earth. Put like that it sounded final and invigorating at the same time.

"Where's the wormhole?" Steve asked plaintively as we got back into the BMW. "I want to see it."

"Two miles to go," Zoe said. "That's all now."

The lorries were first out of the assembly park and onto one of the new tarmac roads that led to the wormhole, with the rest of us following. There was a wide path on the left of the road. Backpackers marched along it, about ten abreast, a constant file of them. I couldn't see the end of the line in either direction. They all had the same eager smile on their faces as they strode ever-closer to the wormhole. Zoe and I probably looked the same.

"There!" Olivia suddenly shouted. She was pointing at the trees on the other side of the backpackers. For a moment I was confused, it was as if a dawn sun was shining through the trunks. Then we cleared the end of the little wood, and we could see the wormhole directly.

The zero-length gap in space-time was actually manifesting as a sphere three hundred yards in diameter. Murray had opened it so that the equator was at ground level, leaving a hemisphere protruding into the air. There was nothing solid, it was simply the place one planet ended and another began. You crossed the boundary, and New Suffolk stretched out in front of you. That was the notorious eye-twister which made a lot of people shiver and even flinch away. As you drew near the threshold, you could see an alien landscape dead ahead of you, inside the hemisphere. Yet it opened outwards, delivering a panoramic view. When you went through, you emerged on the outside of the corresponding hemisphere. There was no inside.

It was early morning on New Suffolk, where its ginger-tinted sun was rising, sending a rouge glow across the gap to light up the English countryside.

We were half a mile away now. The kids were completely silent, entranced by the alien sunlight. Zoe and I flashed a quick triumphant smile at each other.

The road curved round to line up on the wormhole, running through a small cutting. Police lined the top of each bank, dressed in full riot gear. They were swaying back and forwards as they struggled to hold a crowd of protestors away from the road. I could see banners and placards waving about. The chanting and shouting reached us over the sound of the convoy's engines. Things were flying through the air over the top of the police to rain down on the road. I saw several bottles smash apart on the tarmac. Backpackers were bent double as they scurried along, holding their hands over their heads to ward off the barrage from above.

Something thudded onto the BMW's roof. Both kids yelped. I saw a stone skittering off the side. It didn't matter now. The first of our convoy's lorries had reached the wormhole. I saw it drive through, thundering off over the battered mesh road that cut across the landscape on the other side, silhouetted by that exotic rising sun. We were so close.

Then Olivia was shouting: "Daddy, daddy, stop!"

87) Government may not employ more than one manager per twelve front line workers in any department. No Government department may spend more than ten per cent of its budget on administration.

88) Government will not fund any unemployment benefit scheme. Anyone without a job is entitled to five acres of arable land, and will be advanced enough crop seed to become self-sufficient.

89) There will be no death duties. Dying is not a taxable action. Citizens are entitled to bequeath everything they have worked for to whoever they choose.

JANNETTE

IT TOOK US BLOODY hours to get from the station to the wormhole. The Public Responsibility Movement was supposed to lay on buses. I only ever saw two of them, and they took forever to drive around the jammed-up circuit between the station and the rally site. As for the PRM stewards, they'd got into fights with the backpackers streaming out of the station who were asking directions and wanting to know if they could use our buses. The police were separating the two factions as best they could, but the station car park was a perpetual near-riot.

Abbey used the waiting time to stock up at an off-licence. By the time we got on the bus she was completely pissed. She's not a quiet drunk.

As we inched our way across the motorway flyover I could look down on the solid lines of motionless vehicles clotting all the lanes below. There were hundreds of them, thousands. All of them waiting their turn to drive up the off road. Each one full of people who wanted to go through the wormhole. *So many?* Actually seeing how many people wanted to leave was quite a shock. The news says it's like this every day. How can that many people be stupid enough to swallow Murray's promises? I know the country isn't perfect, but at least we're trying to make it progressive, somewhere we're not ashamed to have our kids grow up in.

The bus finally made it to the rally area. A huge Airbus A380 flew low overhead as we climbed out, coming in to land at Stanstead just a few miles to the north. I had to press my hands over my ears the engine noise was so loud. I didn't recognize the airline logo; but it was no doubt bringing another batch of eager refugees from abroad who wanted to join the exodus.

I tracked it across the sky. And there right ahead of me was the wormhole. It was like some gold-chrome bubble squatting on the horizon. I squinted into the brilliant rosy light it was radiating.

"I didn't realize it was that big," I muttered. The damn thing was intimidating this close up.

"Let's get to it," Abbey slurred, and marched off towards the sprawling crush of protestors ahead of us.

Now I remember why I'd stopped going to protests. All that romance about bonding with the crowd, sharing a purpose with your fellow travellers: the singing, the camaraderie, the communal contentment. It's all bollocks.

I got batted about like some cheap football. Everybody wanted to score points by shoving into me. The shouting was loud, in my ear; it never stopped. I got clobbered by placards several times as their carriers dropped them for a rest.

Then we got real near to the police line, and a beer can landed on my shoulder. I jumped at the shock. Fortunately it was empty. But I could see bottles flying overhead, which made me very nervous.

"Let me through you arseholes!" Abbey thundered at the police, using her best I'm-in-charge-here voice.

The nearest constable gave her a confused look. Then she was banging on his riot shield in fury. "I have a right to get past you can't stop me you fascist bastard this is still a free country why don't you piss off and go and bugger your chief constable let me through—" all the while she was pushing up against his shield. I was pressed up behind her. Our helpful comrades behind me were making a real effort to add their strength to the shove. I shouted out in pain from the crushing force but no one heard or took any notice.

Something had to give. For once it was the police line. I was suddenly lurching forward to land on top of Abbey, who had come to rest on top of the policeman. A ragged cheer went up from behind. There were a lot of whistles going off. I was on my knees when I heard dogs barking, and whimpered in fright. I hate dogs, I'm really scared of them. Policeman were moving fast to plug the gap Abbey had created. Several wrestling matches had developed on either side of me. Protestors were being cuffed and dragged off. Clothes got ripped. Those horrible telescoping batons were striking people who weren't even threatening. I saw blood.

Someone tugged the neck of my blouse, lugging me to my feet. I was crying and shaking. My knee was red hot, I could barely stand on it.

A police helmet was thrust into my face. "You all right?" a muffled voice demanded from behind the misted visor.

I just wailed at him. It was pathetic, but I was so miserable and panicky I didn't care.

"Sit there! Wait!" I was pushed onto the top of the fresh earth bank. Ten feet below me backpackers were cowering as they scrambled along the path towards the shining wormhole. They all looked at me in fright, as if I was some kind of demon. That's not right, not right at all. I'm one of the good guys. The vehicles heading for the wormhole were swishing past, their drivers grim as they gripped the steering wheels.

I saw a big Navy-blue BMW 4x4 towing a horsebox. The driver was peering forward intently. Visual recognition kicked in.

"Get your fucking hands off me dickhead this is assault you know I'll have you in court oh shit get those cuffs off right now they're too tight you're deliberately torturing me help help," Abbey was yelling behind me.

"It's Colin," I whispered. "Abbey, that's Colin!" my voice was rising.

"What?"

"Colin!" I pointed frantically. There was Olivia sitting in the back seat, face pressed up against the glass to look out at all the mad people thronging above the bank. Seeing me. We both gaped at each other. "He's taking them. Oh God, he's taking them through the wormhole."

Abbey gave her arresting officer an almighty shove, her weight pushing him off balance. "Get them," she screamed at me. "Move." Three furious policemen made a grab for her. A truncheon was raised. Her shoulder slammed into me. I tumbled down the bank, arms windmilling wildly for balance. My knee was agony. I crashed into a backpacker, and fell onto the tarmac barely a yard from a transit van which swerved violently.

"Grab them back," Abbey cried. "They're yours. It's your right." She vanished beneath her private scrum of police.

The vehicles along the road were all braking. I looked up. Everybody was stuck behind Colin's BMW, which had stopped. The driver's window slid down smoothly and he stuck his head out. We just gazed at each other. A whole flood of emotions washed over his face. Mainly anger, but I could see regret there as well.

"Come on," he said. The rear door opened.

I looked at the open door. I got to my feet. I looked back up the bank at the violent melee of protestors and police. I looked back at the BMW. The wormhole was waiting beyond it. Cars were blowing their horns in exasperation, people shouting at me to get a move on.

I start walking towards the BMW with its open door. I know it's just plain wrong. Morally. Ideologically. I truly believe that. But what else can I do?

IF AT FIRST…

"MY NAME IS DAVID Lanson, and I was with the Metropolitan Police for twenty-seven years. When we got handed the Jenson case I was a Chief Detective, heading up my own team. Not bad going; from outside you'd think I was a standard careerist ticking off the days until retirement. You'd be wrong, I'd grown to hate the job with a passion. Back when I signed on the CID were real thief-takers, but by the time the Jenson case came up I was spending all my time filling in Risk Assessment forms. I'm not kidding, the paperwork was beyond parody. All good stuff for lawyers, but we were getting hammered in the press for truly dismal crime statistics, and hammered by the politicians for not meeting their stupid targets. No wonder public confidence in us had reached rock bottom; the only useful thing we did for the average citizen by then was to hand out official crime numbers for insurance claims.

I suppose that makes me sound bitter, but then that seems to be the fate of old men who're stuck in a job that's forever modernizing. The point of all this being, despite drowning in all that bureaucratic stupidity I reckoned I was quite a decent policeman. That is: I know when people are lying. In those twenty-seven years I'd heard it all, and I do mean *all*: desperate types who've made a mistake and then start sprouting bollocks to cover themselves, the genuine nutters who live in their own little world and believe every word they're saying, drunks and potheads trying to act sober, losers with pitiful excuses, real sick ones who are so cold and polite it makes my skin crawl. Listening to all that day in day out you soon learn to tell what's real and what isn't.

So anyway—We get the call from Marcus Orthew's solicitor that his security people are holding an intruder at his Richmond research centre, and they'd appreciate a full investigation of the 'situation'. That was in 2007, and Orthew was a media and computer mogul then, at least that was the public perception; it wasn't until later I found out just how wide his commercial and technological interests were. His primary hardware company, Orthanics, had just started producing solid state blocks that were generations ahead of anything the opposition were doing, they didn't have hard drives or individual components, the entire computer was wrapped up inside a single hyperprocessor. It wiped the floor with PCs and Applemacs. He was always ahead of the game, Orthew; it was his original PCW's that blew Sinclair computers away at the start of the eighties; everyone in my generation went and bought an Orthanics PCW as their first computer.

But this break in: I thought it was slightly odd the solicitor calling me rather than the company security office; like I said, the longer you're in the game you develop a feeling for these things. I took Paul Mathews and Carmen Galloway with me, they were lieutenants in my team, good people, and slightly less bothered about all the paperwork flooding our office than me. Smart move, I guess; they'd probably make it further than I was ever destined to go. Orthanics security were holding on to Toby Jenson, they'd found him breaking into one of the Richmond Centre labs, which the CCTV footage confirmed. And I was right, there was more to it. We read Toby Jenson his rights, and uniform division hauled him off; that was when the solicitor told me he was a stalker, a twenty-four carat obsessive. Marcus Orthew had known about him for years; Jenson had been following him round the globe, hacking into Orthew's systems, talking to people in his organization, on his domestic staff, ex-girlfriends, basically anyone who crossed his path, but they hadn't been able to do anything about him. Jenson was smart, there was never any activity they could take him to court for, he never got physically close, all he did was talk to people, the hacking could never be proved in law. The Richmond break-in changed all that. As it was Orthew making the allegations, my boss told me to give it complete priority; I guess she was scared about what his magazines and satellite channels would do to the Met if we let it slide.

I went out to Jenson's house with Paul and Carmen. Jesus, you should have seen the bloody place: I mean it was out of a Hollywood serial killer film. Every room was filled with stuff on Orthew; thousands of pictures taken all over the world, company press releases dating back decades, filing cabinets full of newspaper clippings, articles, every whisper of gossip, records of his movements, maps with his houses and factories on them, copies of his magazines, tapes of interviews which Jenson had made, City financial reports on the company. It was a cross between a shrine and a Marcus Orthew museum. It spooked the hell out of me. No doubt about it, Jenson was totally fixated on Orthew. Forensics had to hire a removal lorry to clear the place out.

I interviewed Jenson the next day, that was when it started to get really weird. I'll tell you it as straight as I can remember, which is pretty much verbatim, I'm never ever going to forget that afternoon. First off, he wasn't upset that he'd been caught, more like resigned. Almost like a premier league footballer who's lost the Cup Final; you know: it's a blow but life goes on. The first thing he said was: "I should have realized. Marcus Orthew is a genius, he was bound to catch me out." Which is kind of ironic, really, isn't it? So I asked him what exactly he thought he'd been caught out doing. Get this, he said: "I was trying to find where he was building his time machine." Paul and Carmen just laughed at him. To them it was a Sectioning case, pure and simple. Walk the poor bloke past the station doctor, get the certificate signed, lock him up in a padded room, and supply him with good drugs for the next thirty years. I thought more or less the same thing, too; we wouldn't even need to go to trial, but we were recording the interview, and all his delusions would help coax a signature out of the doc, so I asked him what made him think Orthew was building a time machine. Jenson said they went to school together, that's how he knew. Now the thing is, I checked this later; and they actually did go to some boarding school in Lincolnshire. Well that's fair enough, obsessions can start very early, grudges, too; maybe some fight over a bar of chocolate spiralled out of control, and it'd been festering in Jenson's mind ever since. Jenson claimed otherwise. Marcus Orthew was the coolest kid in school, apparently. Didn't surprise me, from what I'd seen of him in interviews over the years he was one of the most urbane men on the planet. Women found that very attractive, you didn't have to look through Jenson's press cuttings to know that; Orthew's girlfriends were legendary, even the broadsheets reported them.

So how on earth did Jenson decide that the coolest kid in school had evolved into someone building a time machine? "It's simple," he told us earnestly. "When I was at school I got a cassette recorder for my twelfth birthday. I was really pleased with it, nobody else had one. Marcus saw it and just laughed. He snatched one of the cassettes off me, a C-90 I remember, and he said: *state of the art, huh, damn it's almost the same size as an i-pod.*"

Which didn't make a lot of sense to me. Paul and Carmen had given up by then, bored, waiting for me to wrap it up. So? I prompted "So," Jenson said patiently. "This was nineteen seventy two. Cassettes *were* state of the art then. At the time I thought it was odd, that *i-pod* was some foreign word; Marcus was already fluent in three languages, he'd throw stuff like that at you every now and then, all part of his laid-back image. It was one of those things that lingers in your mind. There was other stuff, too. The way he kept smiling every time Margaret Thatcher was on TV, like he knew something we didn't. When I asked him about it he just said one day you'll see the joke. I've got a good memory, detective, very good. All those little details kept adding up over the years. But it was the i-pod which finally clinched it for me. How in God's name could he know about i-pods back in seventy-two?"

Now I understand, I told him: time machine. Jenson gave me this look, like he was pitying me. "But Marcus was twelve, just like me," he said. "We'd been at prep school together since we were eight, and he already possessed the kind of suavity men don't normally get until they're over thirty, damnit he even unnerved the teachers. So how did an eight-year-old get to go time travelling? That was in nineteen sixty-seven, NASA hadn't even reached the Moon then, we'd only just got transistors. Nobody in sixty-seven could build a time machine."

But that's the thing with time machines, I told him. They travel back from the future. I knew I'd get stick from Paul and Carmen for that one, but I couldn't help it. Something about Jenson's attitude was bothering me, that old policeman's instinct. He didn't present himself as delusional. Okay, that's not a professional shrink's opinion, but I knew what I was seeing. Jenson was an ordinary nerdish programmer, a self-employed contractor working from home; more recently from his laptop as he chased Orthew round the world. Something was powering this obsession; the more I heard, the more I wanted to get to the root of it.

"Exactly," Jenson said. His expression changed to tentative suspicion as he gazed at me. "At first I thought an older Marcus had come back in time and given his young self a 2010 encyclopaedia. It's the classic solution, after all, even though it completely violates causality. But knowledge alone doesn't explain Marcus's attitude; something changed an ordinary little boy into a charismatic, confident, wise fifty-year-old trapped in an eight-year-old body."

And you worked out the answer, I guessed. Jenson produced a secretive smile. "Information," he said. "That's how he does it. That's how he's always done it. This is how it must have been first time round: Marcus grows up naturally and becomes a quantum theorist, a cosmologist, whatever... He's a genius, we know that. We also know you can't send mass back through time, wormhole theory disallows it. You can't open a rift through time big enough to take an atom back a split second, the amount of energy to do that simply doesn't exist in the universe. So Marcus must have worked out how to send raw information instead, something that has zero mass. Do you see? He sent his own mind back to the sixties. All his memories, all his knowledge packaged up and delivered to his earlier self; no wonder his confidence was off the scale."

I had to send Paul out then. He couldn't stop laughing, which drew a hurt pout from Jenson. Carmen stayed, though she was grinning broadly; Jenson beat any of the current sitcoms on TV for chuckles. All right then, I said, so Orthew sent his grown up memory back to his kid self, and you're trying to find the machine that does it. Why is that, Toby?

"Are you kidding?" he grunted. "I want to go back myself."

Seems reasonable, I admitted. Is that why you broke into the Richmond lab?

"Richmond was one of two possibles," he said. "I've been monitoring the kind of equipment he's been buying for the last few years, after all he's approaching fifty."

"What's the relevance of that?" Carmen interjected.

"He's a bloke," Jenson said. "You must have read the gossip about him and girls. There have been hundreds; models, actresses, society types."

"That always happens with rich men," she told him, "you can't base an allegation on that, especially not the one you're making."

"Yes, but that first time round he was just a physicist," Jenson said. "There's no glamour or money in that. Now though he knows how to build every post-2000 consumer item at age eight. He can't *not* be a billionaire. This time round he was worth a hundred million by the time he was twenty. With that kind of money you can do anything you want. And I think I know what that is. You only have to look at his genetics division. His electronics are well in advance of anything else on the planet, but what his labs are accomplishing with DNA sequencing and stem cell research are phenomenal. They have to have started with a baseline of knowledge decades ahead of anybody else. Next time he goes back he'll introduce the techniques he's developed this time round into the nineteen seventies. We'll probably have rejuvenation by nineteen ninety. Think what that'll make him, a time travelling immortal. I'm not going to miss out on that if I can help it."

I don't get it, I told him, if Orthew goes back and gives us all immortality in the nineties, you'll be a part of it, we all will. Why go to these criminal lengths?

"I don't know if it is time travel," Jenson said forlornly. "Not actual travelling backwards, I still don't see how that gets round causality. It's more likely he kicks sideways."

I don't get that, I said. What do you mean?

"A parallel universe," Jenson explained. "Almost identical to this one. Generating the wormhole might actually allow for total information transfer, the act of opening it creates a Xerox copy of this universe as it was in nineteen sixty seven. Maybe. I'm not certain what theory his machine is based on, and he certainly isn't telling anyone."

I looked at Carmen. She just shrugged. Okay, thank you for your statement, I told Jenson, we'll talk again later.

"You don't believe me," he accused me.

Obviously we'll have to run some checks, I replied. "Tape 83-7B," he growled at me. "That's your proof. And if it isn't at the Richmond Centre, then he's building it at Ealing. Check there if you want the truth."

Which I did. Not immediately. While Carmen and Paul sorted out Jenson's next interview with the criminal psychologist, I went down to forensic. They found the video tape labelled 83-7B for me, which had a big red star on the label. It was the recording of a kids show from eighty-three: Saturday Breakfast with Bernie. Marcus Orthew was on it to promote his Nanox computer, which was tied in to a national school computer learning syllabus for which Orthanics had just won the contract. It was the usual zany rubbish, with minor celebrities being dunked in blue and purple goo at the end of their slot. Marcus Orthew played along like a good sport. But it was what happened when he came out from under the dripping nozzle which sent a shiver down my spine. Wiping the goo off his face he grinned and said: "That's got to be the start of reality TV." *In nineteen eighty three?* It was Orthew's satellite channel which inflicted Big Brother on us in 1995.

Toby Jenson's computer contained a vast section on the Orthanics Ealing facility. Eight months ago, it had taken delivery of twelve specialist cryogenic superconductor cells, the power rating was higher than the ones used by Boeing's shiny new electroramjet spaceplane. I spent a day thinking about it while the interview with Toby Jenson played over and over in my mind. In the end it was my gut police instinct I went with. Toby Jenson had convinced me. I put my whole so-called career on the line and applied for a warrant. I figured out later that was where I went wrong. Guess which company supplied and maintained the Home Office IT system? The request must have triggered red rockets in Orthew's house. According to the security guards at the gate, Marcus Orthew arrived twelve minutes before us. Toby Jenson had thoughtfully indicated in his files the section he believed most suitable to be used for the construction of a time machine.

He was right, and I'd been right about him. The machine was like the core of the CERN accelerator, a warehouse packed full of high-energy physics equipment. Right at the centre, with all the fat wires and conduits and ducts focusing on it was a dark spherical chamber with a single oval opening. The noise screeching out from the hardware set my teeth on edge, Paul and Carmen clamped their hands over their ears. Then Carmen pointed and screamed. I saw a giant brick of plastic explosive strapped to an electronics cabinet. Now I knew what to look for, I saw others, some were sitting on the superconductor cells. So that's what it's like being caught inside an atom bomb.

Marcus Orthew was standing inside the central chamber. Sort of. He was becoming translucent. I yelled at the others to get out, and ran for the chamber. I reached it as he faded from sight. Then I was inside. My memories started to unwind, playing back my life. *Very* fast. I only recognized tiny sections amid the blur of colour and emotion: the high speed chase that nearly killed me, the birth of my son, dad's funeral, church where I got married, university. Then the playback started to slow, and I remembered that day when I was about eleven, in the park, when

Kenny Mattox our local bully sat on my chest and made me eat the grass cuttings.

I spluttered as the soggy mass was pushed down past my teeth, crying out in shock and fear. Kenny laughed and stuffed some more grass in. I gagged and started to puke violently. Then he was scrambling off in disgust. I lay there for a while, getting my breath back and spitting out grass. I was eleven years old, and it was nineteen sixty eight. It wasn't the way I'd chose to arrive in the past, but in a few months Neil Armstrong would set foot on the moon, then the Beatles would break up.

What I should have done, of course, was patented something. But what? I wasn't a scientist or even an engineer, I can't tell you the chemical formula for Viagra, I didn't know the mechanical details of an airbag. There were everyday things I knew about, icons that we can't survive without, the kind which rake in millions; but would you like to try selling a venture capitalist the idea of Lara Croft five years before the first pocket calculator hits the shops? I did that. I was actually banned from some banks in the City.

So I fell back on the easiest thing in the world. I became a singer songwriter. Songs are ridiculously easy to remember even if you can't recall the exact lyrics. Remember my first big hit in seventy-eight, *Shiny Happy People*? I always was a big REM fan. You've never heard of them? Ah well, sometimes I wonder what the band members are doing this time around. *Pretty in Pink, Teenage Kicks, The Unforgettable Fire, Solsbury Hill?* They're all the same; that fabulous oeuvre of mine isn't quite as original as I make out. And I'm afraid Live Aid wasn't actually the flash of inspiration I always said, either. But the music biz has given me a bloody good life. Every album I've released has been number one on both sides of the Atlantic. That brings in money. A lot of money. It also attracts girls, I mean I never really believed the talk about backstage excess in the time I had before, but trust me here, the public never gets to hear the half of it. I thought it was the perfect cover. I've been employing private agencies to keep an eye on Marcus Orthew since the mid-seventies, several of his senior management team are actually on my payroll. Hell, I even bought shares in Orthogene, I knew it was going to make money, though I didn't expect quite so much money. I can afford to do whatever the hell I want, and the beauty of that is nobody pays any attention to rock stars or how we blow our cash; everyone thinks we're talentless junked up kids heading for a fall. That's what you think has happened now, isn't it? The fall. Well you're wrong about that.

See, I made exactly the same mistake as poor old Toby Jenson: I underestimated Marcus. I didn't think it through. My music made ripples, big ripples. Everyone knows me, I'm famous right across the globe as a one-off supertalent. There's only one other person in this time who knows those songs aren't original: Marcus. He knew I came after him. And he hasn't quite cracked the rejuvenation treatment yet. It's time for him to move on, to make his fresh start again in another parallel universe.

That's why he framed me. Next time around he's going to become our god. It's not something he's going to share with anyone else.

I looked round the interview room, which had an identical layout to the grubby cube just down the hall where I interviewed Toby Jenson last time around. Paul Mathews and Carmen Galloway were giving me blank-faced looks; buttoning back their anger at being dragged into the statement. I couldn't quite get used to Paul with a full head of hair, but Orthogene's follicle treatment is a big earner for the company, everyone in this universe uses it.

I tried to bring my hands up to them, an emphasis to the appeal I was making, but the handcuffs were chained to the table. I glanced down as the metal pulled at my wrists. After the samples had been taken the forensic team had washed the blood off my hands, but I couldn't forget it, there'd been so much; the image was actually stronger than the one I kept of Toby Jenson. Yet I'd never seen those girls until I woke up to find their bodies in the hotel bed with me. The paramedics didn't even try to revive them.

"Please," I implored. "Paul, Carmen, you have to believe me." And I couldn't even say *for old time's sake.*

THE FOREVER KITTEN

◆◆◆

THE MANSION'S GARDEN WAS screened by lush trees. I never thought I'd be so entranced by anything as simple as horse chestnuts, but that's what eighteen months in jail on remand will do for your appreciation of the simple things.

Joe Gordon was waiting for me; the venture capitalist and his wife Fiona were sitting on ornamental metal chairs in a sunken patio area. Their five-year-old daughter, Heloise, was sprawled on a pile of cushions, playing with a ginger kitten.

"Thanks for paying my bail," I said.

"Sorry it took so long, Doctor," he said. "The preparations weren't easy, but we have a private plane waiting to take you to the Caribbean—an island the EU has no extradition treaty with."

"I see. Do you think it's necessary?"

"For the moment, yes. The Brussels Bioethics Commission is looking to make an example of you. They didn't appreciate how many regulations you violated."

"They wouldn't have minded if the treatment worked properly."

"Of course not, but that day isn't yet here, is it? We can set you up with another lab out there."

"Ah well, there are worse places to be exiled. I appreciate it."

"Least we could do. My colleagues and I made a lot of money from the Viagra gland you developed."

I looked at Heloise again. She was a beautiful child, and the smile on her face as she played with the kitten was angelic. The ball of ginger fluff was full of rascally high-spirits, just like every two-month-old kitten. I kept staring, shocked by the familiar marbling pattern in its fluffy light fur.

"Yes," Joe said with quiet pride. "I managed to save one before the court had the litter destroyed. A simple substitution; the police never knew."

"It's three years old now," I whispered.

"Indeed. Heloise is very fond of it."

"Do you understand what this means? The initial stasis-regeneration procedure is valid. If the kitten is still alive and maintaining itself at the same biological age after this long, then in theory it can live forever, just as it is. The procedure stabilized its cellular structure."

"I understand perfectly, thank you, Doctor. Which is why we intend to keep on funding your research. We believe human rejuvenation is possible."

I recognized the greed in his eyes: it wasn't pleasant. "It's still a long way off. This procedure was just the first of a great many. It has no real practical application, we can't use it on an adult. Once a mammal reaches sexual maturity its cells can't accept such a radical modification."

"We have every confidence that in the end you'll produce the result we all want."

I turned back to the child with her pet, feeling more optimistic than I had in three years. "I can do it," I said through clenched teeth. "I can." Revenge, it is said, is best served cold. I could see myself looking down on the gravestones of those fools in the Bioethics Commission in say…oh, about five hundred years' time. They'd be very cold indeed by then.

Joe's affable smile suddenly hardened. I turned, fearing the police had arrived. I'm still very twitchy about raids.

It wasn't the police. The teenage girl coming out from the house was dressed in a black leather micro-skirt and very tight scarlet T-shirt. She would have been attractive if it wasn't for the permanent expression of belligerence on her face; the tattoos weren't nice either. The short sleeves on the T-shirt revealed track marks on her arms. "Is that..."

"Saskia," Joe said with extreme distaste.

I really wouldn't have recognized his older daughter. Saskia used to be a lovely girl, but this creature was the kind of horror story that belonged on the front page of a tabloid.

"Whatcha starin' at?" she demanded.

"Nothing," I promised quickly.

"I need money," she told her father.

"Get a job."

Her face screwed up in rage. I really believed she was going to hit him. I could see Heloise behind her on the verge of tears, arms curling protectively around the kitten.

"You know what I'll do to get it if you don't," Saskia said.

"Fine," Joe snapped. "We no longer care."

She made an obscene gesture and hurried back through the mansion. For a moment I thought Joe was going to run after her. I'd never seen him so angry. Instead he turned to his wife who was frozen in her chair, shaking slightly. "Are you all right?" he asked tenderly.

She nodded bravely, her eyes slowly becoming unfocused.

"What happened?" I asked.

"I don't know," Joe said bitterly. "We didn't spoil her, we were very careful about that. Then about a year ago she started hanging out with the wrong sort: we've been living in a nightmare ever since. She's quit school; she's got a drug habit, she steals from us constantly, I can't remember how many times she's been arrested for joyriding and shoplifting."

"I'm sorry. Kids, huh!"

"Teenagers," he said wretchedly. "Fiona needed two Prozac gland implants to cope."

I smiled over at Heloise who'd started playing with the kitten again. "At least you've got her."

"Yes." Joe seemed to make some kind of decision. "Before you leave, I'd like you to perform the cellular stasis-regeneration procedure for me."

"I don't understand. I explained before, it's simply the first stage of verifying the overwrite sequence we developed."

His smile hardened. "Nevertheless, you will do it again. Without my help you will be going back to prison for a long time."

"It's of no use to adults," I said helplessly. "You won't become young, or even maintain your current age."

"It's not for me," he said.

"Then who..." I followed his gaze to Heloise. "Oh."

"She's perfect just the way she is," he said with a gentle smile. "And that, Doctor, is the way she's going to stay."

BLESSED BY AN ANGEL

◆◆◆

IMELDA LEAVES HER MODEST family home as the evening shade washes over the front garden, a coy smile lifting her maroon glossed lips. She's off to see her lover, a prospect which lifts her heart and enhances her buoyant nature. The sun is slowly sinking behind the gigantic seven-hundred-year-old arcology that dominates the centre of her home town, Kuhmo, casting a shadow which methodically stretches out to darken the town's outlying districts. It is a sharp eclipse which she has witnessed every evening of her seventeen years. Yet the gloaming it brings does nothing to stifle her mood; she's a happy, beautiful girl with an enchantingly flat face and pert nose, her auburn hair flowing below her shoulders. Tonight she's chosen a sleeveless blue and white dress to wear, its semiorganic fabric swirling jauntily around her long legs. Wherever she goes she attracts wistful glances from the boys who linger along Kuhmo's boring streets as they search for something to do before the night is out.

She turns into Rustwith Street, one of the broad thoroughfares which radiate out from the hexagonal base of the tapering arcology. Tall novik trees line this street as they do all the major routes cutting through the civic centre, their woolly blue-green foliage a deliberate counterpoint to the bleak mountainous walls of the arcology. There are vehicles driving down the wide road, primitive vehicles with wheels powered by electric motors. This world of Anagaska has never really benefited from the bountiful wealth flowing among the Greater Commonwealth planets, its citizens seemingly content to bumble along their own slow cautious development route, decades if not centuries behind the more dynamic worlds. And this provincial town is very set in its ways, manacled to the past by the arcology which dominates the local mindset much as it does the landscape.

There are some modern regrav capsules in the air above the roads. Shiny colourful ovoids as big as the cars below, skimming silently along at their regulation fifteen metres altitude which puts them level with the upper branches of the trees.

Imelda pays the traffic no attention as she hurries along to the cafe where she has arranged to meet her lover; like the arcology the buzz of vehicles is a mere background fixture. So she is completely unaware of the chrome green capsule gliding along at walking pace several hundred metres behind her, maintaining a steady distance. The two Advancer Protectorate members inside are observing her through sensors meshed with the capsule's metal skin, and a deluge of scrutineer programs they have scattered across the local net. Their organization might not be official, but they have access to police codes, allowing them to pursue their clandestine business undetected within the town's electronic and physical architecture.

As Imelda turns into the Urwan plaza with its throng of pedestrians several wolf-whistles and raunchy pings are thrown in her direction. The scrutineers examine the pings for hidden code, but the boys and young men who sent them are intent only on compliments and hopeful for a smile. Imelda does smile breezily, but keeps on walking. She is using virtually none of her Advancer functions, the macrocellular clusters supplementing her nervous system are barely interfaced with the planetary cybersphere. Exoimages and mental icons are folded back into her peripheral vision, untouched by her neural hands. Secondary thought routines operating inside her macrocellular clusters monitor several relevant events. She is pleased to see Sabine, her younger sister, has finally reached their aunt's house in New Helsinki, there was a long delay at Inubo station while she waited for the delayed regrav bus connection. Imelda is quietly relieved, she loves her sister dearly, but Sabine is quite a ditzy girl; that kind of foul up was likely to panic her. Imelda's other interest is Erik Horovi, who is not merely on time, but well ahead of schedule, waiting for her in the Pathfinder cafe. An exoimage from the cafe's net reveals him to be sitting at a booth table ordering the stewardbot to stand by. Her neural hands grip the exoimage and expand it, sliding the focus in towards his face. His own clusters must be alerting him to the observation for he grins round at the camera. She sends him a tactile ping, hand-squeezing-thigh, and says: "I'll be there soon, order for me."

His grin broadens at the ping, and he calls the stewardbot over.

It is all manufactured. Erik, his location, his responses, are in fact all being cooked up by a simulacrum program running in a large processor kube on the arcology's seventy-fifth floor. The same suite of abandoned rooms where Erik's unconscious body is lying, fastened to a field-medical cot. But the program has fooled Imelda, she hurries on through the plaza.

Her route takes her out through one of the side paths before turning into a narrow opening between two buildings. The alleys here form a small maze as they link up to the rear of a dozen commercial buildings. But she's perfectly safe. The walls might be high, and old, and dark; there may be rubbish scattered over the concrete, and there may not be any people about, but this is Kuhmo, and she remains linked to the cybersphere. Imelda is a thoroughly modern child of the Commonwealth, she knows that safety and the police are only the speed of a thought away.

A lustrous green regrav capsule descends into the alley ahead of her. It's unusual, but she doesn't hesitate. She's mildly puzzled, because its a large capsule, and she sees it's going to be difficult for her to squeeze round. Just how stupid and inconsiderate is the pilot program?

Her link to the cybersphere falls away. Imelda comes to an uncertain halt, frowning suspiciously at the capsule. She's never been disconnected since the macrocellular clusters became active the year she reached sexual maturity. The cybersphere and beyond that the all-embracing Commonwealth unisphere are her eternal companions; they are her *right*, she thinks crossly. Even now, fear is alien to her. This is the Commonwealth.

A malmetal door expands on the regrav capsule. Paul Alkoff steps out. The Protectorate team's chief is a tall man, over four hundred years old, and twenty years out of rejuvenation; like just about everyone with an Advancer genetic heritage his biological age is locked into his early thirties.

"You're in the way," Imelda protests. "And I think your capsule is messing with reception."

"Sorry about that," Paul says. A quick review of his exoimages show him their kube is producing an optimum digital shadow of Imelda. Friends and family all think she's still walking along the alley en route to the cafe. He holds his left hand up towards her, and the smallest weapon he's wetwired with fires a stun pulse.

Imelda feels nothing. The world shifts round her, and she realizes she's fallen to the ground. There is no pain from the impact, though she knows she hit her head and shoulder hard. She heard the *crack* they made. There is no sensation from anywhere in her body now. She can neither blink nor move her eyeballs. However, her neural hands are not physical, she moves them across icons, triggering every security alert she possesses. There is no response. Shapes appear above her. Men, but out of focus. There is more movement. She is carried into the capsule. It is dark inside. Her mind is screaming, gibbering for help. No one can hear, there is no linkage. She is alone.

The green capsule rises out of the alley and slips back into the designated travel path above the nearest thoroughfare. It is a brief journey to the base of the arcology which now lies deep in the monstrosity's umbra, then the capsule rises up the side until it reaches the seventy-fifth floor and edges its way through a fissure in the outer wall.

At one time, in the decades after the arcology was built, the apartments up here on the upper levels were all packed to capacity, and the central malls buzzed with activity all day long. But that was seven hundred years ago, following the Starflyer war, when the entire population of Hanko was relocated to Anagaska. People were grateful for any accommodation they were given in the terrible aftermath of their homeworld's destruction. Once they had recovered their equilibrium, they began to build out from the arcology, covering the fresh open landscape with new suburbs. Families started to drain away out of the arcology to live in the less confined homes springing up along the new grid of roads. The vision back then was for a town that would continue to grow and establish new industries. Growth, though, proved expensive, and investment on poor old sidelined Anagaska was never abundant. Much cheaper and easier for the town council to refurbish sections of the arcology to keep their community going. In later centuries even that philosophy stalled, and the whole edifice began to deteriorate from the top downwards. Now the giant city-in-a-building is a decaying embarrassment, with no one capable of providing a satisfactory solution.

Dank water from a slimed ceiling drips on the immaculate green skin of the regrav capsule as it settles on a cracked and buckled concrete floor. The cavernous hall used to be an exemplary mall, with shops, bars and offices. Today it is a squalid embalmed memory of the comfortable times long gone. The only light comes from rents in the outer walls, while the ancient superstrength structural spars are sagging as they succumb to gravity and entropy. Not even the town's bad boys venture up to these levels to conduct their nefarious affairs.

Paul and his team member Ziggy Kare carry Imelda from the capsule into one of the abandoned shops. Its walls are dry, if filthy, and the floor is reasonably level. The stun pulse effect is slowly wearing off, allowing Imelda to move her eyes slightly. She sees signs of the new occupants, plyplastic furniture expanded out to form tables and chairs; red-tinged lights, electronic equipment, power cells—all the elements of a sophisticated covert operation. In one of the small rooms they pass she sees a field-medical cot. Erik is lying on it. Her eyes widen in consternation, but her throat remains unresponsive as she tries to shout.

The next room contains a great deal of equipment which she doesn't understand. There is however a face she recognizes. Only a face. Her gorgeous friend's head is sitting inside a transparent bubble with various tubes and cables impaling its neck. The top of the skull has been removed, allowing an invasion of gossamer-fine filaments to penetrate the exposed brain.

A terrified whimper gurgles out through Imelda's numb lips.

"It's all right," Paul says at the sound. "I know you probably won't believe me, but we're not going to harm you. And you'll never remember any of this, we'll give you a memory wipe."

She is placed on a field-medical cot, where plyplastic bands flow over her limbs before solidifying, holding her fast. Tears begin to leak out of her eyes.

Ziggy brings over a sensor stick, and sweeps it above her abdomen. "Damnit," he grunts in disappointment. "She's pregnant all right. Looks like that memory checks out."

"How long?" Paul asks.

"Couple of weeks."

"Can you tell if it's Higher contaminated?"

Ziggy sighs in reluctance, the sound of someone who is forcing himself to do the right thing. "Not from outside, not with our sensors. We'll have to run a detailed pathology scan." His hand indicates a clutter of equipment on a nearby table.

"Okay," Paul says, equally sad. "Take it out, and run the exam."

Ziggy turns to the collection of medical instruments, and picks up a disturbingly phallic device.

Imelda finally manages to scream.

OF ALL THE MEMORIES Paul was able to extract, arrival was the clearest.

The angel clung to the starship's fuselage as the big commercial freighter emerged from its wormhole a thousand kilometres above the bright blue expanse of Anagaska's major ocean.

Dwindling violet light from the wormhole's exotic fabric washed across its face, revealing late-adolescent features that were carefully androgynous. With its firm jaw it would be considered a striking and attractive female rather than classically beautiful, while as a male people would think it inclined to the delicate. The baggy white cotton shirt and trousers it wore offered no clue as to its gender orientation.

As soon as the wormhole closed the starship began to decelerate, chasing down towards the planet where New Helsinki lurked behind the darkness of the terminator. From its position just ahead of the starship's engineering section, the angel could see the archipelagos rolling past beneath. The impression of speed was such that it felt there should be a wind blowing its long honey-coloured hair back. Instead it just smiled across the vacuum at the world which awaited it. Advancer senses revealed the dense electronic chatter of the planetary cybersphere ghosting through the atmosphere, with intangible peaks reaching out to connect with Anagaska's satellite constellation. When the angel accessed the starport's traffic control it could find no hint that their flight was subject to any additional audit, security was light, no intelligent scrutineers were probing the starship's systems. The local Protectorate group didn't know it was here. Not that there was ever any active presence at the starport; but every visitor to Anagaska was quietly recorded and checked; if it had arrived incognito there was a small risk their identity-examiner programs would raise a query. This way was safer, it was playing very long odds against detection.

As soon as the starship fell below orbital velocity, the angel let go. It configured the biononic organelles inside its cells to provide a passive deflective field around itself, one that would surreptitiously warp the active sensor radiation pouring out from the starship's navigation network. The energy sequence flowing through its biononics was even sophisticated enough to disguise its mass, leaving it completely undetected as the starship raced away.

The angel began its long fall to the ground. It expanded its integral force field into a lenticular shape over two hundred metres wide. Electric-blue scintillations slithered over the surface as it caught the first wisps of Anagaska's upper atmosphere, aerobraking in a long curve to subsonic speed. Its descent strategy was simple enough, the majority of its flight was out over the ocean where there would be no one to see the telltale crimson flare of ions against the force field as it sank ever-lower, nor hear the continual thunderclap of its hypersonic passage through the air.

When it reached a three kilometre altitude its downward plummet had slowed to less than a hundred kilometres an hour, thanks to the protective force field which was now over three hundred metres wide and acting like a parachute. It was fifty kilometres out from Olhava's western coastline when it changed the shape of the force field once again, producing the dragonfly wing planform which contributed to its name.

An hour and a half later the angel swooped out of the night-time sky to step lightly onto a sandy beach. It shut down most of its Higher functions, pulled a pair of soft leather sandals from its shoulder bag, and began to walk up the grassy slope to the coastal road.

They'd been lucky, Paul acknowledged, as soon as he'd reviewed the arrival. A lone yachtsman had been underneath the angel as it aerobraked, a man sailing out from Olhava to spend a long vacation amid the archipelagos. A true sailor who knew the seas and the skies. He'd seen the glowing point flashing across the stars and known what it meant, and he had a friend who had a friend who knew a unisphere contact code. Paul and his team had arrived at the coast that morning to begin their tracking operation.

It had taken them a couple of weeks to corner the sneaky creature as it began its mission in Kuhmo. The fight when they surrounded it had taken out three Protectorate members and created a firestorm in the town's college campus, but they'd eventually driven it into a force field cage which could contain its Higher energy functions. They loaded it into a big regrav capsule and ferried it over to the arcology as the flames from the art block building roared up into the night sky behind them.

"I would have just left," the angel said in its pleasant melodic voice as the capsule negotiated its way through the rent in the wall of the seventy-fifth floor. "There was no need for all this."

"That depends whose viewpoint you're taking," Paul snapped back. He was still shaken and infuriated by the deaths; they'd left the bodies behind in the flames and now he was worried the heat might damage his colleagues' memorycells. Once they were re-lifed in replacement clone bodies they could well lose several hours of memories since they last backed up in their secure stores.

"The obvious one, of course," the angel said.

"That's it for you, isn't it? Game over. Shake hands. All go home."

The angel's pale mouth smiled. "It's the civilized thing to do. Don't you approve of that?"

"Ask my three colleagues that you slaughtered back there. They might have an opinion on just how civilized you are."

"As I recall, you fired first."

"Would you have come quietly?"

"So that you could perform your barbarisms on me? No."

"Just tell us what we need to know. Have you contaminated any of us?"

"Contaminated! How I curse your corruptors. You could have lived a rich rewarding life, instead they have condemned you to this poverty of existence."

"Screw you, pal. You Highers want to condemn us to your non-existence. We retain the right to choose our destiny. We *demand* the right."

"Two hundred billion people can't all be wrong. The Central Commonwealth worlds have all embraced biononics, why do you think it is called Higher civilization?"

Paul gave the angel an evil grin. "Self-delusion? More likely: desperate self-justification."

"Why do you resist using biononics?" the Angel asked, its beautiful face frowning disparagingly. "You of all people must be aware of the benefits they bring to a human body. Immortality without your crude rejuvenation treatments; a society which isn't based around industrial economics and its backward ideologies, new vistas, inspiring challenges."

"Challenges? You just sit and vegetate all day long. That and plot our downfall. What have you got to look forward to? Really? Tell me. The only thing that awaits a Higher is downloading into Earth's giant brain library. Why bother waiting? You know that's where you're all heading. Just migrate there and plug yourself into that big virtual reality in the sky, go right ahead and play mental golf for the rest of eternity. I know the numbers downloading themselves are increasing; more and more of you are realizing just how pointless your lives are. We're not designed for godhood, basic human essence cannot be tampered with. We need real challenges to satisfy ourselves with, we need to have our hearts broken, we need to watch our children grow up, we need to look over the horizon for new wonders, we need to build and create. Higher civilization has none of that."

"The Central Commonwealth is our race's greatest creation. To misquote an ancient lyric: Do you think we don't love our children, too?"

"I'm sure you do. But not enough to give them a choice. To be born Higher is to stay Higher, they can't escape."

"They could, they just don't want to. Yet tens of millions of ordinary Advancer humans convert to Higher every year. Does that tell you anything?"

"Yes. It's simply the last step in their adventure. They've *lived* first, they know there are different ways to exist. Only then do they go in for your defeatist digital dreaming; they've decided that they want to die then anyway, so what have they got to lose?"

"Is that what you'll do, Paul? Give in and download your memories into Earth's repository?"

"When I'm finally tired of life, then I might just. But don't expect it for another millennia or ten; it's a big galaxy."

"I am always saddened by how ignorant your views are."

"Is that: *my type*, by any chance?"

"Yes, Paul. Your type indeed, all you reactionary Advancers. Advanced genes have shown you how far you can extend human evolution and abilities; you've extended your lifespan, you're virtually immune to disease, you're naturally integrated with the unisphere, and a lot more besides; all those abilities have brought you half way towards us, yet still you refuse to make the final step. Why?"

"Reactionary my arse. Biononics are not part of us, they are not derived from the genome and cannot be added to it, they are machines. They infect the cells of your body, that is why you have to be born with them to be truly Higher, they have to multiply in tandem with an embryo's natural growth. Only then can they be incorporated by every cell. It's impossible for every cell to be corrupted in an adult. That's the difference, the crucial one. They are alien, imposed."

"Listen to yourself: Infect. Corrupt. Impose. Alien. How small your mind is, how closed."

"I am what I am. I like what I am. You will not take that away from me, nor my children. I have that right to defend myself. If what you are doing is an act of kindness and charity, they why did you arrive here the way you did? Why not be open about it? Every person on this planet can travel to the Central Commonwealth should they wish. Why are you here to spread your culture by deceit?"

"The lies and prejudice you sustain leave us no choice. You're condemning generations unborn to suffering they do not deserve. We can save them from you."

Paul tilted his head to one side, and gave the angel a superior grin. "Listen to yourself," he said with soft mockery. "And the best thing is, I know that you're in a minority among Highers. You disgust the majority as much as you do me."

"And yet they do not stop us."

"The price of true democracy. Now, are you going to tell me what I need to know?"

"You know I cannot do that."

"Then this is going to get very unpleasant. For you."

"That's something your conscience will have to carry."

"I know. But this isn't the first time I've had to break one of you. And I don't suppose you'll be the last." Paul manoeuvred the cage into place at the centre of the hastily prepared interrogation room. Equipment modules began to clamp themselves across the outside of the restraining force fields. Eventually there was no sign of the angel beneath the dull metal segments. Paul gave Ziggy a weary glance. "Let's get on with it."

It took nine days to defeat the angel's biononics. Nine days of negative energy spikes pounding away at the force field which its biononics produced. Nine days draining out its power reserves. Nine days denying it food, water, and oxygen. Nine days smothered inside a sarcophagus of machinery designed to wreck its body and all the Higher functions it was capable of generating. Nine days to send invasive filaments into its brain, preserving the neurones while its ordinary body cells were burned and destroyed one layer at a time. Nine days to kill it.

Eventually, the inert head was removed from the charred remains and artificially sustained on the cusp of life. The filaments linked Paul's thoughts to the angel's undead neurones, allowing him to access memories as if the angel were now a subsidiary brain, nothing more than a recalcitrant storage system grafted on to his own grey matter. Burrowing through the stranger's thoughts was difficult, and not even modern biochemicals could sustain the neurones indefinitely. Decay gave them a very short timescale to work in. There was no neat index. Human sensory experiences were very different to electronic files, their triggers were unique, hard to guess. But Paul persevered, extracting the missing days since its arrival in confused fragments. Piecing together what had happened.

The angel had reached Kuhmo the day after it landed, renting a modest apartment on the arcology's fifteenth floor. It merged easily into the lives of the town's adolescents, signing on at the college, joining several clubs. For two days it studied potential targets.

ZIGGY TAKES LESS THAN an hour to confirm the presence of biononics in every cell of the tiny foetus.

"Son of a bitch," Paul grunts.

"I thought you'd be pleased," Ziggy says. "It means what we did was right."

Paul gives Imelda a guilty glance. The girl is crying silently, her face sticky with tears. Occasionally she lets out a small piteous snivel. Traumatized though she is, he still cannot grant her the comfort of oblivion. There is one question he still has to ask. "I don't like being forced to do what's right," Paul says. "Not this."

"Right," Ziggy says. He slides the dead foetus into a flash furnace, eradicating the last trace of the angel's attempt to subvert their world.

Paul leans over Imelda. "One final thing," he says, "and this will all be over."

Fear squeezes yet more tears from her eyes.

"Did you know you were pregnant?"

The distraught girl opens her mouth and cries out in anguish. "Yes," she sobs.

Studying her face, Paul knows she is telling the truth. There will be no need to use drugs or other stronger methods of enquiry. "Thank you," he says. At last he activates the sleep inducer, and her weary eyes flutter shut.

"We'll need a replacement foetus," Paul says. "I can wipe tonight's memories from her, but if we take away that entire week she spent screwing Erik and the angel she's going to know something happened; that kind of gap can't be covered up. A doctor will find our tampering."

"Not a problem," Ziggy says. "We've got both of them, I can fertilize one of her eggs and re-implant before morning. She'll still have lover boy's baby. There'll be nothing for anybody to be suspicious about."

"Apart from their new friend vanishing."

Ziggy shrugs. "Kids their age, it's hardly unusual. They all have a dozen relationships a year, more if they can. Erik was desperate to bring more girls back to the angel's apartment. You said he was always going on about it; he wanted to bed Imelda's sister for a start. Horny little devil."

"Yeah," Paul says. "It's about time Erik learned he has responsibilities."

ERIK HOROVI WAS A perfect opportunity for the angel. Quite a good looking lad, but still mildly introverted, which left him susceptible to any girl who befriended him. The angel shifted over into full female mode and spent half a day talking to Erik, who was first nervous, then delighted that such a beauty could show any interest in him. He screwed up his courage and asked her out for a date, trying desperately to disguise his surprise when she readily said yes.

The beer and mild aerosol narcotics legitimately available in Kuhmo's bars had a big effect on Erik's inexperienced bloodstream, making him pleasantly inebriated early on in the evening. He talked more easily than he really should have about the Viatak sisters, especially Imelda, the eldest, and how he'd worshipped her from afar. But his alluringly gorgeous new date didn't seem to mind talking about another girl; she was, she said with an eager smile, very liberal when it came to her own sexuality. The haze of subtle chemicals in Erik's head did nothing to dampen his arousal as they both smiled at each other knowingly.

Imelda met the angel the very next day; its memory of the event comprised a confused montage of faces flitting across the main quad in the collage campus, bursts of conversations, scent of the nearby roseyew bushes that decorated the quad. The scent of flowers in full bloom was a strong one leading Paul onward through the memories until he was somehow walking through a city of soaring towers and delightful parks with vegetation that was sweetly reminiscent of Kuhmo's public gardens. Silver-white regrav capsules slipped silently overhead as the pink-tinged sun shone at the apex of a cloudless purple sky. It was Teleba, one of the earliest planets to be settled, now nestling right at the heart of the Central Commonwealth. A world of Higher culture, where there were no urban areas decaying like the entirety of Kuhmo, no economic hardship or market fluctuations to perturb the population, no crime for little was forbidden or withheld—except for the angel's own purpose, but even that was open to its peers. It strode along a boulevard lined by semiorganic treesculptures whose prismatic ever-shifting leaves were modelled on New York's unique ma-hon tree. Information and thoughts from the superdense planetary cybersphere whirled into its mind like particles of a multicoloured snowstorm to be modified or answered, its own questions and suggestions administered into the pervasive flow of knowledge, arguing its ideal and ethic to those who showed an interest. Agreement and disagreement swirled around it as it crossed a plaza with a great fountain in the centre. It felt invigorated by the debate, its own resolution hardening.

The enlightened informed process was the democratic entitlement of all Highers. People didn't have to strive, with their material requirements supplied by Neumann cybernetics and their bodies supported by biononics they could devote themselves to their uniqueness. Human thought was the pinnacle of terrestrial evolution, Earth's most profound success. Now each mind was yoked into the Commonwealth unisphere, collecting, arranging, and distributing information. Whole districts of the city were given over to institutes that delved into science and art, multiplying into thousands of sub-disciplines. Their practitioners communed in mental harmony. Higher culture was reaching for the Divine. *Can you not see the rightness of it, the inevitability? The comfort?*

Paul had to wrench his thoughts away from the guileful desire Trojan. Even in its crippled state the angel's brain was dangerous. There were many elaborate traps that remained empowered amid the waning neurones, quite capable of ensnaring the unwary. He pushed his own mind back into the memories of Imelda and Erik.

There were long lazy evenings spent in the angel's secluded apartment. Bottles and aerosols were imbibed leisurely, their contents complimented by a chemical designed to neutralize any standard female contraception troche. The lights were dimmed, the lovers' thoughts sluggish and contented, bodies inflamed. Paul experienced Erik in congress, his youthful body straining hard against the angel. There were loud, near-savage cries of joy as he climaxed successfully.

Deep inside the angel's complicated sexual organs Erik's spermatozoon were injected with a biononic organelle.

Imelda's smiling, trusting face as she rolled across the jellmattress underneath the now very male angel, unruly hair spreading across the soft pillows. Her sharp gasp of delight at the impalement. Wicked curl of her mouth at the arousal, and piercing cry of fulfilment. A fulfilment greater than she knew as the modified semen was released inside her.

Under the angel's tutelage the eager youngsters experimented with strenuous and exciting new positions night after night. Bodies writhed against it, granting each other every request that was whispered or shouted before granting its single wish. Each time it focused their arousal and ecstasy to one purpose, the creation of its beloved changeling.

IMELDA ARRIVES HOME IN the dead of night after staggering some unknown distance along the street outside. The house recognizes her and opens the front door. She has clearly had a lively evening, her movements lack any real coordination; she squints at most objects unable to perceive what they are; her electronic emissions are chaotic, nonsensical. Every now and then she giggles for no reason. At the bottom of the stairs her legs fold gracelessly under her, and she crumples into a heap. She begins snoring.

This is how her parents find her in the morning. Imelda groans in protest as they rouse her; she has a hangover which is surely terminal. Her parents fuss, and issue a mild chastisement about the state she is in; but they are tolerant liberals, and understand the impulses which fire all adolescents. They are not worried, after all, this is the Greater Commonwealth, citizens are safe at night even in dear old worn down Kuhmo. Imelda is helped upstairs to her bed, given water and some vitamins, and left to sleep off her night of youthful excess.

When she wakes up again, around midday, she quickly calls Erik, who himself is still recovering from his narcotic sojourn. Their questions are almost identical: "What did we do?" As are their answers: "I don't remember."

"I think we met up in the Pathfinder," Imelda says uncertainly. "I remember going there, but afterwards I don't know..."

Erik jumps on this, relieved that one of them has some memory of the evening. "We must have struck a bad aerosol," he claims immediately.

"Yeah, right." Imelda agrees, even though the voice of doubt is murmuring away inside her head. But accepting that easy explanation is so much more comfortable than examining ideas that may have unpleasant outcomes. "You want to meet up again tonight?" she asks.

"Sure, but maybe at my house. I thought we could have a quieter time. And we need to talk about the baby, we'll have to tell our parents."

"It's early days," Imelda says carelessly, she sends him a tactile ping of a very personal nature. "Maybe not too quiet, huh?"

Erik grins in disgraceful delight, last night already forgotten.

NINE MONTHS LATER, ERIK is grinning in an altogether different fashion as he is present at the birth of his daughter. The little girl is perfect and beautiful, born at the Kuhmo General Hospital with an ease that only modern Commonwealth medical technology can provide. Afterwards, Imelda lies back on the bed in the airy delivery room, and cuddles the newborn, lost in devotion.

"We have got to decide on a name," she says dreamily.

Erik idly brushes her mane of auburn hair away from her shoulders. "How about Kerry?" he suggests tentatively. It is the name he knew the angel as; he often wonders where she is now.

"No," Imelda says. There is still some association about Kerry and his abrupt disappearance that she can't shake off.

"Okay, well there's no rush. I'd better go out and see everyone."

The respective families are waiting outside. Imelda's parents are polite; happy that the birth has gone without a hitch, and of course delighted they have another grandchild. However there is a certain degree of strain showing in their outwardly civil attitude towards Erik. His own parents are less formal, and hug him with warm excitement. He goes over to Sabine and kisses her.

"Congratulations," she says.

Erik tenderly brushes Sabine's thick auburn hair. "This doesn't change anything," he says sincerely. Sabine smiles back, grateful for the reassurance, especially right now. She is Imelda's younger sister by forty minutes, and so genuinely doesn't want their special sibling bond soured by any jealousy.

As Erik confessed to Kerry, bedding the sisters was his fantasy since the first moment he saw them. Identical twins is a common enough desire in a hormonally active teenager, and Kerry of course made that particular wish come true readily enough. Even today Erik still has trouble telling his lovers apart, and his memories of them during those wonderful long erotic nights in that apartment on the arcology's fifteenth floor are completely indistinguishable.

Now Inigo wakes up and loudly starts to demand his afternoon feed. Sabine is immediately busy with their infant son who was born in the very same hospital two weeks earlier. She too rejected the name Kerry.

THE DEMON TRAP

WHAT HAPPENED

NOVA ZEALAND WAS THE world chosen for the massacre for exactly the same reason the party of youthful Dynasty members had chosen it as their funtime holiday destination. It barely qualified as H-congruous, capable of supporting human habitation, but that bad geophysics gave it some astonishing scenery which simply begged to be exploited by extreme sports enthusiasts. There was a small population without any real industrial base; its commerce was the leisure industry. Yet in case of a genuine emergency the Intersolar Commonwealth with all its fabulous medical and technical resources was only a single fast train ride away.

The trains came in at Compression Space Transport's planetary station on the north side of the capital, Ridgeview (pop 43,000). They arrived through a wormhole which provided a direct link back to EdenBurg, an industrial planet, owned by the Halgarth Dynasty, and one of the major junctions in CSTs interstellar transport monopoly. None of the trains went any further than the station, Nova Zealand didn't have the kind of road and rail network common to most Commonwealth worlds. All medium and long distance travel was by plane.

It was mid-morning when the train from Hifornia pulled in at the station. The first three carriages were for passengers, while the last two were vehicle carriers. Once it drew to a halt, large malmetal doors on the vehicle carriages retracted and ramps extended out from the platform. The sound of highly-tuned engines firing up was unusual enough to turn the heads of the ordinary passengers as they disembarked. Five customised cars growled their way out onto the ramp. The first a glowing orange Jaguar roadster, with faint blue flames stuttering out of its exhaust pipes as the engine revved. With a final roar of power it sped off the bottom of the ramp with a showy wheel spin. Second was a silver Cadillac that was half bonnet, with front scimitar fins and a rear variable-camber spoiler; then came an eight-wheeled stretched limo; followed by a hundred-year-old V-class Mercedes; and finally a brutish Lexus AT PowerSport; hydroskis retracted against its burnished gold sides.

The convoy raced off out of the station, a show of casual affluence and arrogance which brought grimaces of contempt from those watching. After a discrete minute, the rest of the party's vehicles slid quietly out of the carriage; seven long luxury vans which carried the necessary domestic staff and assistants, along with luggage and sports equipment. The Dynasty members never travelled without their home comforts close by.

Ridgeview's airport was five miles from the planetary station; a disappointingly short journey for the owners of the custom cars, hardly far enough for them to jostle and race along the road. They drove over to the waiting Siddley-Lockheed CP-450, a subsonic cargo/passenger combi plane operated by a local tour company. Inside the vast cargo hold, electromuscle clamps curved out of the floor to secure the fancy cars. Doors opened, and the brash young things sauntered out, filling the air with overloud taunts and calls to each other. Their girlfriends accompanied them, tall slender beauties, terribly young to be dressed in such sensual couture. Stewardesses smiled impassively at the braying sexual harassment they were casually subjected to, and showed their haughty passengers to the upper deck's Imperial Cabin.

The vans purred smoothly into the plane. Staff found their seats in the mid-deck lounge. Within ten minutes, the big rear doors swung shut and the plane taxied onto the runway.

Ridgeview air traffic control cleared them for takeoff to Nova Zealand's arctic continent. It was a nine hour flight that would take them to the notorious Fire Plain. A hundred-kilometre circle of wet swamps just short of the pole itself, whose abnormal climate was created by a ring wall of active volcanoes. Visitors to the resort could watch glowing lava flowing into the constricting cliff of the polar glacier, spurting out phenomenal jets of superheated steam all the way up to the ionosphere. While down in the weird wetlands of giant ferns, huge dangerous creatures left over from an earlier geological era wallowed in the mud and ate anything which moved.

The Siddley-Lockheed CP-450 rose into the air, folding its undercarriage away neatly. It curved towards the north through a clear azure sky, bright blue-white sunlight shining on its green fuselage. Below it, the harsh scrub desert fell away to the sea in long rumpled folds and sharp ravines.

Five minutes after takeoff the plane was climbing through ten thousand feet as the pilot watched the flight management array throttle the duct fans back to cruise power. At which point one of the Dynasty heirs decided it was time to renew his membership of the mile high club. It wasn't in his nature to retire discreetly to the washroom. The rest of the party gathered round his reclining couch to cheer as his obedient girlfriend stripped off. Scandalized stewardesses peeked from the galley, trying not to giggle.

A red star alert flared in the pilot's virtual vision. The plane's array was issuing a proximity alarm. It took the pilot a shocked couple of seconds to analyse the data which the radar was presenting him with. An object barely a metre long was streaking towards them at mach five. Disbelief froze him for another second as he struggled to admit he was seeing a missile. He managed to yell: "Mayday!" into the open channel as he slammed his hands down onto the manual control pads. For someone who hadn't physically flown a plane for over two decades he managed his evasion manoeuvre remarkably well, ramming on the power and initiating a steep dive. It delayed impact by a good three seconds, long enough for everyone on board to realize something was disastrously wrong.

The missile struck the fuselage just below the port wing root. Not even modern super strength materials could withstand the blast. The wing was ripped off, sending the fuselage into a fast spin. It began to disintegrate immediately, scattering fragments and bodies as it plummeted out of the sky.

Before the first pieces even hit the ground, a shotgun message entered the unisphere, attempting to infiltrate the address stores of every person who had an access code—about ninety-five per cent of the human race. The carrier format was new enough to avoid the majority of commercial sentinels, though the unisphere's node management programs soon adapted to the intruder and blocked its progress. Before that happened, it managed to reach several billion people who were annoyed to find the small file slipping into their stores. Most were unisphere-savvy enough to have their e-butlers delete the pest. Those that did open it were shown a simple text.

> *The Free Merioneth Forces announce the eradication of more Dynasty parasites. Our team on Nova Zealand have today successfully struck against our oppressors. Until our planet is liberated from the financial bonds which the Dynasty leaders have shackled it with, our campaign will continue.*
>
> *We urge all Dynasty members to exert your influence and compel your leaders to negotiate with our government. Failure to comply with our requests for freedom and dignity will result in the further elimination of your worthless kind. We will no longer tolerate our taxes being spent to uphold your decadent lifestyle.*

Senior Investigator Paula Myo's e-butler deleted the shotgun as soon as it reached her unisphere interface; it was the newest adaptive version with a real-time update facility to the Serious Crimes Directorate RI, so it knew what it was dealing with. At the time she was trying to be polite with the decorator who was gazing round the lounge of her new apartment, shaking his head as if he'd been confronted with restoring the Sistine chapel.

"Next month?" he suggested with a typical Gallic shrug.

Paula was only surprised he wasn't wearing a beret and smoking a cigarette; he'd certainly polished the rest of the Parisian indifference routine to stereotype perfection. "That's fine." She'd been in the apartment a week, and even she acknowledged it needed sprucing up. It wasn't much: bathroom, bedroom, and a lounge with a tiny kitchen alcove. The building was a typical Paris block, centuries-old with a pleasant central courtyard. She really didn't care about the aesthetics, all that counted was its proximity to the office.

"What colour scheme?" he enquired.

"Oh...whatever: white."

"White?" From his blatant dismay she must have deliberately insulted his French ancestry all the way back to the royal era.

"Yes." A priority communication icon popped up into her virtual vision. She touched it with a virtual hand she'd customized to a red skeletal outline; her physical fingers twitched in mimicry as parallel nerve impulses ran along the organic circuitry tattoos on her wrist.

"Grade one case coming in," Christabel Agatha Halgarth said. "The Director wants us on it immediately."

"On my way in," Paula replied.

"No don't. I'm going for a car now; I'll pick you up. Three minutes."

"All right, transfer the case files over." Paula dismissed the decorator. Perhaps it was because of her carefully controlled mix of Filipino and European genes which had given her such a delightful face he assumed he could bluster and intimidate as he usually did with single female clients. The stare she gave him froze the protest after just a couple of words. He nodded compliance and retreated, counting himself lucky she hadn't actually said anything.

Paula pulled on a grey suit jacket and picked up her small shoulder bag, moving instinctively as the files from the Directorate slipped into her virtual vision. She read the scant details on the plane crash as she hurried down the worn stone stairs to the courtyard below.

One of the Directorate's dark sedans pulled up outside the block's main entrance. The gull wing door pivoted forward, and Paula got in. Christabel was sitting on the rear bench, a brunette with an Asian ancestry a lot stronger than Paula's clinic-manufactured heritage. She was Paula's deputy; they'd known each other since their training academy days.

"Wow, you look great," Christabel enthused. "Positively jail-bait. I'd forgotten how pretty you are when you're young. You shouldn't wait so long between rejuvenations."

"I can't spare the time," Paula said automatically. Her hand went up to sweep her raven hair away from her face. With rejuvenation returning her biological age to late-adolescence her hair had grown very thick again. Every time she was tempted to have it trimmed to a shorter style. But this fitted her, along with the simple-cut business suit and plain black shoes she always wore to work, defining what she was. It was as much her identity as her modified genes.

"Welcome back," Christabel said with a knowing smile. "How are your inserts settling in?"

Paula held up a hand, flexing the fingers. The OCtattoos were invisible against her skin. It was still a relatively new technology, with development houses finding new applications each year. The ones she'd had before rejuvenation were a lot cruder; they'd been eradicated by her treatment, so the last week had been spent at a Directorate facility augmenting her body with the new generation of insert gadgets.

"A couple of glitches left. I'm due a final formatting session on Saturday. Things have come a long way since I had my last installation."

Christabel held up her own hand. Threads of intense blue light appeared, pulsing along her fingers. "You didn't fancy the latest versions then? Function and fashion combined. Not bad, huh? I paid for the customization myself. I can get you a good deal if you like, I've still got contacts in my Dynasty."

Paula gave the glowing strands a curt look. "No thank you."

Christabel laughed.

"We don't seem to have much on the Free Merioneth Forces," Paula said as she continued to open case files.

"No. They're relatively new. Emerged while you were in rejuvenation. This is their fourth strike in five months. Very effective. We haven't arrested anyone yet."

THE DIRECTORATE SEDAN DROVE across Paris to the huge CST station where it boarded a trans-Earth loop train, taking it through a series of wormholes linking the old world's major cities. From Paris the loop led to Madrid, then London before crossing the Atlantic to New York; four more stops, and twenty minutes later the train pulled in at the massive LA galactic station, where they drove over to the Intersolar terminal and onto a direct train to EdenBurg.

Eighty minutes after Paula got into the sedan, it was driving off a vehicle carriage at the same platform which the Dynasty party had used less than three hours earlier. The car's array took them round the Ridgeview ring road, and out across the scrub desert to the north. Paula watched in surprise as a group of wild camels sauntered across the hard-packed sands. They'd been gene-modified to digest the local cacti-equivalent vegetation, but even so it was a harsh environment. After five miles, the track vanished, and the suspension rose up to cope with the rocky ground.

"Hope you brought a hat," Christabel said. She was squinting out of the window at the blazing noon sun. Ridgeview was about as far south as the planet's climate would allow. After another couple of hundred miles the scrub desert gave way to true desolation. Nova Zealand's entire equatorial zone was bare rock, baked by the intense blue-white star; the heat even repelled clouds leaving the land in a permanent shadowless summer where the daily air temperature rose far above boiling point.

The crash site perimeter was still being established by the local police. Wreckage had so far been spotted over seven square miles.

The Directorate car delivered them to a cluster of police vehicles parked together above a wide sandy gully. Helicopters droned slowly through the clear sky above.

Paula reluctantly dug a wide-brimmed hat from her little bag. The door opened, and she immediately held her breath as oppressively hot air swept in.

"Hellfire," Christabel groaned. "Literally."

They climbed out. Paula put on a pair of sunglasses which opaqued up to their highest level. Then she took her jacket off, feeling sweat prickle her bare arms. The arid desert air was burning its way down her throat, drying her sinuses.

"Wouldn't do that if I was you," a man told them. He was dressed in a loose Arabic-style robe with a deep white hood. "Detective Captain Aidan Winkal," he said as he offered his hand.

"Paula Myo."

"I've heard of you, Investigator. But seriously, if you haven't put on screening membrane, five minutes exposure in this sunlight will burn your skin down to the bone."

"Okay," she put the jacket back on.

"Come on, I've got our mobile situation office set up."

It was a big old van with the Ridgeview police logo emblazoned on the side. Five tall heat dump fins sprouted out of the roof, glowing a faint rose-pink. Inside, the air was thankfully cool. A bench table down one side was cluttered with various desktop arrays operated by Winkal's colleagues. Screens and small holographic portals relayed various images from the helicopters and jeeps covering the site.

"What procedures are you following?" Paula asked.

Aidan Winkal had pulled his hood back to reveal a weathered face with silver-fox hair cut short. He appeared hesitant. "Look, we're not exactly used to this kind of thing, you know."

"We're not here to criticize," Paula assured him. "We both want the same thing, to catch the people responsible. The Directorate will assume responsibility for tracking down the group which did this. But site control and recovery is all yours. Now tell me what you're doing, and we'll be happy to provide advice."

"Okay, thanks. We're trying to map the debris area. The larger sections of fuselage are easy enough to find, and so far we've picked up thirty-seven personal emergency beacons. My squads are escorting medical teams out to them. The bodies we've located so far…they're not intact, you know."

"I understand. However, their memorycells should be able to survive the impact. They're designed to withstand a lot worse than this."

"Sure."

"We have a Directorate forensic team en route. Some of their sensor systems will be able to help your search. I'll assign them as soon as we've identified and recovered the missile. Have you located the launch site yet?"

"No. I'm concentrating on the crash, finding those poor people. We're still trying to build a full passenger list."

"Fair enough. Christabel and I will work out where it was fired from. I'll need complete access to the plane's memory. Have you found it yet?"

"Yes. It never lost contact with the unisphere. We know where it is but we haven't actually collected it yet. I encrypted the channel and restricted access."

"Good. I'd also like to see the CST station closed to both inbound and outbound trains. We can do without the reporters who are undoubtedly on their way. Secondly, there's a chance the team which fired the missile is still on the planet. If so, I'd like them confined here."

"I, er, don't really have that authority. I don't even think our Prime Minister does."

"I'll contact my chief right away. But you'll need to post some officers at the station. It might turn ugly once the trains stop running."

"Okay."

PAULA AND CHRISTABEL CLAIMED a couple of fold-out chairs at the rear of the van, and got Aidan to open the restricted channel to the plane's memory. Using the radar data to backtrack the missile's trajectory was easy enough; it had come from a point approximately a quarter of a mile from the coast, five miles outside Ridgeview.

"Wouldn't take long to get to the city ring road from there," Christabel exclaimed as she reviewed a local map in her virtual vision.

"Pull Ridgeview's traffic management records," Paula told her. "Find out what vehicles if any joined the road from outside this morning. I'll also want the air traffic records scrutinizing. They might have flown out."

"Right away."

"What kind of orbital surveillance have you got here?" Paula asked Aidan.

"Eight low orbit satellites for geophysical observation," he told her. "The resolution isn't good. You could see the Siddley-Lockheed, and most houses; but a car would be hard to make out, and individual people are too small."

"Okay. We'll see what kind of images the Directorate RI can pull out of the raw data. Right now, we need to get out to the launch site. This sun is degrading our evidence by the minute. Can you give me a helicopter, please?"

THE DIRECTORATE FORENSIC TEAM arrived in time to join them on the helicopter. Aidan Winkal also elected to come with them. As the coast slipped into view through the cabin window he shook his head in bemusement. "I just got word from the station," he called above the rotor noise. "CST has suspended the train service to EdenBurg. Your Directorate has a lot of clout."

"Three of the holiday party were Sheldon Dynasty members," Paula said. "That'll speed things up a little."

Aidan nodded in understanding.

Christabel leaned in close to Paula. "I give it ten minutes before *someone*'s here to help."

Paula gazed down at the coastline. "You think it will be that long?"

"I've already had two calls from the Halgarth security office. Any assistance we need..."

They circled the zone Paula had identified, seeing nothing but shingle and rock. A scan from the helicopter's radar didn't add anything. Paula's optical inserts were giving her an infra-red picture. Every surface was radiant with heat as it basked in the fierce sunlight. "Anything?" she asked Nalcol, the forensics officer who was with them. He was sitting next to the open side door, aiming a specialist array at the ground.

"A spectral of an unusual airborne carbon residual. Could be the launch booster. Don't know for sure. But we'll need to land clear. I don't want the downwash to screw up evidence."

The pilot put them down three hundred yards away.

Paula, Christabel, and Aidan followed Nalcol and his assistant towards the area where the carbon residue had spread. The forensic people were sweeping their arrays at everything as they went. A little pack of bots crawled along beside them, like foot-long caterpillars with thin antenna strands stroking the ground as they went.

"No sign of any vehicle tracks," Christabel said.

"Tough to see on this terrain," Paula said. Her toe nudged some of the flat shingle. "If Nalcol confirms this as the launch point, we'll seal it off and bring in the rest of the team."

"This is going to be a tough one," Christabel said, shielding her eyes as she scanned the grey-blue sea. The land sloped down towards it like a giant beach. "They didn't leave much for us."

"Actually, this isolation helps us a great deal," Paula said. "When we get back to Paris I want you to put together a team to track down who knew the Dynasty members had booked their holiday here. Get a profile on everyone from the Fire Plain resort staff through the tour company they use, and most importantly the entourage. I want to know if any of them have left recently. Then there's the girlfriends, one night stands, other friends—their families, connections. It'll be a big list, but finite. Cross reference for any connection to Merioneth."

Christabel let out a soft whistle. "I'll assign Basker to lead it. He's good at data analysis."

"Fine." A sound made Paula look up, pushing back her wide hat. "Oh, hello."

A small black helicopter was approaching the launch zone, flying low and fast.

"That's not one of ours," Aidan said in annoyance. "How did it get flight clearance? This is a designated restricted zone."

Paula held back on her smile. The poor police captain sounded quite indignant. "A word of advice, Captain," she said as the new helicopter landed beside theirs. "This is where you get to play with the big boys. If you haven't done this before, don't try and claim jurisdiction on any aspect of this investigation. You really do have to work with them."

"Uh huh," Aiden spat onto the stones. "And if I don't?"

"Your career is over. It's not blatant, but it is effective. If you really annoy them then you won't have much of a life after your next few rejuvenations either."

"And you just let them walk all over your investigations, do you?"

"No," Paula said. "There are boundaries, and with me they know where they stand. But I've spent decades building that political coverage. You haven't."

A man climbed down out of the helicopter as the blades slowed. He was dressed in a robe similar to the one Aiden wore, except he was like the captain's younger, smarter, richer brother.

"Nelson Sheldon," Christabel muttered. "Impressive. Third generation down from Nigel himself."

Paula nodded appreciatively. Nelson was one of the five deputy managers of the Sheldon Dynasty security service, heading up the external threat division. She'd met him on three Directorate cases when their respective interests overlapped; each time he'd been the total professional, and very diplomatic. Rumour had it that he'd be chief within fifty years.

"Captain," Nelson said politely, and offered his hand to Aidan. "I apologize for the interruption, but as you can imagine my family is deeply distressed by this appalling attack on our members. I'm here to offer whatever support you need, practical or political."

There was a moment of hesitation. Then Aiden shook the proffered hand. "Understood," he said. "All of it."

"Ah," Nelson smiled. "The ladies have been telling tales about me. Christabel, nice to see you again. Paula, you look amazing. You'll have to tell me which clinic you use to rejuve in."

"Sorry about your people," Paula said.

"Thank you." Nelson's expression hardened. "They'll be relifed, of course. Everyone on the plane will be, no matter what their insurance status. We owe them that much."

"We'd appreciate a complete list of passengers," Aidan said. "I need to know the full make up of the entourage to help recovery."

"You've got it. I'll liaise with the other Dynasties for you."

The four of them stood together, watching the methodical movements of the forensic duo and the pack of specialist bots.

"So what's the story with your three?" Paula asked. "Anyone special?"

"Hell no," Nelson said. "They're fifth and sixth generation. Standard issue brats who were busy pissing away their trust funds. Never done a day's work in their life. Honestly, the new generations are a real disaster area. As far as I know it was the same for the Brandt boy and the Mandela. There was nothing important about them other than they're Dynasty and goddamn easy targets."

"They were important in terms of propaganda for Free Merioneth," Christabel said.

"Yeah. All this crap about their taxes paying for little tits like our useless descendents is hitting a nerve. You know how financially integrated the Commonwealth planets are. It costs a frigging fortune just to begin settlement these days, and as to building up a decent technoindustrial infrastructure, well... Any planet starting up today is looking to be paying off those costs for the next two and a half centuries—minimum."

"And the Dynasties control the finance houses," Paula observed.

"Along with Earth's Grand Families," Nelson said in a defensive tone. "They haven't been targeted, please note. Not yet, anyway."

"So the start-up costs go back to you, along with interest payments."

"That's the way the universe works, Investigator."

"I can see the emotive force behind targeting the young Dynasty members. We've all seen their antics, or accessed unisphere reports on it. There's not a lot of sympathy out there for them."

"The rich never have any sympathy," Nelson said. "I can live with that. But it doesn't mean you can go around slaughtering them—us!—to advance your political goal. In any case, there were only five Dynasty members on that plane, out of a hundred and thirty people."

"I wasn't agreeing with them," Paula said. "I'm just trying to understand the motivation."

"I'd have said it was justification not motivation," Aidan said. They all turned to look at him. He shrugged. "Everyone knows they're not going to win, right? 'Government does not negotiate with terrorists.' That's been public policy number one since before people ever left Earth. It's not going to change now. So this is just an excuse to give your psychosis full head. Serial killing taken to the next level."

"Could be," Paula said cautiously. Something about the case was bothering her. As Aidan said, the motivation wasn't quite right. But as to the result of Free Merioneth's actions, there was no mistake. Their criminality was her primary concern. Her motivation. Which was unbreakable. Her mindset was aligned through psychoneural profiling; a genetic science comprehensively banned throughout the Commonwealth. The resolution of justice was built into her genes, along with a few other little traits like obsessive compulsive behaviour, which people were extremely uncomfortable with. Paula wasn't. She'd always been perfectly content with what she was. She also quite enjoyed the irony of being a senior Commonwealth law enforcement officer, whilst technically being illegal on every planet except one—her birthworld, Huxley's Haven. Or as the rest of the Commonwealth called it: The Hive.

"Found something," Nalcol called. He was kneeling beside a tough-looking wizened bush cacti, touching the ground with peripheral sensors on his array. Three of the bots were stationary next to the plant's stem, probing its leathery skin. "Could be a urine patch," he said as they gathered round. "Someone from the missile team probably relieved themselves." He pushed a long transparent probe deeper, collecting samples in its spoon-shaped tip.

"Are you certain?" Paula couldn't see any hint of moisture in the crumbly ochre soil. *But then, why send a human out here when a bot is perfectly capable of firing a missile?*

"This goddamned sun," Nalcol complained. "It's evaporating the fluid rapidly, which is how we detected it. The effervescence cloud is distinct to our sensors. But it doesn't leave much to work with." Various graphic displays danced across the array's little screen. "Yep, here we go. Viable DNA. I can get you a positive fingerprint from this."

"Thanks," Christabel said. "What about the missile exhaust?"

"Definite. It's an oxidized carbon trace, with aluminium and several other accelerant compounds."

"What type?"

"All I can tell you is: very crude. No one reported seeing a chemical exhaust, not at altitude, so I'm guessing it incorporated a basic hyper-ram. An intake nozzle that compresses air which is then heated with electron injection or high-frequency induction before squirting that hot air out the back like a rocket exhaust. But you need a booster to get it up to operational speed to start with. Solid chemicals are a primitive but effective method of initial acceleration. Nobody builds that kind of thing anymore. At least, not the commercial armament companies."

"You mean it was homemade?" Nelson asked.

"Probably. Most of the components you'd need are widely available. It just needs a bit of skill to put them together."

"That would take some organization."

"Fanatics do that well," Paula said. "But surely a beam weapon would be more effective, and completely untraceable? Every planet in the Commonwealth produces them."

Nalcol stared up into the hot sky. "Not for this range. That kind of power rating is more specialist. Easier to trace."

"What did the earlier attacks use?" Aidan asked.

"The first two were booby-trapped cars, with standard augmented explosives," Nelson said. "The third was arson in a block of flats in Leithpool, with the fire escapes sabotaged. That killed twenty-three—and only three were Dynasty."

"Two of whom were Halgarths," Christabel said. "The Merioneth team have moved up a level with this."

"This wasn't a team," Paula said. She was looking down slope to the small waves washing ashore. "You only need one person to launch a missile like this. That gives minimum exposure to the rest of the organization. It's also easier for one person to get out. Aidan, how far are we from Ridgeview by sea?"

He gestured at a distant headland. "About seven miles to the docks, there are some marinas closer, though."

"The terrain between here and the ring road is bad," Paula said. "Even if you were on a dirt bike it would take too long, and there's too much that could go wrong. Fall off, puncture, whatever. Let's pull up the satellite imagery and check for a boat."

THE HELICOPTERS TOOK THEM back to the police situation van. Paula sent Nalcol on to Ridgeview. "If we find a boat, I want samples from it," she told him.

Christabel sat down in front of a spare desktop array as soon as they were back inside the van, and started to call up the satellite images. Paula stood at the back, watching her.

"She's good at this," she told Nelson as she pulled her hat off and dabbed at the sweat on her brow. Her hair was hanging limp against her brow and cheeks. Nelson handed her a cup of water from the cooler tower. They both sipped eagerly as Christabel began flicking through images, muttering instructions to the Directorate's RI. "Thank you for shutting down the station," Paula said quietly.

"The least we could do."

"I do require the suspect to stand trial. That means no unfortunate accidents. I will not permit that."

Nelson was watching one of the screens showing two medics leaning over a bloody chunk of gore, inserting surgical tools. "The Sheldon Dynasty has every confidence in you, Paula. That's official. But the perpetrators must be removed from society. The Dynasty will not have its members picked off in this fashion; ideologues must be made to understand that."

"It will happen. However, I will only be going after the team responsible for the actual attacks. Unless we discover complicity or a funding link with their political wing, the rest of the movement will remain untouched by the Directorate. They have a right to free speech no matter how unpleasant their views."

"I am aware of article one in the constitution, thank you; Nigel helped draft it. Leave the politicians to us."

"I still don't understand the point of it," Paula said. "Merioneth is barely self-sufficient. They need continuing investment. They must know that."

"Ideologues aren't rational people."

"A convenient label for us. But—"

"Got a boat!" Christabel shouted out. Everyone in the van craned for a look at her screens. The satellite image wasn't good. It showed the coast next to the launch site, land and sea dividing the screen in half. A small clump of grey pixels formed a blob in the centre. "Time code checks," Christabel said. "This is fifteen minutes prior to the crash." The image changed as the satellite slid along its orbit, showing the coastline further to the east, there was little overlap; the boat was right on the edge of the screen.

"We're going to lose it," Nelson said. "This satellite is moving too quickly. It won't be overhead after the launch. When's the next pass?"

Christabel consulted a display. "There's another satellite coming up in forty-two minutes. So we've got no coverage during the launch. I guess they worked that out, too."

"I don't need to see them fire the missile," Paula said. "I just needed confirmation it was a boat. Aidan, get me access to every camera in every marina in Ridgeview. I want the image files from fifteen minutes before the launch to now. Find me a boat coming in. If they took a direct route it'll be about twenty minutes after the attack. Christabel, start there."

Aidan slipped into the seat next to Christabel, and used his police authorization to establish links into the city's marinas.

"How many trains left between then and now?" Paula asked Nelson.

"Seven."

"Get the station camera records ready for access."

"Way ahead of you," he grinned. "I'm pulling up passenger carriage camera files as well."

It took Christabel another eight minutes to find a boat mooring at the Larsie marina. A man in a yellow shirt stepped off. "Here we go," she said with a trill of excitement as the camera observed him walk along the wooden quay used by Danney's Boat Hire. She froze an image as he was just short of the camera, revealing the round face of a man in his late forties, with flesh starting to build up under his cheeks and round his chin. Dark skin, with stubble. Thinning grey-brown hair dangled out of his blue cap. His yellow shirt was open at the neck, revealing a dark necklace cord.

"Nalcol, get over to the Larsie marina," Paula said. "We've found the boat. Captain, call up the hire company office, tell them it's impounded. It must not be cleaned."

"You got it," Aidan said.

"Nelson, transfer the station files to our RI, it'll run visual recognition on that face. Christabel, get into the hire company's records. Who paid for the boat?"

"Yes, boss."

The Directorate RI took ninety seconds to review every camera record from the station, running each face through a recognition program to identify the man in the marina.

"There he is," Paula exclaimed contentedly as the largest screen in the situation van showed their suspect strolling down the main platform to a waiting train, still wearing his yellow shirt. The timeline was thirty-seven minutes after the attack. They watched the RI follow him through the cameras until he was sitting in a carriage on an express train heading for Earth. The train moved out of the station.

"Let's go," Paula said.

THE THREE OF THEM took Nelson's helicopter back to the station. There was a train already waiting to leave, packed full of passengers angry at the delay. Paula, Christabel and Nelson hurried into the first class cabin and it left immediately, trundling along the track to the big wormhole generator half a mile beyond the marshalling yard. Once it was through, it made an unscheduled stop at a small service platform in EdenBurg's vast terminal. They transferred over to an express heading for Earth.

Nalcol called as they reached the platform. "DNA match confirmed," he told Paula. "The man on the boat was the one who took a leak at the launch site."

"Send the file back to Paris," she told him. "Find his profile."

"He bought his train ticket with a one-time account," Nelson told them. "Untraceable. But we've followed him through LA galactic. He caught a trans-Earth loop, and got off at Sydney an hour ago. Caught a taxi."

"Leave that to us," Paula said. "The Directorate can track him."

They sat back as the express accelerated out of EdenBurg. Five minutes later it was pulling in to LA Galactic.

"Basker just called," Christabel said. "We've got a positive identification; visual corresponding to DNA. Dimitros Fiech. Address in Sydney. Works for Colliac Fak, a software development company. He's a sales rep so he travels round a lot. Oh get this, Colliac's Leisure Division supplies software to the travel industry, including the resort at Fire Plain."

They left the express and started to run through the vast terminal to the platforms serving the trans-Earth loop. "Mine his background," Paula told Christabel, then put a call into the Directorate's Sydney office. "I want a tactical team armoured up and ready when we arrive. Have a helicopter pick us up at the station."

"Yes ma'am," the duty officer replied. "The suspect's taxi dropped him at the Wilkinson Tower off Penfold. We have two officers there now. As far as we know he's still inside."

"Good work, we'll be there in fifteen minutes."

"I'd like to observe, please," Nelson said.

"Yes," Paula said. "But that's all."

"I know."

THE LOOP TRAIN TOOK them to Mexico city followed by Rio, down to Buenos Aires and then over the ocean to Sydney. A Directorate helicopter was sitting on the station security division pad, rotors spinning idly.

Paula and Christabel started putting on their armour as it lifted into the dark sky cloaking the city. Nelson watched enviously.

"If you do need back up…" he said.

"Then the city police will be happy to provide it," Paula said.

He sighed and gave up.

The ancient harbour bridge was illuminated in orange and blue holographic outlines as they flew in parallel to it. A wall of skyscrapers punctured the cityscape behind Circular Quay, their surface illuminations throwing cold monochrome light down onto the deserted nighttime streets below. They landed on the roof of the fifty storey Wilkinson Tower. Five of the Directorate's tactical team were waiting for them.

"Stay here," Paula ordered Nelson as she hopped down onto the roof.

Dimitros Fiech's apartment was on the thirteenth floor, looking inland. The Directorate team were evacuating the residents above and below.

"Fiech is a legend," Christabel said as the lift opened on the thirteenth floor. Three tactical team members were waiting for them, dressed in back armour and holding big ion pistols.

"Basker validates an eighteen month employment record with Colliac Fak, Fiech's CV and general background are false. It'll withstand a standard employment agency search, but our RI burned right through it. Records were inserted, referees are false. He's a genuine undercover agent for someone all right."

"Thanks," Paula said. Her red virtual finger touched a communication icon, opening a secure link to the tactical team. "Be aware, we confirm target is hostile. He has access to weapons, and does not hesitate to open fire. Civilians are not safe. Squad sergeant?"

"Yes ma'am."

"Can you immobilize him?"

"We've got a nerve jangler drone, but we'll have to blow the door open to get it in there. We don't know if it's reinforced."

"Has he rigged the approach?"

"No sensors detected in the corridor."

"All right, let's go. Be careful." Paula called up feeds from the cameras on the suits of the entry team. Seeing jerky images of the corridor as they hurried along. The wooden door to Fiech's apartment was painted a dull green. They gathered round it and quickly rolled an explosive tape along the edges. One camera showed the drone being held ready, a small triangle of grey plastic.

"Go!" the squad sergeant ordered.

The explosive tape detonated, shattering the wooden door. The remnants crashed inwards. Suit sensors went active, cutting through the smoke and dust, producing a sharp black and white image. The drone streaked in. Icons blinked green and amber, showing the nerve jangler field was active. Theoretically it would stun Fiech's nervous system, giving the team time to get in and cover him before he could go for any weapons. Unless he was ready and protected.

The icons turned blue and the entry team charged in. Fiech was sprawled on a couch in the living room, still wearing the yellow shirt Paula had seen through so many camera images. His head was flung back, hanging over the edge of the cushions as his limbs shook from the aftermath of the jangle. Drool leaked out of his gaping mouth.

Paula was running down the corridor, turning the corner. The wreckage of the door was in front of her. Four more team members were charging through it into the apartment. She followed them in. Fiech was still spread out across the couch. One of the suited figures was pressing an ion pistol to his temple. The second was providing cover. The remainder spread out through the apartment, guns held ready, sensors on full power, scanning ahead.

"Clear," the squad sergeant called.

Fiech was given a full deep scan. His body had a few inserts and a couple of OCtattoos, simple unisphere interfaces and a standard memorycell, none of them combat grade. They turned him over and secured his wrists. Two ion pistols remained trained on him. He was white and shaking now, on the verge of vomiting.

Paula removed her helmet, shaking out her hair. Fiech gave her a terrified stare.

"It's going to be rough on you," Paula said. "Even if you cooperate, memory reading is never pleasant. But if you give us the names and structure of your movement we can keep it to a minimum. We'll just verify your information. Trust me, it's worth it."

Fiech started sobbing, tears tricking down his cheeks. "What the fuck is happening?" he wailed. "What is going on?"

Paula gave him a contemptuous look. She'd expected more professionalism. "Take him down to the office. Prep him for a memory read. I'll run it myself."

A whimpering Fiech was dragged past her. Christabel came into the apartment, taking her helmet off to look round. "I'll get forensics in, rip this place apart."

"Sure." A formality, Paula knew. The apartment was part of his cover, it'd be clean.

"Hell of a first day back, boss. What are you going to do tomorrow?"

WHAT I KNOW HAPPENED

I WAS UP EARLY that morning, just like bloody always these days. Damn company is squeezing its staff to husks, always raising our performance targets. You can't keep doing that year after year, people can only do so much.

Anyway...the first wave of commuters were buzzing about on the streets when I left the tower lobby. Poor bastards. Just like me. Squeezed on all sides. You can see it in their null expressions. All that effort and angst etched into their faces, and it was only five past seven.

I walked down O'Connal street to the underground metro station. It's steep ground just behind Sydney harbour, and the skyscrapers are so high you don't see sunlight that time of the morning. Some of my fellow sufferers were gulping down Bean There coffee from plastic cups. I hate that. Food on the run gives me really bad indigestion.

The metro station has a direct line to the CST station on the south side of the city. It took eleven minutes. Three longer than usual. Every bugger is conspiring to make my life worse.

I missed the first train to Wessex. Typical. So I waited on the big platform, with its white wing roof. Me and two hundred others. Time was I used to be excited just being in CST's Sydney station. Think of it. Out there past the end of the platform there's eighteen wormhole generators, each one with tracks leading to a different phase one world. One line goes to Wessex, the junction to phase two space, with another twelve worlds beyond that. They're going to open five more in the next three years. All that opportunity, the potential out there, and what does my life amount to? Bugger all. Corporate drone, that's me. Worlds aren't new starts and fresh hope, all that crap in the brochures. I've been to all of them. They're just more developments that I've got to flog Colliac Fak's bloody software to. We're covering every H-congruous planet in the galaxy with concrete; building little nests with a window we can look at the neighbouring squalid skyscraper with. Yeah, we're a really progressive species, us humans.

So I got the next train to Wessex. Standard class coach, and I just managed to grab a seat next to a window. Beat some woman to it, who looked real pissed at me when I slipped in ahead of her. *Gotta learn, lady. Survival of the fittest on this route. Every route, every day.*

The Wessex station made its Sydney cousin look small. Three big passenger terminals with gold and scarlet roofs curving high over twenty platforms apiece, you could probably fit my apartment skyscraper inside one of them. And a marshalling yard that sprawled over fifteen square miles, a giant zoo of cybernetic machines and warehouses.

I had to switch terminals for the train out to Ormal. That's a five minute trip on a pedwalk, then I had to find the right platform. The insert that provides my virtual vision has interface problems now, so the guidance icons I was picking up from the station management array were blurred. Nearly misread the damn thing. Finished up on platform 11B waiting with a big crowd for the train. These people weren't so stressed and desperate as the ones back in Sydney. More prosperous types, with suits a lot more expensive than mine. They had neat little leather designer arrays edged in gold or platinum tucked into the top pockets. You could see their fingers flicking about minutely as they shunted icons around their high-rez virtual vision. I even saw a few of those new OCtattoos, the ones that light up, tracing colourful lines across their skin. One woman had green and blue spirals on her cheeks.

The carriage wasn't so crowded, so I got a seat by a window again. I guess most of my fellow travellers were up in first class. Trip to Ormal was a simple eight minutes. We rolled out from the end of the platform and across the marshalling yard. I could see the row of wormhole generators up ahead like a metallic cliff, bloody huge great rectangular buildings side by side with a wormhole gateway at the end, like the mouth of an old-fashioned train tunnel. Only these ones had light shining out of them; alien suns spreading a multitude of subtle shades across the rusting jumble of the marshalling yard.

Our train headed straight for a pink-tinged hole, and I felt the tingle of the pressure curtain across my skin as we passed through. Then we were rolling along a couple of miles of track surrounded by open countryside with strange bulbous grey and white trees before we reached the CST planetary station.

Harwood's Hill, the capital, was small, barely half a million people. But it was beautiful, one of those places which had banned combustion engines. It was spread across a big slope that rose up out of a freshwater sea, with green spaces outnumbering buildings five to one. If I could afford it, I'd probably move there. You knew this world was making an effort to get things *right*. But it cost to grab a chunk of a dormitory planet for the upper-middle classes. For Christ's sake, real estate here was more expensive than back on Earth.

My train had arrived late evening. I took a taxi out to the airport using the company card. Even the taxi cost more than the return train fare. I watched the yachts out on the lake, trying not to be all sour and envious, there must have been hundreds coming in to port, their sails all lit up by the sinking sun. Didn't anyone in the city work?

The flight to Essendyne was another three hours. At the other end, the airport was little more than a flat patch of grass with a strip of enzyme-bonded concrete down the middle like it was left over from an experimental road building project.

Essendyne itself was a little town of stylish houses at the end of a valley. The surrounding mountains were impressive, too. In winter they have over a metre of snow. It is perfect for skiers.

I took another taxi out to the resort, a forty minute ride. The place was only half-finished, with the main building a mass of scaffolding crawling with construction bots. Some of the cabins had roofs, but the insides weren't fitted. I got that shitty sinking feeling as soon as we arrived. The office had told me the whole thing was in its final stage of completion, with the staff busy getting ready for guests. All that was left to do was a bit of landscaping. Complete crap.

The taxi dropped me outside the site manager's office. She wasn't available, some crisis out there among the scaffolding with a malfunctioning bot. Her assistant had the grace to look embarrassed as he explained that the hand-over date had been put back three months. It was difficult to get the materials out to Essendyne from the nearest train station, two hours drive away along a narrow road. No one from the resort company was even on site, let alone available to meet me.

Fucking pricks! Nobody back in Sydney had even bothered to check. Bastard scum! So I'd wasted an entire day on a trip to a client that didn't even exist yet. I wanted to bill the dicks back home for the commission I'd lost and the expenses I'd built up.

The taxi took me back to the airport. And of course the plane back to Harwood's Hill didn't leave for another five hours. I hit the bar in the concourse—grand way to describe a hut with a glass wall. After an hour, when the anger was really peaking, I called Sydney and told the dick of an office manager what I thought of him. I didn't wait for him to say anything back, I cut the channel and got my e-butler to block all incoming calls. There was a seafood bistro next to the bar. I went in and tried some of the local food. Not bad. Waitress was kind of pretty, too. Then I went back to the bar.

I remember one of the stewardesses helping me onto the plane. Great looking chick with flaming red hair and a cute smile. I told her so, too. Then we took off and I was poorly. She helped clean it up. I slept the rest of the flight.

Harwood's Hill was a grind. Strange city, small hours of the morning, with a mother monster hangover. Took a taxi to the CST station. Managed to find a little store that was still open and bought some cleaner tabs. I don't take them often, they're worse than the hangover if you ask me. But they do only last an hour before your body stabilizes. I was back in Sydney by then. Cold, depressed, with bones that ached. Couldn't eat, and felt real hungry thanks to the cleaners. And absolutely fuck all to show for my time.

I went home. Bugger the expense, I took a taxi. I was kind of surprised my company card was still working by then. You know I thought that was my low point. Then the bloody next thing I know, the police are blowing up my door. I don't know what they hit me with when they stormed in, but it was like my whole body was on fire. I just wanted to die. I mean, how could the universe do this to me?

WHAT THE COURT DECIDED

IT WAS THE BIGGEST case ever to be heard in a Nova Zealand court; in fact it was the biggest anything to happen on Nova Zealand, period. Reporters from every unisphere news show flooded into Ridgeview, with their companies block booking entire hotels. Those unable to snag a room had to park their mobile homes on the ring road where they were jostled by curious camels brought to the planet by Bedouins eager to recreate their ancient culture out in the freedom of the vast deserts. While in town, the narrow streets with their broad white canvas awnings rapidly became clogged by giant mobile studio trucks.

Paula was given a room in the city Attorney's office. It was cramped, with desks shoved against the wall, and a noisy water tower, but better than trying to catch a train in each day.

When the case was opened in front of judge Jeroen, Paula was surprised when the defence lawyer, Ms Toi entered a plea of not guilty.

"Is she going for some kind of technicality?" Paula whispered to Stephan Dorge, the Directorate's prosecutor.

"I don't see how," he whispered back. "They didn't ask for a deal."

"What about the memory deposition?"

"Nah, we can prove it's an implant."

When Paula looked at Ms Toi, she thought the lawyer seemed uncomfortable.

Prosecution opened with the forensic evidence from the launch site. The DNA match between Dimitros Fiech and the urine sample. Skin analysis taken at the Directorate's Sydney office immediately after the arrest revealed traces of the missile's chemical rocket booster exhaust on his arms and face; there were also plume traces on his yellow shirt. The jury was shown camera pictures from the Larsie marina and Ridgeview's CST station. Additional corroboration was skin cell DNA taken from the boat.

"The evidence which places Dimitros Fiech at the launch site is incontrovertible," Stephan Dorge concluded. "He fired the missile which killed a hundred and thirty eight people. And for what? To push his perverted ideological platform."

In the docks, Dimitros Fiech shook his head in disbelief.

Defence called Paula Myo. "I'd like to concentrate on the deposition of Dimitros Fiech's memory on the day concerned?" Ms Toi asked. "You ran the memory read yourself, did you not?"

"I did," Paula said. "They contained no recollection of the missile launch. We believe false memories of his day on Ormal were inserted at the same time his true memory of the attack was erased."

"False memories? You mean someone created them in a studio like a Full Sensory drama?"

"No. An accomplice went to Ormal in his place to provide an alibi. That experience was recorded, then loaded into Fiech's brain."

"You believe someone like the defendant went to Ormal. How do you know it wasn't him?"

"Because he was on Nova Zealand firing the missile."

"But the person, the *personality,* sitting here in this courtroom today did not fire the missile, did he?"

Paula gave the defence lawyer a small smile. "Nice try. The defendant's personality arranged for the current memory to be implanted, therefore he is what he wants to be."

"But what he is now is not the original personality?"

"Who knows? There is no test that I'm aware of for identifying personality; in any case as any first-year psychology student will tell you, personality is fluid, it changes as you age, some say it matures. Just because you don't remember committing a crime, doesn't mean you're innocent of it. That precedent was established when the first memory erasure techniques were developed. The Justice Directorate suspension chambers are full of criminals who removed inconvenient incriminating memories. I'd point out that Fiech has erased his entire life prior to joining the Colliac Fak company; which has very neatly blocked our investigation into the Free Merioneth Movement, and we all know what that's led to in the last six months. To me such behaviour is the personality trait of a real fanatic."

"Objection," Ms Toi exclaimed. "Speculation. I want that struck from the record."

"You asked for my opinion on his personality," Paula countered.

"I'll allow it to stand for the moment," Judge Jeroen said. "It was a legitimate answer to your line of questioning, defence."

"Your honour," Ms Toi bowed to the judge. "Investigator, you said that memory erasure is common when a crime has been committed."

"That is correct."

"Have you ever known alternative memory for the time of the crime to be implanted?"

"I haven't come across it before, although the technique is relatively straightforward. You just need a colleague like the one Fiech had to record his day."

"So if I implanted the memory of firing the missile into your brain, would that make you guilty?"

"No. Because I didn't do it. The rest of the physical evidence would support that."

"So in fact, Investigator, this boils down to two sets of opposing evidence. Both equally valid."

"Valid but not of equal credibility. That is correct."

"Please describe to the court the efforts which you undertook to establish that the person on Ormal was not Dimitros Fiech."

"I retraced the route myself, and interviewed everyone he remembered encountering. Security camera images were recovered and analysed."

"What did they show?"

"A man with similar facial features to Dimitros Fiech travelled to Ormal. We assumed he underwent a cellular reprofiling treatment."

"But you can't prove it. The man sitting here in the dock could have been the one on Ormal, and his made-up doppelganger could have fired the missile on Nova Zealand. Am I right?"

"No. Under my instruction, a Directorate forensic officer analysed the seat cover on the plane which flew from Essendyne back to Harwood's Hill. It had been cleaned, but we found large traces of vomit containing DNA. It did not correspond to Dimitros Fiech's DNA, yet it was the seat he remembers using and being sick on. It wasn't him on Ormal."

Ms Toi gave Paula a startled look. "I see. Thank you, Investigator."

"No!" Dimitros Fiech yelled. "No, you can't believe that. I didn't do it. Damn you, I didn't." He turned to the jury and gave them a wild stare. "It wasn't me. I wasn't there. I know I wasn't."

Judge Jeroen banged his gavel. "Be seated Mr Fiech."

"I'm being framed." He turned to Ms Toi. "Do something!"

She winced.

Paula quietly left the witness stand as Fiech continued his tirade. Two large court officers moved forwards into the dock as the judge banged his gavel repeatedly.

AFTER ANOTHER DAY AND a half of evidence the jury retired. They took an hour to reach their verdict of guilty. Judge Jeroen sentenced Dimitros Fiech to two-thousand-seven-hundred-and-sixty years life suspension, twenty years for each of the people who suffered bodyloss in the crash.

PAULA WAS PACKING HER bag when Aidan Winkal rapped his knuckles on the office door. "Hello," she said.

He grinned. "I just came to say goodbye."

"That's very kind of you, Aidan. You've handled yourself well while we were putting this case together, and I know this hasn't been easy. I expect your Chief will be promoting you."

"Probably. I gather Christabel got her promotion."

"Yes. Chief Investigator at last. I'll miss her. There'll be a party in Paris tonight when we get back. You're welcome to join us."

He scratched at his short hair. "Go to Paris just for a party. That's a real city dweller thing. An Earth city."

"Come on, you're not such a small town boy. I'd dance with you."

"I can't believe how thorough you were. I really thought the defence was going to nail you with that question about evidence from Ormal. I guess she didn't realize how methodical you are."

Paula shrugged and dropped her spare jacket into the bag. "It's what I do. I have to be certain for myself. And Ms Toi should have known, I'm notorious enough for my diligence. He was badly represented."

"So you're convinced he did it?"

"The Dimitros Fiech sitting in the dock this morning was the physical person who launched the missile, I have no doubt of that."

"Now there you go, see: a real lawyer's answer."

"I concede defence did have a point about what constitutes a whole person. Body and memory are the two halves of being human."

"But Fiech's memory of the attack has been wiped. It's over. We got what we could of him."

She smiled reassuringly. "Yes, we did. And he got the sentence he deserved."

Christabel and Nelson appeared behind Aidan. Neither looked as jubilant as they should have done. Aidan gave Paula an uncomfortable smile. "I'll leave you guys to it."

"Try and get there tonight," Paula told him. "I meant it about that dance."

A sheepish Aidan shuffled out past Christabel who did her best not to laugh at his schoolboyish delight.

"Is he really your type?" Christabel asked.

"I don't have a type," Paula said. "But he is an honest policeman. I value that."

Nelson looked at Christabel then Paula. Took a breath. "Anyway… I'm also here to deliver my Dynasty's thanks. We appreciate the effort involved in securing the verdict."

"You're welcome," Paula said. "It's a shame we couldn't use Fiech to uncover his co-conspirators, but that memory wipe was very efficient. There is nothing left of his life prior to his arrival in Sydney for that job. Until we finally arrest the entire Free Merioneth Forces we're not going to find out who he is."

"Was," Christabel corrected.

Nelson's expression turned bitter. He made a show of closing the door. "That's unlikely to happen. Not now."

"What do you mean?" Christabel asked.

"Confidentially: my Dynasty along with several others has agreed Merioneth will become an Isolated world."

Paula let out a hiss of exasperation. She'd suspected something like this would happen. The last few months while they'd assembled the case against Dimitros Fiech had seen the Free Merioneth campaign expand to alarming proportions. After the Nova Zealand plane, the movement had been steadily refining their operations, developing into more sophisticated assassins. The results were dramatic. Their targets were now dispatched with cool efficiency, and the number of collateral casualties was significantly reduced. In the last twelve attacks, thirty-nine Dynasty members had suffered complete bodyloss. The new generations were now running very scared, with few of them leaving their mansions on the private family worlds. "You gave in," she said in frustration.

"We couldn't afford it," Nelson said with equal chagrin. "The cost of providing upgraded security for every member of every Dynasty was completely unrealistic. Far beyond writing off the investment costs in Merioneth."

"There's more at stake here than money," an annoyed Christabel snapped.

"I know that," Nelson said. "Of course, it won't appear to be any kind of climb down. We wouldn't allow that. We negotiated the terms of Isolation with the new Nationalist Party that sprung up on Merioneth. The terrorists stop their attacks, and in a couple of years we close the wormhole. They'll be on their own. Forever."

"It'll come back to bite you," Paula said. "You've shown your opponents a weakness. It can be used every time someone wants a concession out of a Dynasty."

"That was one of the reasons we agreed," Nelson said.

"I don't understand."

"We don't have other opponents, not in this category. The Intersolar Commonwealth is a relatively civilized place. Sure we can all disagree with each other; politicians on half of the planets we've got aren't speaking to the other half, but there's only a tiny minority who want to leave, and an even smaller number who resort to violence to obtain their ends. This whole succession notion is ridiculous. An Isolated planet will never benefit from the advances the rest of us make. Their social and economic development will be stunted, hell, Merioneth will probably regress. When we announce the wormhole is to be closed we're expecting a lot of its ordinary residents will rush back to the Commonwealth before Isolation begins. Our analysts have reviewed this; they're not sure Merioneth will even be able to maintain basic rejuvenation technology levels, not in the short-to-medium term. I sure as hell wouldn't want to live there. Bodyloss will become death again."

"And the Dynasties consider that a big plus point," Christabel reasoned. "Anyone who doesn't like the Dynasties and what they represent will be free to emigrate to Merioneth."

"Then we slam the door shut behind them," Nelson said. "It's a bolt hole for malcontents the Commonwealth over. Everyone is better off afterwards."

"An old fashioned pressure valve for hotheads," Paula muttered.

"So the Dynasty leaders decided," he admitted. "It still galls me that the real culprits behind the attacks won't be brought to justice. But that's a political price, and it gets set far above our heads."

THE CLUB WAS UNDERNEATH a twenty-second century retro-Napoleonic building on the Left Bank. It was chic enough, though there were far more expensive places in Paris, but aside from Christabel herself no one from the Serious Crimes Directorate office could afford an evening partying with the truly wealthy Grand Family members who colonized such establishments—and Christabel never pushed her heritage on anyone. Until tonight.

It was dark inside the annular vault, a gloom punctured by holographic blobs oscillating with naughty subliminal vibrations. Paula flinched as she walked down the stairs to the floor, the sound system was like a de-rated sonic weapon. Glass galleries enlivened by violet light ran round the high stone walls at two levels, linked by curving glass stairs. People thronged along them, Paris's eternal clique of bohemians, wearing clothes of semiorganic fabric embossed with elaborate patterns that merged seamlessly into the vivid OCtattoos on their skin. It was hard to tell what was fabric and what was flesh. Feathers were the current merging trend, curving fronds longer than ostrich quills that sprouted from the spine. Six months ago it had been membrane petals. Several men displayed their plumage as Paula walked by, having it fan out on either side of their shoulders like wings. One was pure angel white, with a divine body to match. She smiled modestly and walked on, immune to such raffish peacocks.

Christabel was close to the bar inside the central circle of pillars, knocking back a tall glass of Ritz Pimms. Her lips were microlayered gold. Whenever a hologram floated across her they sparkled dazzlingly.

"You made it!" she shouted at Paula.

Paula snagged a glass from a waitress. "Cheers!"

"Is he here?"

Paula shrugged, pretending not to understand. But there was a specific reason she was wearing a traditional little black dress with a semi-organic hem that swirled about of its own volition. In her newly youthful body it made her look hot, and she knew it. Several junior Investigators were staring in a way they'd never dare back at the office. "Congratulations," Paula said. "Traitor."

Christabel laughed. "I've served my time. And I made Chief Investigator on merit alone. That's what I needed. For myself if not the Dynasty."

"You'll be a loss to the Directorate."

Christabel leaned in a fraction. "The Dynasty is going to need me. Our entire concept of security is going to have to be revised thanks to our idiot founders giving in to Merioneth. I heard that everyone is now pouring funds into researching personal-sized force fields generators. And they're all beefing up the defences on our private worlds."

"Typical. So am I allowed to ask what department you're joining?"

"Deputy-manager EdenBurg protection."

"Wow. Big field."

"Yeah. Give me a couple of decades and I'll make it to chief of the division. After that..." she trailed off and drained her glass.

"You'll be locking horns with Nelson."

"Nhaaa. He's too smart. We'll get on, at that level you have to."

"Speaking of which—"

"Of course. We'll dataswap. Happy to. Unless dear old grandma Heather actually kills someone—then I'll be helping to cover her arse."

"It's not your Dynasty's founder I'm interested in."

"Oh?" Christabel plucked another glass from the bar.

Paula thought she looked defensive. *How quickly alliances shift.* "If you get the chance to access your Dynasty's file on the Merioneth Isolation, I'd appreciate a summary."

"That kind of thing never gets put in a file, as you well know. What are you looking for? We got Fiech, for God's sake. Two and a half millennia in oblivion! It doesn't get better than that."

"Why did he do it?"

"What?"

"I don't understand his motivation."

"To liberate Merioneth from Dynasty oppression," Christabel recited viciously. "And the bastards won."

"Yes, they did, but Fiech didn't. He was utterly committed to his cause, so much so that he perpetrates one of the worst atrocities in modern history. One which almost killed his precious movement stone dead. People were repelled by what he did, even his old colleagues realized that was too much, which is why they quickly got professional. That's how they won. Continuing to wipe out the Dynasty kids and keep bystander bodyloss to an absolute minimum was smart. It bought pressure to bear exactly where it was needed. Yet Fiech will never see the end result, he'll never live on his free, liberated Merioneth. Motivated people simply don't commit suicide, which is effectively what he's done. By the time he comes out of suspension, the Commonwealth won't be recognizable, even if it still exists. Damnit, we'll probably all be post-physical by then. He's sacrificed himself for something he'll never know. That does not make any sense."

"Fanatics never make any real sense to anyone except themselves. Don't look for logic here, you'll only be disappointed."

"There *was* logic behind this, I just don't understand it yet. And that bothers me, it means we've overlooked something.

Whoever set this up expended a huge amount of effort. The Directorate ran checks on every planetary medical database in the Commonwealth, nobody has any record of the doppelganger's DNA, which is extremely unusual for this day and age. The nearest we can do is identify family traits; he has ancestry within a mix of Celtic, Northern Spanish and Saudi ethnicities. We found what we believe is a possible cousin on Piura, it was certainly the closest genetic match. But the poor girl didn't recognize Dimitros. I ran her family tree as best I could, but if he's on it I couldn't tell. We just don't know who he is. If we can't find out, then he's either the most important man in the Merioneth independence movement, or an absolute nobody. I don't believe either."

"Maybe you're right with the first one, and his pals in the Free Merioneth Forces are planning on springing him out of suspension just before CST shuts the wormhole."

"Not going to happen. Nothing and nobody can break into the Justice Directorate suspension facility."

"So what are you going to do?"

Paula saw a nervous-looking Aidan appear at the top of the stairs. She smiled. "What I always do; keep the file open, solve the case properly."

Christabel followed her gaze. "Of course, you always get your man."

"Yes. Always."

WHAT PAULA FOUND OUT

NELSON SHELDON WAS RIGHT about the timing. Twenty-one months after Fiech's court case, and three weeks after a planetary referendum officially denounced as a shambolic farce by Intersolar observers, the Senator from Merioneth stood up in the Commonwealth Senate to declare that her planet was regretfully withdrawing from the Intersolar Commonwealth to 'pursue our future independently'. The Speaker wished her well, and there was a chilly silence as the Merioneth delegation dramatically walked out of the full chamber. CST immediately announced that the wormhole link to Merioneth would be withdrawn in three months, leaving enough time for anyone on the planet who didn't wish to be Isolated to return to the Commonwealth.

Out of a population of seventeen million, the number wanting to remain part of the Commonwealth was just over nine million. It took an awful lot of trains running round the clock to bring them out. Which made travel to Merioneth extremely easy, with an inbound train arriving every ten minutes. When Paula caught a train to Baransly, the capital, three weeks before the wormhole was due to be shut she was the only passenger in first class. Most of the carriages were vehicle carriers. Émigrés favoured big trucks crammed full with their possessions. Local shipping companies were charging a fortune to transport containers of larger items. And the emergent national government was getting difficult about letting industrial machinery leave. The latest batch of restrictions covered all types of agribots; a lot of farmers were heading back to the Commonwealth.

Paula stared out of the long window as they emerged through the wormhole's pressure curtain. It was winter outside, with flecks of snow drifting through an iron-grey sky. The landscape here outside the capital was arranged into neat fields given over entirely to row after row of some vine equivalent; with brown leafless stems stretched along wire frames. Hundreds of small agribots rolled slowly down the lines, their plyplastic tentacles pruning the vines back to their regulation two-metre length.

Baransly itself was a sprawl of housing estates and industrial zones clustered round a commercial centre that had already started to put up skyscrapers. The architecture was a little bleak and functional perhaps, but the city's size was an excellent example of successful development for a world that had only been open to settlement for eighty years.

By the time the train reached the marshalling yard outside the station, there were signs of law and order beginning to break down. Streets were clogged with abandoned cars and vans. The crates and boxes that they'd carried were now strewn everywhere, broken open to spill their contents onto the icy enzyme-bonded concrete. It was as if the goods of a hundred department stores had been scattered across the district by a real live cargo cult god. Gangs of kids and some adults were foraging the bounty. Then the train drew into the marshalling yard itself, and Paula's view of the city vanished behind walls of metal containers stacked taller than the surrounding buildings, all waiting shipment out. Men in thick jackets with the Merioneth Nationalist Party logo on their sleeves patrolled the aisles.

The train drew in at one of the ten platforms under the cover of a sweeping green crystal canopy. Every square metre of the platforms and concourse was occupied by a bad tempered crowd. Armour-clad CST security guards patrolled along narrow clearways, their jangler guns carried prominently.

Paula slipped off the carriage to be greeted by Byron Lacrosh, chief aide to the Prime Minister, Svein Moalem, who was also leader of the Merioneth Nationalist Party. Byron and an armed police escort guided her down one of the clearways. A large limousine took them from the CST station to the Parliament building along roads that were still being cleared of discarded vehicles. Every few minutes they passed crews of men and bots lifting cars onto big tow-trucks.

"You won't need to worry about mining any new metal for a few years," Paula observed.

"Material resources aren't our prime concern," Byron Lacrosh said. "We hope to establish a culture which isn't as technology-based as the Commonwealth."

"You're going to go the agrarian route?"

"We favour divorcing ourselves from the consumerist monoculture that dominates the Dynasty-ruled worlds, yes. We don't shun technology, we just don't see the necessity to incorporate it in every aspect of life."

"Appropriate sustainability, then?"

Byron gave her an interested look. "You understand the philosophy?"

"It's hardly new. My birthworld is based on it."

"Oh yes, of course. I'd forgotten where you came from, Investigator Myo."

The Parliament building was a concrete and glass monstrosity, intended as a vigorous statement of a new planet's identity and prosperity. The result was the kind of design-by-bureaucrat-committee that Paula always found depressing, representing the exact opposite of the ethos it had originally been commissioned to promote.

Svein Moalem's office was on the fifth floor, with a curving glass wall that opened onto the hanging rose garden—famous locally for its cost overruns and leaky troughs. He sat behind a dark desk made from native kajawood. A broad-shouldered man ten years out of rejuvenation, with a neatly trimmed beard—following current local tradition. His light-blue eyes were strongly contrasted with dark skin and mousy hair. Paula saw tiny luminescent green lines flickering along his cheeks to curve round the back of his neck. More OCtattoos shone on his hands. When she ordered her inserts to scan the office she found a considerable amount of encrypted electromagnetic traffic emanating from him, to be exact the necklace of flat opals he wore. It was the kind of emission level she usually associated with sensory drama actors, allowing the unisphere audience to experience their body's sensations. The two people, a man and a woman, sitting in front of his desk were also broadcasting an unusually large amount of data, from similar necklace arrays. Paula suspected every aspect of her interview was to be recorded and analysed. A high capacity cybersphere node was discreetly incorporated into the floor to ceiling bookcase behind the desk, but apart from that and several security sensors she couldn't detect any other active hardware. Not that she expected any weapons to be active.

"Thank you for agreeing to see me, Prime Minister," she said.

Svein Moalem nodded graciously, but didn't get up. He gestured to an empty chair directly in front of his desk. "I asked for two representatives from the Attorney General's office to be present."

Paula glanced at the two lawyers flanking her as she sat down. "I'm not here to arrest you. In fact, nobody really knows if the Intersolar Commonwealth has jurisdiction here at the moment. You've declared independence, and we've agreed to recognize it in three weeks time. Anything between those dates is a very grey legal area."

"Yes, but nonetheless they will insure my reputation is protected from unfair allegations."

"Allegations are for tabloid shows. I'm only here to ask questions."

The green lines under Moalem's beard scintillated. "As a friend of the Commonwealth I'm happy to oblige; we have nothing to hide from you. And of course, who can resist your personal notoriety? So let's get started, shall we? I can spare you thirty minutes."

"I am the appointed Investigator for the Dimitros Fiech case. Did you know him, Prime Minister?"

"I know of him, sadly. His misguided organization was one of the main inspirations behind setting up our Nationalist party. Of course, we completely repudiate the use of violence to achieve independence."

"So you didn't know him personally?"

"No. My party's goals were achieved by legitimate democratic ends."

"I accessed the report from the observer team on your referendum. They wouldn't agree."

"Biased vitriol from those who have a vested interest in our continuing dependence and integration with their monoculture."

"Whatever. Fiech and his colleagues proved exceptionally resourceful, and they certainly learned quickly from their mistakes. He is the only member of the Free Merioneth Movement we have apprehended so far. What they did required a large amount of money at the very least. Is your government aware of where that finance originated from?"

"Your pardon, Investigator, but right now the treasury department has more pressing concerns than examining bank transactions from two years ago. Little matters like making sure we have a valid currency in place for the cut off. You understand."

"Their money must have originated here."

"I'm sure you're right. If we find out in the next three weeks, we'll be sure to inform your Directorate."

"Could it have come from the same source as your Party's money?"

"We are not dignifying that with an answer," the female lawyer said sternly.

Svein Moalem gave Paula a small mocking shrug to say *out of my hands.*

"You set up your party after Fiech's organization had already won Isolation from the Dynasties," Paula said.

"Interesting allegation, Investigator." Moalem glanced at the female lawyer. "Do you have proof of this?"

"At the moment I'm purely interested in motives. As someone who embodies the Isolationist dream, can you tell me why Fiech sacrificed himself?"

"I'm sure old Earth history is full of martyrs; all neatly documented if you are that interested. But I suspect he believed as I do. And those who truly believe in the cause of freedom will go to any lengths to see it become reality. I commend his bravery, though of course I cannot condone his method."

"Yet his methods secured your goals."

"They helped focus the imaginations and aspirations of everyone on this planet. He woke us up to the oppression we laboured under."

"I don't believe the people of this planet are inspired by monstrous violence. Over a hundred and thirty people suffered severe bodyloss on the Nova Zealand plane alone. Your citizens would want justice for them and all the others whose blood was spilt."

"Justice, yes. But we equally disapprove of the vengeance we've seen your Directorate unleash."

"Excuse me?"

"Who did you find guilty of the Nova Zealand crime, Investigator? Not the person who pulled the trigger, at least not the whole person. The man you have in your suspension facility lived a different life on that day. Your prisoner is not guilty of bringing down that aircraft. You hold a prisoner of conscience. A patsy whose sole purpose is to satisfy the masses to the benefit of your political masters."

"Dimitros Fiech committed that crime," Paula said, doing her best to hold her temper in check. She knew the Prime Minister was provoking her, trying to throw her off track. "There is no question of that."

"So already we see the difference between your culture's rigid nature and our more liberal, progressive quality. Your laws cannot adapt to new circumstances."

"Fiech's memories are an alibi, nothing more. It's no different to using cellular reprofiling to change your facial features."

"It is completely different; it is his mind. The mind of the person you have suspended knows he was on Ormal during the crime. You said it yourself in the deposition: He knows his office screwed up sending him there, he knows he paid the taxi fare in Harwood's Hill, he was the person who watched the land roll past through the plane's window, he was angry and frustrated when he arrived at the resort, he tasted the vodka at the airport bar, he fancied the redhead stewardess who helped him on the plane, he had the hangover. That was Dimitros Fiech. Nobody else. *His* personality. Him! Your imprudent freedom fighter was someone else."

"Who was erased by his colleagues. And I will find them," Paula growled out. "In order to do that, I need to comprehend the psychology behind all of this. So tell me, help mitigate Dimitros Fiech's sentence: why exactly do you want Isolation? What can you possibly achieve here that requires this drastic severance from the Commonwealth?"

"That's a very long list, Investigator. Starting with removing the contamination of a morally bankrupt, decadent society."

"At the cost of medical benefits? Your industrial capability is going to be reduced drastically."

"Not as much as your propaganda insists. We shall live here peacefully, and progress in our own way. A way not dictated by the Dynasties or the Senate. Many people are attracted to such a notion. Millions, actually. Do you really begrudge us such liberty?"

"No. I just don't see what ideology can't be pursued within the umbrella of the Commonwealth. It is not as oppressive as your party claims, as *you* are well aware. A great many reduced-technology communities flourish on Commonwealth worlds. What you have engineered here is radical. I'm trying to understand its rationale."

Svein Moalem sat back in his chair and gave Paula a thoughtful stare; very much the politician trying to convert another wavering voter. "You of all people struggle to understand? Forgive me, but that is hard to believe."

"Why?"

"You were created and birthed on Huxley's Haven, the most reviled planet in the Commonwealth. How the illiberal classes hated its founding. A world with everyone genetically predisposed to their job, a society in which everybody has a secure place. It is living proof that alternatives can work. Surely that's a concept to be welcomed and admired?"

"Its functionality is admirable. However, even I don't approve of its static nature. Those humans can no longer evolve."

"Yet they live perfectly happy lives."

"Yes," Paula said. "Within the parameters established by the Human Structure Foundation."

"You would want Huxley's Haven broken up and abandoned?" he sounded very surprised.

"Certainly not. Its citizens have a right to their existence. It is pure imperialist arrogance for outsiders to propose alteration."

"You see, Investigator, you make my argument for me. That is your answer. The right to self determination is a human fundamental. Such a thing is not possible while under the financial hegemony of the Dynasties and Grand Families."

"Everything comes down to money in the end," Paula offered.

"Quite."

"I still can't believe some abstract ideology is enough for Fiech to sacrifice himself."

"Hardly abstract," Moalem waved at the city outside. "His wish has become our reality."

Paula pursed her lips, following his gesture. "I hope it's worth it."

"It is."

She stood and gave him a small bow. "Thank you for your time, Prime Minister."

"You're welcome, Investigator. In fact, I'd like to offer you a place here with us. Our police forces will need a substantial reorganization after the cut off. Who better to manage that? You are celebrated and respected on every world in the Commonwealth. Your honesty and devotion to justice have broken the hatred and prejudice barrier. In a way, you are what we aspire to be."

"That's very flattering, but the answer is no."

"Why not? Indulge me, please, I am curious. You left Huxley's Haven. The only one of millions ever to do so. You found the Commonwealth more attractive. Why not us?"

"I didn't leave," Paula said, feeling her shoulder muscles tense up. "I was stolen from my birthing clinic. The political activists who took me wanted to make a point in their campaign to 'liberate' Huxley's Haven. Consequently I was brought up in the Commonwealth. I chose to stay."

"You found it more desirable than the most secure civilization ever established?"

"I was created a police officer; it is what I am. There is more crime in the Commonwealth than on Huxley's Haven, and it is the culture I was brought up in. It was logical for me to stay. Here I would never lack for challenges."

"So the activists were right then? The manufactured people of Huxley's Haven would be able to settle in the Intersolar Commonwealth?"

"They could physically settle. Intellectually, I doubt they would be able to integrate. Myself and other police officers are a very small minority of the population. The exceptions. I understand that after my 'batch' the Foundation changed the psychoneural profiling. Huxley's Haven police officers are no longer as liberal as me," she licked her lips in amusement. "A notion which discomforts the Commonwealth even more. Can you imagine a less forgiving version of me, Prime Minister?"

"That's a tough one, I admit." Finally, he stood, a faint smile on his lips. "Good day, Investigator."

TWO DAYS LATER, PAULA woke up to a call request from Christabel flashing in her virtual vision. She yawned. Stretched. And told her maidbot to bring some tea. Then her virtual finger touched Christabel's green icon.

"You made it back okay," Christabel said. "I heard it's getting tough in Baransly. CST asked for a week's extension before they switch off the wormhole; they're worried they won't be able to get everyone out before the cut off."

"There's a lot of people there," Paula said, remembering the trip back to the CST station, the way her police escort had to force their way to a train for her. "What did the Merioneth government say?"

"No."

"Figures. Moalem has worked hard to reach this moment. He's not going to allow anything to stop it now. Especially now."

"Especially now? Did you get some useful information?"

"Very. He was the alibi memory. Svein Moalem went to Ormal and spent the day living Fiech's life."

"*What?* You've got to be fucking kidding me."

"No. I'm not."

"How do you know that?"

"He fancied a redhead."

"Come on, talk sense to me."

"Moalem told me the stewardess on the plane Fiech flew on from Essendyne back to Harwood's Hill was a redhead. He's right, too." Paula closed her eyes, recalling the memories that didn't belong to her, the ones she'd read from Fiech's brain. Seeing wavery images of the attractive woman in her neat blue and green uniform, Celtic-red hair all tied up with leather clips. Trying to smile as she supported his body up the stairs, and amazingly still calm when she deposited him in his seat and he made a crude drunken pass.

Paula had interviewed the woman a week later as she retraced the alibi, confirming the memory.

"So?" Christabel asked.

"That detail wasn't in the memory deposition filed with the court. I just said a stewardess."

"He could have found out."

Paula pulled the straps of her slip up properly on her shoulders as the maidbot came in with a large breakfast cup of green Assam tea. "Why would he?"

"Because they're obviously all part of the same group of Isolationists. He'd want to know everything connected with the case."

"No, this was a casual detail. I know it was. He was the one on Ormal."

"Oh bloody hell, so now what?"

"Obviously, he has to be arrested. He was a major part of the crime. If he was as deeply involved in the Free Merioneth Forces as I suspect, he could well expose the others with a memory read."

"Not going to happen. There's only two and a half weeks left to Isolation. You'll never get clearance for that. It would take a small army to go in there and arrest their new Prime Minister. Actually...how come you didn't try while you were there? I know you. You cannot stand back."

"I know. It's engineered into my nature. But the probability of a successful outcome if I'd tried to arrest him on the spot was zero. They would simply have eliminated me."

"So natural self-preservation is stronger than the rest of you after all. That's a relief to know."

"It was simply a decision based on common sense. I am going to arrange a meeting with Nelson. He may be able to secure me the return ability I need to complete the case."

"Damn, that's a long shot."

"Yes, but what else have I got? The Directorate won't be able to lift Moalem from Merioneth."

"I wouldn't count on the Sheldons doing it either. The political fallout would be too great. Lifting someone from an Isolated world and making them stand trial here all because they assassinated Dynasty members. That won't look good for the Dynasties, Paula, not politically. Isolation was the end of this, the deal."

"I know, but Nelson is the best option I've got." She sipped some of the tea. "What were you calling me about?"

"I've been digging round where I shouldn't have, as you asked. I'm not sure how relevant this is now, but the Dynasties know who's been backing the whole Merioneth independence movement."

"Who?"

"Now promise you won't shoot the messenger."

Paula grinned and took another sip. "I won't."

"The Human Structure Foundation."

The surprise made her start. "Damnit!" she struggled not to let the tea spill onto the bed.

"You okay?"

"Yes yes." Beside her, Aidan stirred at the commotion.

"Look, I can maybe make some enquiries at this end, see if my Dynasty will go along with a covert extraction. The Free Merioneth Forces hurt a lot of Halgarths. Heather was not happy about giving them Isolation. We could put together an operation with the Sheldons."

"That's more like vengeance," Paula said quietly. "Not due process."

"You're running out of options."

"I know. I need to make a few more enquiries about this. I'll get back to you."

Aidan blinked round, lifting his head off the pillow. "Something wrong?"

"No," she ran her hand through his dishevelled hair. "Early start, that's all. Something unexpected came up. I've got to take a trip."

"Where to now? Other side of the Commonwealth again?"

"The Caribbean, actually."

THE NEAREST CITY ON the trans-Earth loop was New York. When she arrived at the Newark station, Paula took a cab over to JFK and flew a Directorate hypersonic parallel to the east coast then on south to Grenada. The Human Structure Foundation campus occupied a broad stretch of rugged land behind a series of curving beaches whose pale sand was just visible in the low moonlight. A circular white-glass tower formed the centre, silhouetted by liquid bifluron tubes embedded in the structure. The long sodium-orange web of streets radiating out from the base revealed the surrounding village of elaborate bungalows. Foundation members didn't reside in any of the island's ordinary towns; in the last century few ventured out beyond the heavily guarded perimeter strip. It was a micro-nation of genetic ideologues, despised by just about everyone, yet continuing to operate under Senate-imposed research restrictions. Restrictions which had grown ever stronger since the establishment of Huxley's Haven.

Paula was familiar enough with the set up, though she'd never actually visited before. The notion of walking round the place which conceived her—intellectually and physically—was an experience she simply didn't want.

Her plane landed on a circular pad by the tower. Long plyplastic petals unrolled from the edges to form a protective shell over her little craft. An astonishingly attractive woman called Ophelia escorted her up to Dr Friland's office on the top floor of the tower. On the way through the atrium lobby, people stopped and stared at Paula. It was three o'clock in the morning local time; the tower should have been deserted. She was used to attention, but this was akin to religious respect. Some looked like they wanted to bow as she walked past. The effect was unnerving—and she wasn't used to that feeling at all.

"You're the living proof that the concepts for which we stand have been successful," Ophelia murmured as they walked into the lift. "There have been many sacrifices down the decades, so please excuse their wonder."

Paula sucked in her cheeks, unable to meet any of the ardent stares as the lift doors slid shut.

According to his file, Justin Friland was born towards the end of the Twentieth century. Meeting him in the flesh, Paula couldn't tell, and she normally prided herself in spotting the telltale mannerisms of the truly old. He didn't have any. His effusive good-nature matched his handsome adolescent appearance perfectly. Like the Foundation members down in the lobby, he gave Paula an incredulous smile as she came into his office.

"Director, I appreciate you seeing me," Paula said. "Especially at this time of night."

"Not at all, this is an absolute honour," he said, shaking her hand too-vigorously, and beaming a wide smile.

"Thank you," Paula said gently, and removed her hand from his grip.

"I spent twenty-five years on Huxley's Haven helping to establish the birthing centres," Justin Friland said. "And seeing you here is..." he spread his arms out. "Astonishing. We never thought one of you could adapt to life offworld."

"One of *me*?" Paula arched an eyebrow.

"Sorry, sorry! It's just—we took so much shit over the Haven. Even fifty years ago the perimeter here was surrounded by protestors. However, the days of the ten-thousand-strong mob have long gone. We still do have a hard core camped to the side of our main entrance. They're not...*pleasant* people. My thoughts are still in war-mode. My fault."

"I see."

"Please, sit down," he hurried over to a wide couch. "What can I do for you?"

"I need information."

"Whatever I can provide," he was nodding enthusiastically as Paula sat beside him.

"There is a rumour that the Foundation financed Merioneth's Isolation."

"Not us," Friland said emphatically. He brushed some floppy chestnut hair from his forehead. "However, the Foundation has undergone considerable schism during the last quarter century. I now lead what you'd probably call a Conservative faction."

"What of the other factions?"

He sighed. "The person you want to talk to is Svein Moalem."

Paula gave Friland a surprised look. "He's a Foundation member?"

"An ex-colleague, yes. Now the leader of the New Immortals."

"We didn't know that. We don't have access to Merioneth files now."

"Wouldn't have done you any good. The New Immortals have coveted their own planet for some time. They did a lot more than simply finance the Isolation revolution on Merioneth. They infiltrated its civil service quite some time ago. Any records you did access through the unisphere merely say what they want them to say."

"And you didn't feel obliged to tell us this?"

"Us?" Justin Friland smiled faintly.

"The Intersolar Senate. The Serious Crimes Directorate."

"Ah. Your government? No. Pardon me, Paula. I wasn't about to come running to the organization which officially condemned my projects as the work of the devil. Besides, up until they started killing Dynasty members, our Immortal brethren didn't actually do anything illegal. Political shenanigans are perfectly permissible under our oh-so liberal Intersolar constitution. Manipulating public data for ideological ends is common practice. I assume you have better statistics than I do on the subject."

Paula thought about arguing, but decided against. The information might be useful later, if the Directorate decided to press complicity charges against Friland. "The New Immortals?" she asked. "I assume it's a relevant name. What method have they adopted? And why does it need an Isolated world?"

Julian Friland looked distinctly uncomfortable. "It's a modified version of today's re-life memory succession, which eliminates the requirement to rejuvenate a body."

"Thank you. You've just told me nothing."

"If you suffer bodyloss today, your insurance company grows a clone and downloads your secure memory store into it. Many people regard that as death. It's a question of continuity, you see. In rejuvenation, your body simply floats in a tank while its DNA is reset. The you which comes out is still the you which went in a year before, so there's no doubt about originality and identity. What Moalem and his group proposed was operating continuous bodies. A mental relay, if you like, with a personality twinned between an old and young version of the same person."

"So when the old physical body dies, the young one carries on."

"With continuity intact," Friland emphasised. "I acknowledge the concept is an elegant one."

"Not entirely original," Paula said, thinking about the emissions she'd detected coming from Moalem. She frowned, trying to follow the idea through to its conclusion. "Surely the two bodies would have to be close together. If they started to diverge, see and react to different things, then the personality would also start to fraction."

"Good point. The New Immortals claimed that was actually a desirable outcome. Moalem decided that a singular personality input-point was a primitive notion. The human mind should be able to expand to encompass many bodyforms, all inputting their experiences to the unifying mind."

"That has to be unstable. Bipolar disorder and multiple personalities are notoriously erratic."

"I've been through these arguments so many times with Svein. He maintains that inherent mental illness is completely avoidable in these circumstances, that the human mind can evolve in conjunction with its physical environment. The host personality has to be willing and receptive to change, to want to learn how to be different. He's probably right."

"I'm sorry, I don't follow. You say the Foundation split because of this? I thought you were all about exploring new forms of human existence."

"We are. I set up the Foundation to advance humanity through genetic modification. But change in isolation is not a desirable thing. Hence Huxley's Haven. Not only are its citizens perfectly adjusted to their jobs, the entire society is designed to be stable so that only the professions and abilities we have allowed for are needed. There are human clerks who make electronics, especially computers, redundant. Engineering is constitutionally fixed to equal early-Twentieth Century development, so mechanics are capable of performing all repairs, rather than writing software for maintenance bots. It's a level which was specifically chosen to give everyone a decent quality of life without dependence on cybernetics. Which is what makes Huxley's Haven a perfectly integrated society. It doesn't change because there is no requirement for change. That is what Commonwealth citizens found so disturbing, it's also why it works. Within the Foundation we had a very large debate as to whether we should Isolate it once it was established."

"Why didn't you? A society like that can only be challenged by an outside force, so why risk continued exposure? There are plenty of idealists even today who would like it stopped."

"I don't believe we had the right. Maybe in a few hundred years time, the Haven will choose to isolate itself from what the Intersolar Commonwealth will become. Who knows?"

"And if it starts to fail, you can fix it," Paula guessed. He had that kind of egotism.

"That's what the freethinkers are for," Friland said. "And to a lesser degree the police such as yourself. All societies should include a mechanism for self correction."

"You're distracting me," Paula said. "Why the split with the New Immortals?"

"Very well," Friland said. "I owe you of all people that explanation, if nothing else."

"How ironic for you, having to explain yourself to your creation."

"I'm not a Frankenstein, Investigator."

"Of course not. The split?"

"Firstly, the prospect of a hive mind is one I resist. Call me old fashioned, but I don't regard it as a human goal. Yet there is that danger. Svein knows that you need more than two bodies to guarantee life-continuity. The more you have, the higher the personality's survival probability. There is no theoretical limit. He can possess hundreds. Thousands, of bodies. More still. Exponential growth rates are a favourite politician's scare image, and I don't like to use it, but something close to exponential expansion is a very real threat in this case. What happens to individual, normal humans if a New Immortal expands its nest of selves? An Immortal by his or her nature becomes focused on survival. That will trigger competition for resources, possibly as bad as it was in the twenty-first century before Ozzie and Nigel developed wormhole technology. Would the singulars survive? Would they be allowed to survive? And what about other nest Immortals? One route is merger. The universal monomind. Again, something I instinctively shy away from. Svein was not complimentary about what he perceives as my outdated reactionary thinking."

"That must have been painful for you."

"Quite. The other problem I have is the method which the New Immortals have chosen. It is not pure genetic evolution, which is our creed."

"Now you've really lost me."

"If you have children, Investigator, they will remain true to your nature. They will inherit the genetic and psychoneural profiling that make you the perfect law enforcement officer. We fixed the traits which make you what you are, they are dominant. Even if all our fabulous society should fall, if the wormholes are closed, the factories break down, electricity ceases to flow; if the human race enters into a new age of barbarism—what the Foundation created will remain. Our heritage is written in our genes. When we define an advancement, we incorporate it in our DNA. It can never be lost. An equal science can remove it, but our advances would endure a dark age. Svein's system will not. He shares his thoughts and memories with his other bodies via the unisphere. He needs OCtattoos and inserts to transmit and receive. He needs clone vats to grow new bodies. His is a cybernetic, technological, future. It is a very short step from what he wishes to become, and simply downloading your thoughts into a machine like today's uniheads do with the SI. After all, a machine can be made far stronger than human flesh. This is not the route I wish the Foundation to go down. At the far end, it is not a human outcome which awaits."

"Surely that's all contrary to the stasis of Huxley's Haven?"

"The Haven provides us with a proof of concept. We know we can match our genetic and societal requirements synergistically. That sets the stage for our next advances."

"Which are?" she asked sharply.

"Development along all fronts. Extreme longevity—ultimately self rejuvenation. Increased intelligence. Huge disease resistance."

"Bigger. Stronger. Better," she murmured.

"Yes. These advances are slowly seeping into the human genome. Parents have baseline procedures carried out on their embryos to give their offspring healthier physiques. Reprofiling is commonplace in rejuvenation tanks, at least for those who can afford it. We are a slow revolution, Paula. People find our long-term aims uncomfortable, but they continue to incorporate our immediate successes into their very selves. Given such development, society will inevitably adapt and evolve. Which is why I reject the obsessional goal of the New Immortals. I will happily continue my rejuvenation treatments every thirty years because they will ultimately be temporary. In four or five hundred years' time, I will be beginning my senior lifespan, which will be measured in millennia. Can you imagine what kind of culture that will play host to?"

"Even if I could, I obviously wouldn't have a place in it. I'm just a half-way stage experiment, remember."

"Oh no, Paula, you've become much more than that. You've humbled us by showing how adaptive humanity is. You are an inspiration that we can all exceed our perceived limits."

"How very lovely for you," she said acerbically, and stood up.

Justin Friland looked up at her. "What will you do to Svein Moalem now you know what he is?"

"I'm not sure," she replied truthfully. "I'm sure I'll *adapt* my nature somehow, and bring him to justice."

He smiled sadly. "We're not adversaries, Paula, not you and me."

"Not yet. Not quite. But keep on going the way you are, and we'll wind up facing each other in court. The Senate has strict laws concerning genetic manipulation outside designated human parameters."

"I know. And I'm very tired of them, which is why we're finally leaving altogether."

She narrowed her eyes. "Are you going to Isolate another world?"

"No, we don't have to. The Commonwealth is desperate to make a success of Far Away; the Senate spent so much money getting there they have to justify it to the taxpayer. It's a blank canvas of a world, thanks to the solar flare that eliminated its indigenous life. My remaining colleagues are moving there with me. The Senate's authority and its laws are confined to one city; out in the wild we'll be free of the petty regulations that restrict us here, and we can design a new biosphere environment to compliment whatever enhancements we build into our bodies. The ultimate synergy, eh?"

"That sounds like a project that will keep you occupied for a few decades."

"We would be honoured if you'd join us. You would be an enormously valuable asset to any community, Paula."

"Thank you, but no. I have work to do in this society." She started towards the door.

"There could be tens of him by now," Friland called out after her. "You'll never get them all."

"Nonetheless, he will face justice. You know that. That's how you made me."

WHAT HAPPENED NEXT

THE COUNTRYSIDE OUTSIDE BARANSLY was certainly a lot more hospitable in summer. A warm G-class star shone in a deep ocean-blue sky. High wispy clouds laced the horizon ahead as Paula walked down the narrow farm track that cut through the big fields, pushing her lightweight p-bike over the scattered stone. The air was thick and warm, heavy with the sugary scent of the fireflower vine. She knew the name now. It was the district's main crop. In the summer's warmth and humidity the rows of wire frames were transformed into long dunes of vivid crimson flowers with thick yellow stamen. Petals were already starting to crisp and brown at the edges as midsummer approached; in another month the fruit would ripen to fist-sized globes a dull purple in colour. The pulp was a local staple, equivalent to meatpotato; though the fruit could be crushed for oil as well.

She reached the concrete road at the end of the track, and straddled the p-bike. There was no traffic. She twisted the throttle, and set off towards Baransly's outskirts, five miles ahead.

The city's traffic management network was still functioning. It registered her p-bike as she crossed into the official city boundary. By now she was on Route Two, one of the main highways into the city, with the mid-afternoon traffic starting to build up around her. She told the network she wanted Lislie Road, and received a route authorization. Her vehicle licence had been accepted as current.

Lislie Road was in the middle of a pleasant residential suburb, with small dome-roofed houses grown out of air coral. Paula turned off the tree-shaded road itself onto the broad pavement, and started peddling the p-bike. That way she was no longer monitored by the traffic network. She stopped outside number 62, and wheeled the p-bike up to the front door. It accepted the code she put in, and swung open for her.

Nelson Sheldon had paid Terrie Ority, the previous occupant, a handsome sum for his codes; just as he'd paid another Merioneth refugee for a bike licence. The preparations had taken over a month. Paula and Nelson had put the operation together on Augusta, the Sheldon Dynasty's industrial world. It was the first time in nine decades that Paula had taken a holiday from the Directorate. She'd accrued eight years leave. The personnel office was delighted—her director curious.

Inside number 62 the air was musty. Terrie Ority was a fussy man, he'd turned off all the power before he left. He had also left behind most of the furniture. Paula switched the air conditioning back on, and ran the taps to cycle the plumbing system. A couple of ancient maidbots were sitting in their alcoves, fully charged, so she ordered them to start cleaning.

She spent the rest of the day establishing her legend identity in the civil and commercial systems. Her bank account was opened and loaded from a card. She registered with several local stores and had food delivered. Then she sat back and accessed the planetary cybersphere, with her e-butler extracting news summaries to build a picture of Merioneth after the wormhole had closed five months earlier.

It was like losing a short, brutal war. With half the population gone, whole towns had been abandoned. New consumer items were hard to find; not that it mattered, people simply reclaimed and recycled products from deserted homes. Food hadn't quite been rationed in the winter, but a lot of favourites were no longer commercially available. She was interested to see that medical services including rejuvenation clinics had been nationalized on a temporary basis, so they could be reorganized for fair and equal distribution. Whole fleets of bots, especially civic ones, were breaking down; there were too few service and repair companies to keep them functional. Public transport was patchy, with priority given to maintain strategic links. Cars and lorries were also in need of maintenance, but again there was a huge number of abandoned vehicles which could be utilized. But on the plus side, this summer's crops were going to produce big surpluses—nobody would go hungry. The tidal and hydro power stations were all functioning efficiently. Local currency was stabilizing after months of disastrous inflation. People were starting to adapt to their new life.

She started to research Svein Moalem. He was still Prime Minister, with his Nationalist Party holding two thirds of the remaining seats in parliament. There were due to be elections in two years, when the new constituency boundaries had been established. The party had spent the months since Isolation revoking a whole host of 'oppressive Commonwealth restrictions'; the majority of which were regulations covering genetic modifications and cloning. Helpfully, Moalem's office provided a diary listing events he was due to attend.

The next day Paula started observing his movements within the city. They were typical of any high-ranking politician. Speeches to civic and community leaders, meetings with party officials. Parliamentary debates. Voter-friendly visits to schools, hospitals, and selected business. Trips to provincial towns.

He had bodyguards, of course, good ones. When he was due at an event, crowds were scanned using feature recognition software to check for repeat observers. The traffic network was analysed for any vehicle which kept cropping up in his vicinity. If he took a train or plane, passenger lists were reviewed. All well-established mid-level protocols.

As a consequence she kept her distance, content to follow his routes via some very sophisticated software her e-butler manipulated in the planetary cybersphere.

After a week she'd confirmed he would often abandon his official residence next to the Parliament building in favour of a grand private house in Baransley's most exclusive LakeHill district, where the last remaining multi-millionaires resided. It was a perfect place for his nest to operate from.

On the eighth night, with her monitor routines confirming his presence at a late-night Cabinet session, Paula broke in.

The perimeter alarm circuits and sensors were utterly ineffectual against her superior software and the active stealth covering of her light-armour suit. She started walking through the formal grounds, tracking the sentinel dogs prowling round. Spinneys of local trees provided excellent cover. The house was squatting on the summit of a mound which had been sculpted with high terracing. To Paula's suspicious eye the mound would be perfect cover for an underground complex.

She climbed the dry-stone wall of the last terrace. Ahead of her the house was a three story construction of dark-grey stone, crowned with a lantern tower. The lawn between her and the wall was completely devoid of cover, and dotted with sensors. She used her inserts to neutralize several in her path. Her e-butler told her that several motion trackers up on the eves were locking on as she jogged forwards. Data traffic in and out of the house began to increase.

Paula scurried up to a large French door and used a compact power blade to cut a circle through the glass. She found herself in a big hall which followed the principals of High Renaissance architecture, with square columns and a vaulting ceiling of decorated panels.

The lights came on when she was half way to the vast curving stairs at the far end. Five security staff with high-rated maser rifles were lined up behind the polished stone banister.

"Hold it right there."

More armed security staff scurried in from ground floor rooms and surrounded her. Their armour suits were a lot heavier than hers. She raised her hands as eleven energy weapons lined up on her, any one of which could probably cut through her protection.

"Do not move. Deactivate all your systems."

Paula switched the shimmering stealth layer off, then slowly reached up and removed her helmet. One of the armoured figures up on the stairs stood up, lowering its rifle. Paula's inserts detected a large emission of encrypted data emerging from him, and suppressed a smile.

"Investigator Myo," he said, taking off his own helmet. There was no resemblance to Svein Moalem in his features and his skin was the pale brown of a North African.

"Correct," she said. "And whom am I addressing?"

"Agent Volkep. I'm in charge of the Prime Minister's security." He walked down the stairs. Paula's e-butler told her the nodes in the house had closed their links to the cybersphere. More suppression shielding came on, sealing up the hall from any communication.

"That's convenient for you," Paula said archly as Volkep stood in front of her. His expression gave nothing away.

"Take her over to the holding centre," he told the armed squad. "I want a full scan for weapon inserts; and be very thorough, hell knows what her Directorate equipped her with. Then bring her down to secure facility three. I'll interrogate her there."

Two electromuscle-enhanced gauntlets gripped Paula's arms, almost lifting her off the ground. She turned her head to look at Volkep as she was hauled away across the hall's marble flooring. "Nice seeing you again, Svein," she called out loudly.

That brought a flicker of annoyance to his face.

The holding centre was a simple concrete room with a cage door and a single medical-style chair in the middle. It was equipped with malmetal restraints.

Four of the armoured bodyguards came in with her, powered up and shielded. They ordered her to strip. Paula obediently removed her own armour. "Keep going," they told her. She pulled off her sweatshirt, and slipped her long shorts down her legs. The OCtattoo glowed sapphire and jade on her abdomen, a circle encasing a tight geometry of intersecting curves that undulated slowly. Four gun muzzles lined up on the gentle light.

"What's that?"

"Sensory booster," Paula said. "It's wetwired into my nerves so I can receive a bigger sensation when I'm accessing porn from the unisphere. Don't you have them here?"

"Just get the rest of your clothes off, lady."

She shrugged out of her bra and took her panties off. One of the suited bodyguards dropped all her garments into a big bag and carried it out. Paula was left standing in the cold concrete cell with the remaining three agents.

"Not bad," one remarked.

"You wouldn't need a booster for anything with me," his colleague said. The others laughed.

Paula gazed at his blank shiny helmet and gave a small snort of contempt. Perhaps she had given the secret service agents too much credit after all.

A female technician came in, followed by a trollybot loaded with sensor equipment. She frowned when she saw Paula's OCtattoo. "Put her in the chair."

The malmetal manacles flowed over Paula's wrists and ankles. Sensor pads were applied to her skin over the twisting luminescence. More scans swept across her limbs and torso. Then her skull was given a thorough examination. The woman took samples of her blood and saliva. Nails were tested for toxins. Even the air she exhaled was sampled for any abnormality.

Finally, the technician nodded at the armoured figures. "She's clean. Her inserts are sophisticated, but they're all sensors, memory chips, and processor systems; no weapons of any kind. You can take her down to Volkep."

"So what's that thing?" one of the agents asked, pointing at Paula's abdomen.

"Receiver circuitry wired into her spinal cord, just like she said."

Paula was marched back through the grandiose hall to a room at the back of the house. A lift took her deep underground. She wasn't at all surprised when it opened on a junction of corridors. Volkep took over, dismissing the bodyguards. He took Paula by the arm and led her to a simply furnished office. Svein Moalem was waiting there, his opal necklace just visible inside the open collar of his shirt. Two other youths were with him, one obviously a full clone with identical features to Svein, just five years younger, the other had East Asian features; the one thing they had in common was a necklace. Volkep was still in his armour, so she couldn't tell if he was wearing any kind of array.

"I like the whole underground citadel thing," Paula said, looking round the office with its drab ceiling and dilapidated couch. "Quite the retro Criminal Mastermind secret headquarters." Her abdominal OCtattoo showed her the four of them were exchanging data at a huge rate, all of which originated from the ornamental arrays round their necks. She opened the additional bioneural chips in her cortex and started recording their emissions.

"Why are you here?" Volkep asked.

"I talked to Dr Friland."

"Ah," Svein said, an exclamation simultaneously uttered by his youthful clone.

"You fired the missile on Nova Zealand," Paula said.

"Well that's open to debate."

"In fact I suspect your nest *is* the Free Merioneth Forces in their entirety."

"Not completely. My Foundation colleagues are fully supportive in every respect."

"I see."

"Would you like to arrest them as well?"

"I might get round to it."

"I'm fascinated how you got here. Did you come back before or after the wormhole closed?"

"After. You killed a lot of Sheldons."

"Old concept," the East Asian youth said dismissively. "They're all alive today."

"Interesting," Paula said. "Did you know your inflections are the same?"

Svein walked round in front of her. "Did you know I don't care? Why are you here? Even with Sheldon support you can't possibly expect to snatch all of me back to the Commonwealth. After all, you don't even know how many of me there are."

"True. Did you get hot while you waited for the plane to take off? I did while I was out there. That desert has a terrible climate."

"You'd have to send a small army here for that, and even if Sheldon was determined enough there's no guarantee he'd succeed. Were you sent to try and find out how much I've grown?"

"I don't care how many there are in your nest. Was the missile heavy when you lifted up and aimed it at the plane?"

"What do you mean you don't care? Why are you here? Why did you break in to my home? Is it to snatch data on me?"

"I have all the data I need. It was the reason for the Isolation which puzzled me. Now I know it wasn't a financial or political ethos it makes perfect sense. Did you build the missile here? Did it kick when you launched it? Was the exhaust plume loud?"

"Not political?" Svein said it, but all four of the nest raised their eyebrows in unison, sharing the same slightly mocking expression. "What could be more political than developing a new kind of life, effectively a new species?"

"Friland called you obsessional," Paula said. "I think he's right. Did you actually watch the plane falling out of the sky? I bet you did. Who could resist that, no matter what type of human you are."

"Paula," all four of him assumed a mock-indignant expression. "Are you trying to *provoke* me?"

"Did you feel satisfaction when it exploded?"

"Two can play this game. Did Friland tell you we're related, you and me?" The Svein body grinned.

The Volkep body stood beside Svein. "And he was the original," Volkep said, tapping Svein on the shoulder. "Our minds are rooted in the same ancestor, Paula."

"I didn't know that," she admitted. "Were you nervous when you ran back to the boat? That was a weak point. Someone might have seen you."

"Friland originally funded the Foundation from the clinic he used to run in Granada back in the twenty first century," Svein said. "He sold baseline germ treatments to wealthy Westerners whose own countries banned such tinkering. That way he amassed a massive germ bank, a good percentage of the wealthy and powerful people of the day came to visit at some time and have their children enhanced. Their money and DNA was a good foundation for his Foundation."

"Standing on Ridgeview station platform waiting for the train, you must have been buzzing on adrenaline," Paula persisted. "You'd know me or someone like me would have the trains stopped. You might have been stranded there, with the police closing in. No way to get back to Sydney and establish your alibi."

"I looked up the records in Granada. Our ancestor is Jeff Baker, apparently he invented crystal memories. A famous man in his time. A very smart man, too. Friland needed that level of intelligence in his research team, which is why I was created from Baker's old sperm samples. You, I imagine, require a similar analytical ability. A lot of other sequences were included, which is where we start to diverge, but genetically he's equivalent to our grandfather. Which makes us cousins, Paula. We're family. And you always thought you were unique, isolated and alone. You're not, Paula. We not only share flesh, we think the same."

"Were you watching when my Directorate team arrested your Fiech body? Some clever little vantage point nearby, perhaps?"

Svein pressed his face up close to Paula, his mouth parting with an angry snarl. "That *obsession* you mock in me is exactly the same one that runs through you, Investigator Myo. Friland didn't have to sequence it in to your genome quite as much as you were led to believe. It's not artificial, it's you. It's your heritage. It's my heritage. It's what we are. And this is our world. You're home Paula. Welcome back."

She smiled lightly. "I know what I am, and I know where my home is. Good luck finding yours."

The Svein body took a half step back from her. All four of the nest were frowning in annoyance now. "Why are you here?" they demanded in unison.

"To ensure the sentence passed on Fiech is carried out in full," Paula told them.

"I thought it had been," the Volkep body said coldly.

"It hasn't been yet, because you made sure that part of you didn't remember. But memory's a funny thing, it's triggered by association. And your mind is shared," Paula gestured around at the empty air. "It's all around us, if you know how to look." Her virtual hand touched Nelson's communication icon.

"I've got enough," she said out loud.

"What..." all four nestlings grunted.

The wormhole opened behind her, expanding out from a micron-wide point to a two-metre circle. Bright light shone through, silhouetting Paula's naked body. She stepped backwards, crossing the threshold to be enveloped by the light. Lost her footing as Augusta's slightly heavier gravity claimed her, and fell on her arse in a completely undignified manner. Svein and his nestlings never saw that. The wormhole closed the instant she was through.

She was sitting in the middle of the alien environment confinement chamber of the CST Augusta Exploratory Division, a huge dome-shaped chamber with dark radiation-absorptive walls. In front of her was the five-metre wide blank circle of the wormhole gateway, its grey pseudo-substance emitting strange violet sparkles. Half-way up the curving surface behind her was a broad band of reinforced windows with the big operations centre behind it. Nelson Sheldon was pressed up against the superstrength glass, grinning down at her. Behind him, the hundred-strong staff controlling the wormhole were peering over the tops of their tiered rows of consoles, curious and eager to see the conclusion to their oddest operation ever. Tracking her movements on Merioneth and keeping the wormhole close by had stretched the machinery to its limit.

"You okay?" Nelson's amplified voice boomed down from the ceiling.

"Yeah," Paula said, climbing to her feet. "I'm okay."

WHAT I KNOW REALLY HAPPENED

THE COURT GUARDS WERE utter bastards to me. After that idiot judge passed sentence they dragged me down to the holding cell while I shouted that I was innocent. They just laughed as they slung me inside. I heard them later. Deliberately. They said that the Justice Directorate had developed a suspension system that allows a tiny part of your mind to stay awake during the sentence, so you're aware of each long year as it passes. It's part of the punishment, knowing all the opportunities you've lost, the life you've missed.

Not true. Just another unisphere myth.

After they put me down on the bed in the preparation room. No. I'll be honest. After they held me down. I fought them, *Damnit* I'm innocent. I was a classic case of someone who went down screaming and kicking. They won't ever forget me. It took six Directorate orderlies to hold me in place while the malmetal restraints wrapped round my limbs. And after that, I still shouted. I cursed them and their families. I swore vengeance, that in two and a half thousand years I'd become the killer they wrongly thought I was, and I'd hunt down their descendents and torture them to death.

No use. They still infused the drugs. Consciousness faded away.

I woke up. The room which slowly came into focus around me was very similar to the preparation room I'd gone to sleep in. Stupidly, I was bloody grateful that I hadn't known all that time flowing round me. The waste of my potential lives. But I was alive. Warm. And pleasantly drowsy.

There was something round my neck which seemed familiar somehow, something from the time in my life I'd lost. Icons in my virtual vision were blinking green, showing the memorycell channels into my neural structure were wide open.

Then that queen bitch Paula Myo came in. I tried to get up to throttle her. That's when I found I was still restrained, with malmetal coiled round my arms and legs.

"What the fuck is this?" I shouted. My voice was weak.

"I had you woken," Myo told me. "I have something for you. Something you've forgotten."

"What? What is this?"

"You," she said, and took off her suit jacket. Something was glowing underneath her white cotton blouse. I could see shapes moving.

"Help," I cried. "Someone. Help me." The coloured shadows on her abdomen began to writhe faster and faster. My virtual icons changed from green to blue, showing incoming impulses.

"What is that?" I whispered in fright.

She glanced down, as if only becoming aware of the light. Her smile made her face ugly. "A kind of prison, I suppose. You know, in ancient time necromancers used to draw pentagons to trap demons in. They thought that if they were imprisoned they could use their powers. A very misplaced notion, I suspect. In this case geometry isn't important, I simply had to have a large receiving element. Your thoughts are big, after all. But I managed to catch them. Not all of them, just the right ones. Those that were relevant to the crime."

"My thoughts?" The icons expanded abruptly, wiping out my sight. Then faces emerged through the blue mist. Four of them in some kind of dilapidated room. Faces I knew. Svein. I remembered him. I remembered...being him.

I was the one standing in the desert outside Ridgeview while the rest of me lived our life. It was hot out there. Bloody unpleasant, actually. The sun burned my arms and face. I took a leak against some local plant. That way if the forensic team were any good, they'd find it and confirm the Fiech body's DNA.

Then the air traffic control data playing in my virtual vision showed me the plane was taxiing to the runway. I took a breath and got the missile ready. A simple thing really, three of me had built it in the engineering centre under the Lake Hill house. Most of the components were off-the-shelf, and the custom ones were easy enough for the bots to manufacture. We built quite a few.

The finished product was a simple blue-grey launch tube over a metre long, with a shoulder saddle and a handle. It was heavy when I rested it on my shoulder; I squatted down on the stony sand to make the weight easier. I could see the big old Siddley-Lockheed lift into the sky, with its engine rumble faint in the hot desert air. It took what seemed an age to climb up to its cruise altitude, curving round the city in a wide arc. The passenger list said it was just about full, over a hundred and thirty people. It would be quick. Death in such a fashion always is. And the passenger list confirmed the Dynasty scum were on board. The missile's sensors locked on. There wasn't anything else in the sky to confuse them.

I fired the missile. The bloody launch tube slammed into my shoulder. If I hadn't been bracing myself it would have knocked me down. The roar of the solid rocket booster was obscenely loud. For a couple of seconds I was overwhelmed. It was like being hit on the side of the head. Smoke was seething all round me. I crouched, staggered about. Then I recovered enough to stand still and look up into the wide open sky. The hyper-ram had kicked in, which made the missile just about impossible to see.

I expected the explosion to be bigger. This was just a white pinpoint flash, no fireball. But behind the blaze, the plane started to disintegrate, tumbling out of the sky. Dark fragments twirling away from the main body.

There was no way I could move. Actually, my whole nest of bodies froze up as I watched the spectacle. There was something obscenely beautiful about the sight, and better still was the knowledge that I had created it. If I could do this, I could do anything. I'd be able to force through Merioneth's isolation now. I had the courage and determination.

The first fragments hadn't even reached the ground when I turned and hurried down to the shore where the boat was anchored. This point was critical. The whole area would be swarming with people. The unisphere was already flinging out alarms. Rescue crews and police would be dispatched within minutes. And any local citizens nearby would no doubt rush to help. My Volkep body released the warning message into the unisphere as I reached the shoreline.

After that it was a quick trip across the sea to Ridgeview. I waited on the station platform for my train back to Earth. It was an eerie experience. Everyone round me was accessing the unisphere reports of the plane crash. Nobody said anything, they were all too shocked at the disaster just outside town.

When I got back to Sydney I took a cab straight back to the apartment. The rest of me were a pleasant sensation of reassurance as I took the memory wipe drugs. The Volkep body took the array necklace from my neck, and smiled proudly. I could feel the connection with myself reducing, darkness replacing the joy and colour of my true memories. One contact remained, a single thread of experience: the alibi trip to Ormal. Damn, that stewardess was great-looking, I wish I hadn't been so wrapped up on a mission.

Then I was alone. And the drugs kicked in, I knew nothing more.

Then I was without one of me. Just for an instant I felt regret. But I am many. The loss of a single body is irrelevant. That's what I am, a New Immortal. That's why I am. I continue even after the loss of one, or more. I live.

I was shivering when the glare of colour and sensation subsided into simple knowledge. Paula Myo was looking down at me, pulling her suit jacket back on. The flare of activity within her OCtattoo was subsiding.

"Bitch!" I couldn't sense me. For the first time since I nested I was devoid of myself. One body with a single mind, completely alone.

"Goodbye," said Paula Myo.

"No. No!" a Justice Directorate orderly had entered the room. He was carrying an infuser. Paula Myo nodded at him. "Carry on," she ordered.

"Why have you done this to me?" I cried. "This is inhuman!"

She turned in the door, her face blank as she stared at me. "You are the person who committed the crime. The whole person, now. This is your sentence. The sentence you tried to avoid. Justice has prevailed."

The orderly pressed the infuser against my neck. I screamed, my mind crying out to the rest of me, to help me, to comfort me. There was no answer.

WHAT HAPPENED AFTER

NELSON SHELDON WAS WAITING in the entrance hall of the Justice Directorate as Paula came out of the lift. "How did it go?" he asked.

"Successfully. The true Dimitros Fiech is now serving his sentence."

"Shame about the rest of him."

"Not really."

"Oh?"

"When suspension was first introduced, the Justice Directorate examined the idea of leaving convicts aware while their bodies slept. It was abandoned almost immediately. The experience was too much like sensory deprivation. The minds went insane very quickly under such circumstances."

"So how does that help us?" Nigel asked curiously.

"Dimitros Fiech is now unaware of his predicament. He'll sleep soundly for the next two and a half millennia, and he'll be offered extensive therapy when he gets out—assuming the Commonwealth is still around. Meanwhile on Merioneth..."

"Ah. Svein Moalem's nest knows part of him is in suspension. And as an Immortal..."

"He'll endure those two and a half thousand years aware of the Fiech body's state. The punishment is shared. Or rather, it isn't, because it's all his. Just experienced in different ways."

Nelson smiled. "We can live with that."

"Good, because I have no intention of returning to Merioneth."

"Thank you for going in the first place," Nelson said. "The Dynasty is most grateful. We don't forget who are friends are."

Paula grinned back shrewdly. "I'll remember that."

MANHATTAN IN REVERSE

◆◆◆

IT WAS FIVE DAYS after Easter and Paris was soaking up the heat from an unseasonably bright sun. Paula Myo, Deputy Director of the Intersolar Commonwealth's Serious Crimes Directorate, slipped her shades on as soon as she emerged from the marbled archway of the Justice Courts. Her escort squad pushed past the unisphere reporters crammed on the broad stone stairs. The clamor of shouted questions merged into a single unintelligible wall of noise. Even if she'd wanted to comment on the verdict she would never have been heard. It always amazed her how stupid reporters were, as if any one of them could have gained an exclusive under this kind of circumstance.

Not that her opinion would've been welcomed by the large crowd of protestors shouting and jeering behind the cordon which the city gendarmes had thrown up across the big boulevard outside. They'd certainly picked up on the Easter theme. Glaring holographic placards demanded RESURRECT OSCAR NOW. FREE THE MARTYR. OSCAR DIED FOR US, SAVE HIM FOR OUR SINS.

Her deputy, Hoshe Finn, was waiting at the foot of the broad stairs beside the Directorate's dark Citroën limousine. "Congratulations, Chief," he muttered as the malmetal door curtained open for her.

Paula took one last glance at the snarling faces of the protestors, all directing their venom at her. It wasn't what she was used to. Disapproval and not a little bigotry because of what she was, certainly; as the single person from Huxley's Haven, otherwise known as The Hive, to live in the Greater Commonwealth, she had long since accepted her own notoriety. Like all of Huxley's residents, she was genetically profiled to excel at her job, which in her case was police work. It was a profession which normally resulted in a decent amount of approval at the conclusion of a successful case.

Not this time.

The long Citroën turned smoothly into the Champs Élysées and headed for the Place de la Concorde.

"You know, even I'm wondering if I did the right thing," Paula said quietly.

"I doubted," Hoshe said. "Until you brought the families into the office to prepare our case. You were right when you said time doesn't diminish the crime. Their children still died: a real death, not just bodyloss."

"Yeah," Paula said. Doubt unsettled her. It wasn't what she was supposed to feel, not with her psychoneural profiling. Everything should be clear cut, leaving no room for messy little emotional distractions. *Perhaps the geneticists who designed me didn't know quite as much about DNA sequencing as they thought they did.*

Ten minutes later they drove down into the modern underground garage that had been cut out below the ancient five-story building which housed the Directorate's Paris office. Secure gates unfurled behind them. She wasn't really worried about anyone trying to confront her physically, even though the number of displaced from the worlds lost during the Starflyer War was still alarming eleven months after the war had ended. The number of homeless and destitute people roaming the streets was too high, despite the city authority's sincere efforts to find them places in restart projects on the fresh worlds.

A lift took them up to the fifth floor and the open-plan office she commanded. Her team were all behind their desks, which was unusual enough. They shot her concerned looks, as if they were sharing a collective guilt.

Alic Hogan was rising to his feet. "Sorry, Chief," he said, "he didn't have an appointment but we couldn't really say no...." Alic trailed off with a surreptitious glance toward Paula's own office.

The door was ajar, revealing someone sitting in front of her desk.

There weren't many people in the Commonwealth who could walk into the Directorate building without being invited, let alone get all the way up to the fifth floor. And fewer who would want to. Paula was quite pleased with herself as she went in and shut the door behind her. She'd narrowed the probables down to a list of three names; Wilson Kime was the second.

"Admiral," she said cautiously.

Wilson rose and shook her hand courteously. But then he was more than three and a half centuries old, with manners from a bygone era; she wasn't expecting an angry altercation. "So it really is true," he said ruefully. "You always get your man."

"Do my best," she said, annoyed with herself for sounding defensive. She was what she was, and why should she ever apologize for that? "Though your lawyers were good."

"Best that money could buy. But you threw up a hell of a case, Paula."

"Thank you."

"That wasn't exactly a compliment. Oscar Monroe sacrificed himself so the human race could survive a genocidal attack. Doesn't that count for anything with you?"

"Yes. But not at the intellectual level at which I work. I can't allow that to influence me."

"Jesus," Kime muttered.

"I did recover his memorycell myself," Paula reminded the old war hero. She didn't go into how risky that had been; Kime's own sacrifices during the final showdown with the Starflyer went far beyond hers.

Millions had suffered bodyloss on the worlds invaded and obliterated during the conflict. Clinics across the Commonwealth were overwhelmed with people undergoing re-life procedures in which their force-matured clones were integrated with memories taken from their original bodies. Even so, a place could have been found for one of the human race's greatest selfless heroes. Oscar's personality was still intact in the memorycell she'd removed from his shattered corpse. It just needed a body to animate.

Instead she chose to put him on trial for previous crimes, namely a terrorist action at Aberdan Station decades before which had killed dozens of innocent people. Defense counsel had argued that the young Oscar had been indoctrinated by extremists, that the passenger train wasn't the actual target. The lawyer Wilson had retained was good, adding pleas for clemency from serious public figures including Wilson himself. But Paula had prepared her case with equal proficiency. Time did not lessen the severity of the crime, she argued, and she presented testimony from the victims, the parents of children killed at Aberdan, all of whom were too young to have had memorycells. They hadn't bodylossed, they'd died real deaths.

The judges had found Oscar guilty by a majority of three to two. He'd been sentenced to one thousand one hundred years' suspension; as he was currently bodyless, the senior judge ruled he shouldn't be re-lifed until after the sentence was served. The defense team was already planning to challenge that judgment when Paula walked out of the court.

"I hope you're not here to ask a personal favor," she said to Wilson. "You know I can't help with that."

"I know," he said.

"What's your next move? Appeal to the President for clemency and a pardon? I suspect you have the political clout to bring that off."

"Something like that. I'll get him back, Paula. I won't let him face the fate you have in store for him."

"The courts decided. That's the trouble with this case—everyone thinks it's personal. I don't do personal."

"So you said."

"So what do you want?"

"I'm here to ask a favor."

"Ha!" She took a seat behind the desk.

Wilson gave her a small smile. "Look, you need a break. We all do after what we went through on Far Away."

"I'm okay now, thank you."

"You've got half the human race gritting their teeth in scorn and anger when they see your face. Politically, you need to keep a low profile right now. Maybe do something else for a while."

Paula opened her mouth, ready to explain.

"Yes!" Kime said. "I know you have nothing else other than your work, that it's how you were profiled. And that's why I'm here. You remember Michelle Douvoir?"

"No."

"One of Jean Douvoir's daughters. She was living on Sligo when the Prime fleet hit it. She was lucky to get off."

"Yeah. Hoshe was there, too. He said it was tough."

"She didn't want any special treatment, though God knows she could have had a mansion in any city on Earth if she'd asked. We owed her that much after what her father did. But I made sure she got to Menard; it's one of the planets in phase three space which the Farndale company is fast-developing. Everything got accelerated after the war to give the refugees from the Lost23 worlds somewhere to stay. It's a decent enough place: not too heavy on industry right now, of course, but somewhere she can start over."

"Glad to hear it. So why come to me with this?"

Wilson Kime gave her a small grimace. "There's a problem brewing on Menard. Maybe 'problem' is too strong a word, but something's odd. And it's causing trouble. Michelle called me directly about it."

"What sort of problem?" Paula told her e-butler to call up a basic file on Menard. Planetary data ran across her virtual vision, infinity-focus neon graphics partially obscuring Wilson.

"Michelle is living in Lydian—that's a town on the Jevahal continent."

The map image shifted in Paula's virtual vision, showing the second-largest continent. Its northernmost tip jutted out to straddle the peninsula. Various colorful symbols swarmed the land areas: provisional Farndale corporation development designations. "Arable country," Paula observed.

"Great soil, good rainfall, warm climate, minimal intrusive native microbial ecology; it's perfect for farming. And if the planet is going to accommodate a good percentage of the refugees from Lost23 worlds, they're going to need to eat. Farming is a priority for us. We need to get as much of those big open plains under the plow as possible."

Paula gave him a critical glance as the virtual imagery faded to a shadow spectre. "Didn't we try that in the Amazon Basin once? The Environment Commission is still running restoration projects in that part of the globe."

"This is an emergency situation, Paula. We have the Lost23 populations to resettle now, and those from the Second47 planets can't be held in temporal hiatus forever. Building replacement worlds for their emergence is going to cripple our economy for decades to come. Sometimes we have to take shortcuts."

"Sometimes?"

Wilson gave her an exasperated stare. "I'm not here to argue corporate politics with you. This is something else entirely. The natives on Jevahal are attacking the homesteads. The whole settlement project around Lydian is starting to stall. It can't go on, Paula, and it certainly can't be allowed to spread across the whole continent."

Paula hesitated. "Natives? You mean the original pioneer landowners."

Wilson Kime took a long breath, clearly ill at ease. "No, Paula, I mean the indigenous life."

"Aliens?" she asked in shock. "There are sentients there? Wilson, what have you done?"

"Nothing," he said quickly. "The animals concerned are called onids. Think fat kangaroos with spider legs and you're getting close."

Her e-butler was already retrieving the small xenobiology encyclopaedia files on the onid stored in the unisphere. The image did just about match Wilson's description, once you'd thrown in dark-purple fur. "Your xenobiology team classified them as non-sentient," she read. "They were in a hurry, weren't they? They had to open the planet for settlement for the Lost23 refugees. Farndale's board put them under pressure."

"No. Categorically not. Check the dates. Menard was cleared for settlement before the Starflyer War began. It was a legitimate assessment by the xenobiology team, and they're independent, they have to be."

Paula shot him a suspicious glance. She knew just how impartial things became when a company as vast as Farndale was involved. The amount of money involved in opening up a planet for settlement was phenomenal. There wasn't much which could prevent the awarding of an H-congruent certification once the process had begun. Certainly not an independent scientific team with a foolish case of integrity.

"Believe me, Paula. Farndale didn't override anything here. That classification was genuine."

"All right, so what's happened?"

"That's the billion-dollar question. It began about three weeks ago, with the onid raiding some of Lydian's outlying homesteads. Now it's getting more serious. Packs of them are attacking any human they can find. Nobody's going outside the town. Our local governor is asking the Farndale board for a squad of marshals with enough firepower to eradicate every onid herd in the territory. And each day he's asking louder. So far we've kept this out of the media, but that won't last...." He gave her a forlorn look. "We've just had a war that nearly ended in genocide. We stopped that, Paula, you and me. We played our part. We know better than anyone that that kind of situation cannot be allowed to happen again."

"What the hell do you want me to do?" she exclaimed. "It's hardly a crime in the conventional sense. Someone screwed up the classification. You're going to have to pull out of Menard."

"But why now?" Wilson asked. "Humans have been there for nearly ten years; first a batch of science teams running tests, then preliminary construction crews building infrastructure. The onid didn't even notice us."

"They reacted because there's more of us now?" Paula ventured. "That always happens when new lands are conquered; the natives eventually realize what a threat the invaders are and start to fight back."

"How would they know how many of us there are? How would they know we're spreading out across the continents? They're animals, they don't have any communication. They live in isolated herds."

Paula spread her hands in a gesture of futility. "How would I know? I'm not a xenobiologist."

"No," Wilson said softly. "But you are a puzzle solver."

"Oh, please!"

"You have to admit it's fascinating, almost paradoxical."

"I find it mildly interesting—in the abstract. I also happen to believe the solution lies with your original classification. Either way, it doesn't matter. This is not a Directorate problem, unless you do give that governor what he's asking for. If that were to happen I would order a very thorough investigation."

"Which nobody wants, and if you personally were to shut down a new planet to immigration, especially at this time, your meager popularity would hit zero and then fall off a cliff."

"I'm not in this job for popularity."

"No, but you know very well that to function properly at the level your cases run at you have to have political influence. Securing that verdict against Oscar lost you every credit you won during the war. You can get that back with this case."

"It is not a case."

"Take a break, Paula. Christ knows you've accumulated enough leave time over the last century. That would leave you free to do whatever tweaked your curiosity. I could appoint you to any position you wanted in Farndale. Advisor to the Lydian territorial governor, for instance."

"You have got to be kidding."

"It's practical. It's logical. It's different. And you'd be helping a lot of people—actually, two species. I'm amazed you're even hesitating."

She wanted to tell him why but couldn't actually come up with a valid reason. The wretched thing was, the situation on Menard *did* intrigue her. For all his faults, Wilson Kime was an honourable man. If he thought, or knew, that the xenobiology team had screwed up, he wouldn't be here. "I really can't afford more than a couple of days," she said weakly.

"That'll be all you need," Wilson said with a grin.

THE NEXT MORNING PAULA took a trans-Earth loop train from Paris through the connecting wormhole to Madrid, then London, New York, and into Tallahassee, where she caught the express shuttle to Los Vada, an industrial world owned entirely by Farndale which served as their manufacturing and financial base. Total time elapsed: forty-two minutes, which wasn't bad for the notoriously piss-poor timekeeping of loop trains.

It was just after midnight local time on Los Vada when she arrived. The CST station there was enormous, a junction to over fifty worlds in phase two and three space; the commerce it had to carry was phenomenal, with over a thousand freight and passenger trains charging through every hour. There were five passenger terminals to cope with the volume of people: two for passengers arriving and departing Los Vada itself, the others for connecting travelers. Paula got off at the fourth and took a small transfer capsule over to terminal five, which handled all the trains to planets in phase three space.

Her train left from platform 49H: eight fat carriages crammed with refugee families, people who had fled their homeworlds after the Prime assault wrecked the biosphere outside their city force fields. Since then they'd either been living with generous family members or enduring spartan accommodation in a Government emergency transit center. Only in the last few months had the Commonwealth government finally started to get on top of the displaced populations problem by accelerating the opening of phase three planets that had been in their provisional stages of development back when the war broke out.

The train trundled across the dark yard outside the huge terminal buildings, then slowly accelerated towards the distant cliff of machinery producing the wormholes. Over half of the circular rifts across interstellar space were open onto the daylight continents of their respective worlds, which shone an impressive variety of star-spectrums out into Los Vada's moonless night. Menard was close to Sol's standard white, with just a hint of violet staining the thick beam which the train track curved round to line up on. They slid in behind a long freight train whose open cars were carrying big civil engineering bots and construction machinery along with a host of infrastructure systems vital to support a planet whose population was currently expanding at a rate of thirty thousand a day, with a bump up to fifty thousand scheduled in four months' time. According to Paula's e-butler, trains were being pushed through with barely a minute's separation. *That's a lot of traffic*, she acknowledged. Empty freight trains were hurtling past on the return track.

Then they were through. The pressure curtain tingled across her skin like some fast phantom drizzle and then raw sunlight was blazing through the carriage windows. There was no sign of the wide open lands which Wilson prized so much on this world. Instead the two-mile length of track between the wormhole and the station ran straight through the marshalling yard, stacks of containers forming a near solid wall on either side. They formed their own mini-city, with avenues sliced by tracks where big old fission-powered shunters trundled along day and night. Giant loader gantries slid above the ever-changing stacks on eight-story legs, malmetal tentacles reaching down to pull individual containers out of the stack and place them on the flotilla of trucks rolling along behind.

The CST planetary station was extremely basic, consisting of just five platforms, all prefabricated, and sheltering beneath a tinted polymesh dome which did absolutely nothing to cut down the intensity of the equatorial sun.

Gary Main, who introduced himself as an aide to the Planetary President, was waiting for her on the platform as the train pulled in. He was a fourth-life Englishman five years out of rejuvenation, with a spiderweb of glowing purple and yellow OrganicCircuitry tattoos mottling his face.

"Wilson Kime assigned me to you for the duration," he shouted over the noise as everyone else thronged down the platform on their way to local trains. It was Farndale's policy simply to shunt all the new arrivals on to the lands they were due to occupy as soon as they arrived. Nobody wanted a huge out-of-work population occupying the capital.

"Thanks," Paula shouted back. "How do I get over to Jevahal?"

"We have a plane waiting for you."

Several people in the nearby crowd paused to give them a look; a couple must have recognized Paula, judging from the frowns. Or it could have been envy at her transport. They were all facing a month on trains and ships and buses before they got to their promised patch of frontier dirt.

WILSON HAD ARRANGED FOR a ten-seat corporate hypersonic jet at the city's single airport. Paula had to smile at that. He really was giving her mission top priority. A cruising speed of Mach eight gave them a flight time of two hours, which Paula spent reviewing the xenobiology team's report on the onid. After an hour's reading she reluctantly concluded that the team's original certification might have been correct, at least based on the research data provided. The onid showed no sign of sentience; they were basic herd animals roaming the plains and forests of Jevahal. Each herd had its own territory, of which it was fiercely protective. The onid demonstrated neither elementary tool-building nor language. Their only communication was a few hooting sounds to alert each other to any danger. However, they did bury their dead. Each herd had an area set aside for its graves. They weren't particularly neat, just holes scraped out of the soil, but the team had recorded them dragging bodies a long way from where they'd died to the herd's burial ground. There were a lot of speculative notes on group identity and rudimentary community awareness, a theory backed up by the fact that every onid was buried with a totem: a stone or stick. They weren't carved or shaped, but something was always dropped into the grave as the soil was scraped back over the corpse. As a presentience marker, it didn't qualify within any methodology the Commonwealth used to determine emerging awareness.

Paula didn't know enough to make a judgment, but she certainly followed the tribal cohesion argument in the appendix. The conclusion was that the use of the totems was simply an instinct, like peeing on a tree to mark territory.

The hypersonic landed on a field just outside Lydian's latest boundary. The town had been in existence for only five months, and its entire history could be measured, like tree-years, in rings of construction activity. Farndale had shipped in every building along a laser-straight highway of enzyme-bonded concrete that led all the way back to a port on the coast. The same colossal JCB roadbuilders that had extruded the highway had stayed on to lay out Lydian's concentric grid. Silver-colored housing was now erupting across the long curving blocks: bungalows whose walls and roofs had been flatpacked together in giant containers that could be assembled by a minimum number of bots. The larger civic buildings were also modular, clipped together to sprawl across the ground. Nothing was over a single storey high. Why bother? Land here cost next to nothing, and vertical assembly was an additional expense.

Lydian's purpose, like that of a hundred other towns springing up across Jevahal, was to be a transport and market center for the homesteads that were busy converting the plains to arable country. Soon there would be a railway for the prefabricated station already built on the western side; the tracks were only three hundred kilometers away now, and approaching at the rate of two kilometers a day. With them would come a whole new level of prosperity. Concrete foundations for the grain silos were laid ready, their metal load pins marking circular outlines where the giant cylinders would dominate the town's skyline for decades to come.

Like a smaller version of the capital, Lydian was destined to receive the busloads of recently arrived settlers and ship them out across the eternal plains to their new lives. During the hypersonic's approach Paula had seen several roads radiating out from Lydian, a simple spiderweb pattern of concrete that gradually devolved into thick dirt tracks. She hadn't noticed much traffic on them.

The local Farndale office provided a Marque 12 Land Rover, which they drove into town. Governor Charan was waiting in the territorial administration building, the largest structure in Lydian.

"No disrespect, Investigator," was his opening line, "but you weren't what I was expecting the board to send me."

"And the last thing you wanted," she concluded for him.

Charan shrugged eloquently. One of Farndale's senior political managers, he was two years out of rejuve, giving him the appearance of a healthy twenty-five-year-old. His build was large, emphasizing the image of a no-nonsense administrator accustomed to dealing with the kind of real physical problems posed by pioneer territories. He wasn't going to waste his time with corporate bullshit. "Frankly, I don't see what you can do," he said levelly. "I've got a whole herd of onid kicking the crap out of my homesteaders, and they're tough families."

"Just one herd?" Paula queried. That wasn't quite how Wilson had pitched it.

"So far. They're running loose somewhere over towards the Kajara Mountains, and that's rugged country. Lot of valleys and forests, which gives the vermin plenty of space to hide. Maybe you can work out where their refuge is, track them down somehow. That hypersonic you came in on, does it have area denial weapons?"

"No," Gary Main said hurriedly. "It's an executive passenger jet."

"Then I'm sorry, but you're wasting my time as well as yours. I have a situation here which needs resolving, and fast."

"Violence isn't the answer," Paula said.

"So much you know," Charan snapped. "You've been here twenty minutes. Not even that old biology guy, Dino, has offered me anything worthwhile, and he's been out there well over a week now. Look, again, no offense, but if the board isn't going to help I'm going to put together a posse and issue them with some heavy-duty weapons. Something that'll finish this permanently. I can't afford other herds turning rogue on me."

Paula shot Gary Main a look. "Who's Dino?"

"Bernadino Paganuzzi," Charan said. "He was working over in the capital when it hit the fan. Turned up right after the first few attacks."

"Why?" Paula insisted.

"He was part of the original xenobiology team that classified the onid as nonsentient," Charan explained. "Went off after the herd ten days ago, saying he was going to try and find out what's got them stirred up. Hasn't been in touch since. Probably got himself bodylossed, silly old sod. Looked like he was due a rejuve a decade ago."

"I'd better get after him, then," Paula said, quietly enjoying the annoyance spasming across Charan's face.

"Investigator, as near as we can make out there's over two hundred of them in that herd. You might want to consider some backup. Why don't I assemble the posse, and you can lead them? That way, if there is no nice and quiet solution, you'll be in a place when you can eradicate the herd for us. With all your experience, you'd make a perfect commander for this kind of operation. Everyone respects you."

You don't, she thought. "I'm not having some group of trigger-happy farmers riding round with me. Nothing will get solved that way. I need to conduct this investigation by myself, thank you."

"I'll be coming with you," Gary said as they left the governor's office. "That was part of my brief."

"No," Paula said. "I need you here to keep Charan contained. The first thing he's going to do now he knows the board isn't sending his marshals is put together that posse, officially or otherwise. You outrank him, and you've got Wilson's ear on this. Your job is to give me the clear space I need to work the case."

"Case?" Gary asked as they left the administration block behind.

"Case," Paula confirmed. She pushed her shades on against the hot sunlight. "As the Governor said, something agitated the onid. People are the only new factor in their environment. One way or another, we're to blame. We've done something wrong. That makes it a case."

COMMUNICATION WAS POOR OUTSIDE Lydian. No uniform planetary cybersphere existed, only small individual nets serving each settlement. Twenty miles from town, Paula's connection to the local nodes was operating on minimal bandwidth. Thirty miles, and her OCtattoos could barely maintain a link to the primitive relay towers that had been put up. Not that there were many of them. The five com platforms Farndale had placed in geostationary orbit were basic antenna providing little more than a guidance function; they were still waiting for upgrades to supply universal coverage. Out here it was emergency signals only. If you were lucky.

The Land Rover trundled up into the higher rugged ground to the east of town. At first the homesteads were a brochure image of what frontier life should be: neat silver-white bungalows surrounded by lush fields with their first crops a lustrous dusting of emerald green atop the rich loam. Then after thirty-five miles the enzyme-bonded road ran out. The vehicle's drive array advised her to take manual control as the ground beneath the tires turned to stony dirt. Her e-butler sent an acknowledgement, and the steering column slid out of its recess. She gripped it tight, her fingers making contact with the i-spots. OCtattoos on her skin completed the link, connecting her nervous system directly to the drive array.

She tried to keep going at thirty miles an hour, but more often than not she crawled along at fifteen or twenty as the suspension lurched over the rough surface. It had been a while since she'd driven manually, and her implanted memory skill was slightly foggy. Her main concern was the horsebox she was towing, which sought any opportunity to fishtail behind her. Homesteads were still visible, bungalows identical to those in town but set back a good mile from the road on either side. For the first hour she watched tractorbots ploughing up the pale red-green grasslands in big neat squares. Wide craters of ash illustrated where clusters of trees used to be.

After a while the dirt track bled away to ordinary grassland. Tall marker posts stretched ahead, strobes flashing weakly under the afternoon sun. Trees were once again prevalent on the rolling landscape. The lumber clearance crews had been among the first to retreat when the onid went rogue. Native vegetation had gloomy green leaves suffused with dark maroon veins. Trees shaded close to black. Thick clumps of willow-equivalents overhung small streams while larger hardwood spinnies colonized hollows, their flaky trunks packed close to present an impenetrable fence to any animal larger than a terrestrial dog.

By now, human activity had dropped off altogether. The homesteads strung out along the marker line were uninhabited. Expensive tractorbots were parked outside, motionless. The scene had an uncomfortable resemblance to the Lost23 worlds, abandoned so fast that possessions were discarded without thought. Finally, all she saw were big cargo containers dropped off in the middle of the wild, their contents unpacked and unassembled.

Sixty miles from town the land had become so rugged that the Land Rover was just crawling along. Paula switched it off and went around to the horse box. The horse Charan had found her was called Hurdy, a chestnut-colored mare he promised was gentle with novice riders. Paula deliberately hadn't told him that she'd spent a lot of her early childhood on ponies and horses at her parents' home out in the countryside. Sure enough, Hurdy was skittish until Paula got the saddle on and mounted up. Then the mare realized that Paula knew what she was doing and didn't try to assert herself further.

Paula set off over the empty, undulating land towards the long band of forest that smothered the foothills to the southeast. Rising up behind them were the Kajara Mountains, their snow-covered peaks gleaming brightly under the hot violet sunlight. Something in the local grass-equivalent oozed out a musky cinnamon scent which made the humid air even more oppressive. Away from the Land Rover's air conditioning, she was sweating in minutes.

The Gorjon family's homestead was her first point of call. It had been attacked two days ago, a turning-point event which caused most of the remaining settlers to head back to Lydian to shout at Charan. If she could find any clue as to what was happening, it would be there.

She reached it after forty minutes' riding. The attack method was interesting. Examining the ground outside the depressingly standard bungalow, Paula decided that it had been completely surrounded. Every curly blade of grass-equivalent was trampled and mashed into the soil by three-clawed hoofs. Stones had been dug up and flung at the building. All the windows were smashed and the heat-reflective pale silver coating of the walls was shredded, the tough composite itself scarred and stressed from thousands of impacts. The ground around the building was piled high with loose stones and clods. Peering through the broken glass, she saw that the floor inside was also littered with stones.

It was all the onid had, she realized, their single method of attack. The xenobiology team report had mentioned how their teeth lacked a sharp edge,the relative strength of their forelimbs, primarily used for clawing at the soil so they could reach their base food, the marak root.

Two hundred of them flinging stones at the same time would be frightening for humans caught at the center even if they had been equipped with a decent weapon to shoot back. Yet all Farndale allowed its homesteaders was a weak maser to kill off vermin. The last thing anyone wanted was any kind of range war out here.

Paula circled the battered bungalow. There were no onid corpses. A vermin maser wasn't a difficult weapon to handle, and its beam would have caught a few of them, she was sure. The onid must have dragged the dead herd members away for burial.

But why had they attacked? She couldn't see anything out of the ordinary about the homestead that might have antagonized the onid. She remounted up and rode Hurdy over to the patch of ground which a tractorbot had been ploughing. Like the bungalow, the tractorbot had been victim to a barrage of stones. Stones had wedged into the wheels and axles, where they'd jammed various mechanisms until the safety limiters had cut in. Paula walked away from the forlorn machine until she was in a patch of freshly ploughed land. The tractorbot hadn't ripped up any marak roots. Even with retinal inserts on high resolution and her e-butler running visual pattern recognition programs, she couldn't spot the long gray-speckled leaves of that particular plant anywhere.

So it's not about food. That left territory. Staring out across the vast rumpled land, she couldn't quite credit a nonsentient working out that the arrival of humans constituted an invasion. *A protosentient might have been able to figure something was wrong, but then why would this be the only trouble spot? No other herds on this continent had reacted similarly. It had to be something specific to this area.*

She rode Hurdy in a wide circle until she found the herd's tracks. They led toward the sprawl of forest dominating the foothills, which were at least half a day's ride away. Hurdy started off down the path of battered grass, with Paula keeping an eye on the darkening clouds now twisting above the southern horizon.

After a couple of hours the clouds were thick in the sky, the front of the storm now visible as it slid in from the south. Paula had already retrieved an oiled leather riding coat out of its roll at the back of the saddle, ready for the deluge. Then her e-butler received a weak emergency signal.

"From where?" she asked.

"The Aleat homestead," her e-butler replied. A map slid up into her virtual vision. She was three and a half miles away.

"Nature of the emergency?" *As if I don't know*, Paula thought in excitement.

"Unknown. It is a high-power beacon emission. Standard issue to all homesteads."

"Come on, girl," she told Hurdy. The horse began to pick up speed, galloping across the dark grass-equivalent.

She was still several hundred meters away when she heard the sound. The onid were warbling away loudly in a weird tenor mewling, a din frightening in its intensity. They might not have had a language, but their cries expressed their mood with shocking clarity. They were angry. Very angry.

Hurdy cleared the last ridge. Ahead of Paula, what looked like a small dense typhoon of dark particles swirled above the homestead. The onid herd members were circling round and round, moving at a startlingly fast run for creatures with so many limbs. Charan had seriously underestimated their numbers; there must have been close to five hundred of them. As they ran, each onid bobbed down in a smooth motion, high forelimbs ripping something from the ground each time—a stone or chunk of tough dried earth—then flung it at the homestead as hard as they could.

"Ho crap," Paula grunted. Hurdy had come to a stop, allowing her to scrabble around and extract the maser carbine from its saddle holster. Even now she was reluctant to shoot.

Then a human wail pierced the air, carrying above the onids' angry racket. Paula knew it was female, probably quite a young girl. Her OCtattoo sensors helped her work out the direction.

The homestead's tractorbot. Apparently stalled, it stood alone two hundred meters from the bungalow. More than twenty onid were already circling it. Stones were tumbling down on the curving red bodywork. And Paula caught sight of the petrified girl squeezing herself into the small gap between the rear wheel and the power casing.

Her OCtattoos were telling her that someone was firing maser shots out of the bungalow's broken front door. Peripheral vision caught a couple of onid falling.

"Dammit," she yelled. She didn't want to fire on the onid around the tractorbot; if they had anything like the herd mentality of terrestrial animals they'd probably charge her, which would leave her no choice. She did have enough firepower, but...

Then another horse was racing in towards the homestead from the opposite direction to Paula. Her OCtattoos tracked a couple of small objects streaking away from it, arcing through the sky towards the herd. A deafening soundblast erupted. She had to jam her hands over her ears. Hurdy reared up in fright. Paula lost the carbine in a desperate attempt to hang on. With her ears now unprotected, the sound hammered like a lance against her brain. The mare began to canter away from the homestead. Paula clung to Hurdy's neck with one arm, trying to turn the mare's head with the reins wrapped tight round her free hand.

She caught snatched views of the onid herd. They'd broken from their circular stampede to stream away from the bungalow. In less than a minute they'd all gone, racing away in panic from the noise.

The vicious screaming cut off. It was like an implosion, sucking all sound from the plains. Paula couldn't hear a thing. She tried to soothe the frightened mare as best she could. Eventually Hurdy calmed enough to allow a safe dismount. Paula still couldn't coax her closer to the homestead. She tethered her to the stem of a bush on the ridge, retrieved the carbine, and hurried off down the slope towards the bashed-up bungalow.

Paula could see the other rider chasing after the fleeing herd on the far side of the tractorbot. *Bad idea*, she thought, and hesitated on her downward charge. She still couldn't hear anything other than a nasty sharp buzzing in both ears. That meant the other rider wouldn't hear any shout to stop. Her retinal inserts zoomed in for a closeup, seeing the figure on horseback raise a small fat gun. OCtattoo sensors tracked the projectile he fired. It was a lot larger than a normal bullet and considerably slower. It hit one of the onid, who didn't even seem to notice the impact.

The rider reined his horse in and watched the retreating herd as he slotted the strange gun back into a holster. A man and a woman came sprinting out of the bungalow, heading straight for the tractorbot. The little girl sagged out of the narrow shelter and collapsed onto the ground. From what Paula could make out, she was about eight, and sobbing helplessly.

By the time Paula joined them, the girl was hugging her parents with wild strength. They were clutching her just as hard, arms tight around her as all three of them wept.

"Are you okay?" Paula yelled at the Aleats. She could barely hear herself through the persistent buzzing in her ears.

The man nodded sharply. He glanced at the carbine in her hand. "Did you scare them off? Did the governor send you?"

She shook her head. That was when the second rider trotted up, dismounting with a smooth practiced motion that belied his apparent age.

"Dino?" Paula shouted.

He plucked small green plugs from his ears. "What?"

"You must be Dino, the biologist."

"Good guess. Xenobiologist, actually. But no need to screech." Biologically he was in his late fifties, shorter than average with thinning dark hair turning gray. When he grinned at her she couldn't help but grin back; his face held that kind of happiness. An errant thought flashed through her brain: when he was rejuved he'd probably be quite handsome. "I'm Paula Myo," she said, trying to judge a normal volume. "What did you use to scare them off?"

"Screamers. Standard issue for xenobiology exploration teams. Very humane. Most animals shit themselves when the things go off; they can't get clear fast enough."

"Ah. Right." Sonic weapons were hardly standard issue for Directorate field equipment packs.

Dino glanced back towards the onid herd. "I should get after them."

"What!"

"Will you stop shouting."

"I'll try. Why? Why go after them?"

He gave her that grin again. "I want to know where I went wrong. I need to find out what's going on."

Paula eyed the shaken homestead family. "Humans provoked them."

"Okay. How?" Dino's hands swept round the land, gesturing at the solitary bungalow.

"I don't know. That's..." *what I'm here to find out.*

"*The* Paula Myo, huh? I'll enjoy working with you, Investigator."

"I work alone."

"Oh. So are you getting a signal from your tracer? I am from mine, it's attached to the rump of that onid I shot."

Paula looked out towards the distant foothills, but the herd had vanished from view amid the folds in the land. She sighed. "You need to get back to town until this is over," she told the three Aleats. The girl pushed herself closer to her mother, seeking comfort.

"Town?" The father spat. "Back to town! I'm getting off this whole bloody planet. And I'm going to sue Farndale. We nearly died out here. You're my witness."

Which made Paula give the heavens a brief resentful glance. Actually, she supposed, his reaction was a sign of civilization. *Nobody reaches for a gun anymore, just for their lawyer.*

When she dropped her gaze back to Dino, he was trying not to smirk. "All right," she said. "What sort of range does that tracker have?"

THE RAIN WAS A great deal heavier than she'd been expecting. In fact she'd been on few planets which produced such a downpour. Her broad-brimmed hat and range coat with its high collar were almost irrelevant. The water hit so hard it seemed to be soaking straight through the coat's guaranteed waterproof layers. It was cold, too, making her shiver even though she could still see the late-afternoon sunlight pouring down from a clear sky on the western horizon.

Snorting and steaming, both horses plodded forward through the deluge, their heads hung low. Her OCtattoos were showing the tracker barely fifty meters ahead of them now, somewhere within a rambling stone outcrop. Without a word, she and Dino dismounted simultaneously. They both hunched down and crept forwards.

In these conditions infrared vision was next to useless. They slithered among the thick stone spines, Paula scanning around as far as the sensor inserts on her arms and head could reach—which in this weather wasn't much beyond two hundred meters. No other onid showed up in any spectrum she had available, though admittedly the inserts weren't configured for this kind of work. The herd must have left the tagged one behind. *But why?*

Twenty meters. The signal was perfectly steady, coming from behind a big chunk of flaky sedimentary rock nearly twice her height that leaned at a slight angle away from her, forming an overhang where the tagged onid must be sheltering. Water ran down the rock's sides, making them slick. Even the streaks of gray-blue moss in the crevices had turned to soggy sponge.

She pointed to Dino to take the left side and held up her janglepulse pistol, which theoretically should work on onid nerve fibers. Dino moved surprisingly fast, and Paula rolled herself round the rock, guided by targeting graphics to bring the pistol into perfect alignment on…

"Shit!"

There was no onid. The little tracker pellet lay on the mud, its adhesive side still sticking to a strip of flesh.

Frowning, Dino picked up the small neutral-gray pellet, wrinkling his nose at the dangling flesh. "This was torn off," he exclaimed.

Paula could just about hear him clearly now. The buzzing in her ears had declined to a nasty tinnitus ringing during their pursuit across the grasslands. "Why would they do that?" she asked.

Dino's shrug was eloquent, even under the bulky coat obscuring his shoulders. "Wrong question. How did they know it was there?"

"If something whacks you in the arse, you tend to know about it."

He shook his head. "Naah, don't believe it. Not an animal. It wouldn't know this from a nut dropping off a tree. Besides, the tracker is designed to flex on impact, reduce the smack so as not to arouse suspicion."

"So you're saying a protosentient might manage to work out that the tracker was something bad?"

"Even if we ballsed up the classification and they are proto, how would it know?"

Paula shoved the pistol back in her holster. "Simplest solution applies: Someone told it."

"Really? Someone sat down and explained the principles of encrypted digital radio tracking to a creature who commands a total of two grunts, one for 'food' and another for 'danger'?"

"You classify by vocabulary?"

"It's a big part of the assessment process, yes. Communication is the bedrock of sentience; as an indicator for self awareness it has yet to be beaten. The greater your comprehension beyond the range of simple instinctual triggers, the higher up the scale you are."

"Okay, so how did it know to get rid of the tracker?" She gave the device and its incriminating flesh another look. "And it must have really wanted to get rid of it—tearing that off must have hurt like hell."

Dino started examining the mud around the rock. "They don't have good teeth," he mumbled. "So... Ah, here we go." He fished a slim shard of rock out of a puddle and held it up, squinting. "Interesting. My inserts can just detect cellular material on the edge here. Rudimentary knife, I'm guessing."

Paula winced. The "edge" wasn't that sharp. "So they do know tools?"

"Possibly. We never saw any evidence of tool usage before. It's probably just an instinctive solution."

"I'd say you'd have to think about a solution like that."

"Good job you're not the expert filing these reports, then. Dropping a snail on a rock to crack its shell: sign of tool usage, or instinct?"

Paula gave him a *look*, doubtless wasted with her skin soaking wet and sodden ebony hair plastered to her cheeks. "We need more information."

"Of course we do. That's why we're here."

She couldn't work out if he were deliberately being rude or just unconsciously talked down to non-xenobiologists. "We can set up camp here for the night. I seriously need to get dry," she said. "Their trail will be easy enough to follow in the morning."

"Did you bring a tent?"

"I'm sure my assistant remembered to pack one for me."

PAULA WAS PLEASED TO see that the xenobiologist didn't oversleep. Like her, Dino was up at dawn, ready to begin the day. Not a classic academic, then.

Her hemispherical plyplastic tent shrank back down into a ball barely larger than her fist while she got on with triggering the thermal tabs on her breakfast packs. Chilled orange and mango smoothie to start with, then hot tea with a smoked salmon and scrambled egg bagel.

"Creature comforts, eh?" Dino said as he folded away the more traditional lightweight tent he'd spent the night in.

She grinned as she bit into the bagel. At least he wasn't trying to light a Cro-Magnon campfire and spear something to eat. "We've spent centuries building up the benefits of civilization. Why abandon them now?"

"My tent is simple yet perfectly adequate. Yours is the extreme end of consumerism technology. Ten times the cost, and you can't patch it up if you puncture it."

"Plyplastic doesn't tear easily. It's not a balloon."

"You've reinvented the wheel."

"We've refined the wheel. We took your circle of wood and gave it a tire and suspension. Because that's what we do: improve things."

Dino pushed the last of a bacon sandwich into his mouth. "I wonder if the onid agree with that."

"If they philosophize about that kind of thing, then they're definitely sentient."

"Yes." He started strapping various packs onto his saddle.

"So are they? Something alerted them to that tracker. They knew it was wrong, or dangerous. Doesn't that indicate a rational analytical process?"

"I don't know, okay? I spent most of last night trying to put this together, and I got nowhere. There's nothing in any of our data which could have anticipated this behavior. We're missing something."

"All right then, let's go and find it."

The herd's track was easy enough to pick up. After leaving the Aleat homestead they'd headed for the Kajara Mountains, cutting a straight line of trampled grass-equivalent across the land.

"Do they have some kind of home we can track them to?" Paula asked. "A nest, or warren, or something?"

"The burial ground is always the center of their territory," Dino said. "That's what I've been doing out here: trying to find a fresh trail which would take me to it. I was lucky to find them raiding the homestead. Herds don't normally stray too far from their territory, just enough to graze for food."

"They're strictly herbivores, then?"

"Yes."

"So they don't have an instinctive attack methodology?" Paula mused.

"Correct," Dino said as he mounted up.

"They're sentient, then," she said insistently. "They worked it out for themselves."

Dino just shook his head dismissively and kicked his horse.

Paula let out a small curse of dismay as Hurdy plodded on beside him. She could see that Dino's team had got the onid classification wrong, even if he refused to admit it. At the very least, everything she'd already witnessed would force an official re-evaluation.

It would be hellishly difficult to evacuate every human off the planet, she knew. Or more likely impossible. The people who'd flooded across this world in the wake of the war to build themselves a better life had an edge to them, a determination the Commonwealth hadn't seen for a couple of generations. They wouldn't bow down and accept some distant government's well-meaning law allowing aliens a chance to develop freely, not these days.

And I'm the one who is going to be reporting the wrong classification. Knowing full well how much vilification that would bring down on her, she wondered briefly if Wilson had set her up. *Payback for the Oscar case?* But no; even as she considered it she knew it wasn't true. Plunging Menard into chaos, ruining the lives of millions of refugees along with depressing the already fragile Commonwealth economy just to settle a personal score, was not something Wilson Kime would consider, let alone instigate.

How ironic, then, that he'd chosen the one person in the galaxy who would not shirk from delivering the bad news of the onids' true status to Commonwealth authorities. *Because it is the correct and legal thing to do.* Her psychoneural profiling ensured she would always do what was right and proper. It was what she was.

"Horses," Dino said.

Paula reined in Hurdy and scanned around. Her inserts couldn't find anything moving across the rustling grasslands.

Dino gave her a smug look and pointed down. "When you've done as much fieldwork as I have, you aren't completely reliant on sensors and recognition programs."

Paula zoomed her retinal inserts on the patch of ground he was indicating, finding the pile of horse dung just beside the track the herd had left.

"Three or four days old," Dino said. "Judging from this trail I'd say there were four of them, and riding quite fast. See how far apart the broken blades are? That's some speed, almost a flat-out gallop."

Paula dismounted and studied the ground. Now that she knew what she was looking for, the riders' trail was clear and obvious. It joined the onids' tracks here, but before that the riders had galloped along not quite parallel to the herd's flattened path.

"I think we just found what we're looking for," Dino said.

Paula glanced over at the Kajara Mountains. The foothills and their broad skirt of forests were only five miles away now. Turning the other way, she tried to work out where the horse tracks were leading. Some large stretches of woodland in the distance were the only distinguishing features. According to the map her e-butler threw into her virtual vision, that whole area of the plains was empty; there were no claims, no homesteads allocated. Nothing. Not even the marker posts had reached that far yet.

"Yes," Paula agreed reluctantly. "The riders have stirred them up. But why? What are they doing?" She gave Dino a sharp look. "What does onid meat taste like?"

"That can't be it," he said quickly. "They're biologically similar, but not compatible. The cellular proteins are all wrong for us, and the nitrogen content is way too high as well. Barbeque one of these little beauties, and best case, you'd spend the next day throwing up. That's not your answer."

"What do they excrete?"

"Ah, nice try, Investigator. You're thinking it might be valuable, like guano?"

"Something like that."

"Again: no. Their poop is nothing special. There's a high-ish iron content, but that's from the marak root. It's all in the report."

Paula scanned the foothills with their verdant covering of trees. "So what's in there that is so valuable to someone that they risk all this?"

"This is what I love about my current job," Dino said. "So much unknown to explore."

"Let's go do your job, then," Paula countered, and climbed back up on Hurdy.

Both sets of tracks ran to the fringe of the woods. Under the trees the straggly undergrowth was hard to read, so much had it been churned up by horses and onid. "It's a general thoroughfare here," Dino declared.

"That's good for us," Paula insisted. "All the tracks are leading in the same direction." They dismounted and started leading their horses past the fat trunks. Hooves crunched loudly on the flakes of bark carpeting the ground. Paula's inserts started scanning, alert for any onid moving about in the forest. After forty minutes the trees thinned out again, revealing a wide river flowing swiftly through a long open valley. The foothills which built up the top end of the valley were quite steep, with a great many streams churning down their rugged, boulder-strewn slopes.

Paula stood in the shade of the last clump of trees, running a wide scan across the valley. Several onid were visible, moving slowly as they bent down and scrabbled for marak roots. She slipped behind a trunk.

"Now this is what I expect to see," Dino said, peering round the tree next to hers. "All very tranquil. There's nothing here that anyone could want."

"Let's see what we can find," Paula muttered. She led the way back to where they'd tethered the horses. The only way they'd be detected now was if an onid walked directly into them, a chance she was willing to take. She opened one of her saddlebags and took out a slim case with eight eyebirds in it. The little gadgets were disc-shaped, five centimeters in diameter, comprising a slim outer ring crammed with sensor systems and a central contra-rotating fan. Their motors spun up silently and they rose out of the case to hover in front of her as her e-butler loaded in a search pattern. As soon as the procedure was complete, they swarmed off into the valley, rising up to a level fifteen meters' altitude.

Images slid up into Paula's virtual vision. The eyebirds were crammed with an astonishing array of sensors; if there were any kind of abnormality to be spotted, she was sure they could find it for her.

It would be a tough search, she admitted after the first five minutes. The valley seemed a pleasant, bucolic place. None of the eyebirds could detect a large thermal source that might indicate some type of predator. It was a theory quite high on her probables list that humans had lost some kind of animal, possibly one of the endangered terrestrial species. She knew that cheetahs and panthers and lions and several other types were bred in secret colonies on several worlds. You paid a small fortune for the privilege of hunting them, but there were always people with that kind of money. And a world like Menard would be the perfect place to set up such an enterprise.

"I've got the burial ground," Dino said. "Eyebird three, look. But what's happened to it?"

Paula, who was accessing the feeds from eyebirds eight and five, switched her attention over to three. One of the long stretches of meadowland at the base of a tall rock cliff was the heart of the herd, with the graves showing as small mounds of earth. It needed to be a big area; there were a *lot* of the mounds, she realized, and the oldest were almost flat. The majority were covered in the local grass-equivalent, but a good fifth of them had been dug open. It hadn't been done neatly; long spills of fresh earth were scattered around each one. Whoever did it had been in a hurry.

"Are you sure there are no native predators around here?" Paula asked.

"We never saw any. There's a beast in the northern part of this continent, a gruganat, which is close to a terrestrial lion but a lot faster. They feed on onids and other animals. But none have been spotted here."

"Could this be the first one? Human are settling in the north, too; we could have driven them out of their traditional hunting grounds."

Dino pulled a sour expression. "Gruganats prefer fresh meat. And they wouldn't have any problem killing it here."

Paula moved eyebird two to cover the burial ground in more detail, directing it down to hover over one of the opened mounds. It wasn't a particularly deep excavation, and the decomposing corpse was just visible at the bottom of the shallow oval hole.

"It wasn't a carnivore doing that, then," Dino said. "The body hasn't been touched."

"Agreed," Paula said. "And look at the edges of the hole. They're clean, straight. That was a spade. This is what those riders have been doing."

"The totems," Dino exclaimed in a shocked tone. "They've taken the totems. Each onid is buried with the tribe's totem. No wonder they're so angry."

"Why? What would anybody want with the totems? Your report said they were just stones."

"They are. Pebbles, sticks, even a flower once; each herd has a different one. All they do is reinforce the herd identity, that's what we thought."

"What does this herd use?" Paula asked.

"I've no idea. Each herd seems to choose something that's abundant in their territory."

Paula moved eyebird two over to an intact grave. Its sensors gave the mound a fast sweep. "There's some kind of metal in there." She read the results table that slithered across her virtual vision. "Definitely metallic, a small lump."

"Metal?" Dino asked. "Are you sure?"

She sent the eyebird over to the next grave. Sure enough, it also contained a lump of metal; the signature was almost identical. "Metal detecting is about the oldest science there is. I can't determine the composition, unfortunately. There's only so much you can pack into an eyebird." She raised her hand in front of her face. The slim lines of an OCtattoo materialized across her skin, as if her veins were being invaded by quicksilver. "I need to get a bit closer for a decent readout. I don't want to desecrate anything the way those riders have."

"Where does the herd get metal from?" Dino murmured, puzzled.

"I don't know. But it's got to be valuable to humans somehow." She couldn't think how. "Maybe an alien starship crashed nearby, and they're picking up the wreckage."

"Is that likely?"

"Not really," she admitted. "We'll have to get down there to find out for sure."

"We can't risk getting caught," Dino said. "The herd's upset enough as it is."

"Are they heavy sleepers?"

Before Dino answered, eyebird six sent an alert; several solid objects were airborne below it. They weren't large, and they didn't rise quite high enough to strike the eyebird, but another barrage was rising.

Paula looked directly through the eyebird's camera. A dozen or so onid were clustered below it, flinging stones. She hurriedly instructed it to increase altitude. When it was thirty meters above the ground, she paused it. The onid were still there, still throwing stones. More were joining them. Their hoots of alarm were spreading across the valley.

"How the hell did they see it?" she asked incredulously. "It's silent, the fan balances on superconductor bearings, and the color is dehanced-grey." She glanced up at the clouds scudding past the mountain peaks. "It's practically impossible to see it against a sky like this. Do they have some kind of ultra-vision?"

"No," Dino said, "their eyesight isn't even as good as ours."

"Then how..."

"I don't know." He looked back towards the edge of the forest. "We really need to know what's in those graves."

Paula focused back on the images from eyebird six. There were twenty onid below it, scraping stones from the ground and flinging them skyward. She instructed the eyebird to fly slowly down the slope towards the river at the bottom of the valley. The onid followed as if it was their guru. "How?" she whispered.

The question would have to wait. The situation provided her with a perfect tactical opportunity. She quickly directed four other eyebirds to join up with number six, sending them low over the ground, weaving about so they passed close to various groups of onid. After half an hour the five eyebirds had joined into a loose V formation. Below them—hooting, squealing, and still hurling their ineffectual missiles—were more than a hundred onid, with what looked like every other member of the herd heading across the valley towards them.

The eyebirds drifted towards the end of the valley and the forest beyond. Holding station five hundred meters above them, the remaining three eyebirds watched the burial ground and the surrounding land. It was now devoid of any onid.

"If they were sentient, they would have left guards," Dino said as they rode out of the forest close to the burial ground.

"Yes," Paula conceded. Hurdy trotted along the base of the cliff, keeping to the thick shadow it was throwing. If the onid did have poor sight, as Dino claimed, they'd be hard to see in such shade. Even so, she eyed the fissures in the grey rock warily, holding the carbine ready for any ambush.

They dismounted as soon as they reached the first of the little mounds. The silver lines of Paula's OCtattoo appeared again over her hand, spreading a delicate lacework down her forearm.

She knelt beside the first grave and slowly waved her hand over the wispy grass-equivalent.

The results of the scan materialized in her virtual vision, tight bright graphics superimposed over what she was seeing. "Holy crap," she gasped.

IT WASN'T DIFFICULT TO track the riders' trail across the open grassland. Paula and Dino took four hours to reach the thick woodland it led into. She sent another small flock of eyebirds flitting through the trees as they walked forwards cautiously, the airborne sensors scanning round for any sign of human activity. Three more of the little gadgets zoomed high above the wood and produced an almost immediate result. The trees were crowded around a lake. Right in the center was some kind of crude raft with a plyplastic tent for a cabin. Sensors saw a couple of people moving around. Paula hurriedly withdrew the eyebirds, certain the riders would have some sensor systems of their own, although they'd be very different to the eyebirds. After all, they must have been ordinary prospectors before they hit their unexpected motherlode.

"Now what?" Dino asked.

Paula put on her force field skeleton suit over her clothes and ran a fast integration and function check. "I go and deal with them," she told him, and pulled the carbine out of its saddle holster.

Dino gave her an uneasy look as she clipped more weapons hardware to her belt. "Deal with them how, exactly?"

"Take them into custody and fly them back to the capital for trial."

"Right." He eyed the janglepulse pistol she was checking. "Okay, so what do I do?"

"Wait here. This is what I do. Trust me."

"And the totems?"

"Once I've recovered them, we'll return them to the herd. You might want to think about how we do that."

"Paula... I saw the eyebird images of the raft. That was a big tent, and there are four horses we know about. They'll be armed. Maybe we should get Charan's posse out here to help."

"I don't need help, but thanks for your concern."

For a moment it looked like Dino might object, but he just threw up his hands and said: "Your area."

"That it is."

PAULA SKIRTED THE LAKE, walking parallel to the shore until she found the outflow stream. The ground on either side of the gurgling water was sodden, more sludge than mud, bubbling with the most noxious gasses imaginable, farts from as-yet unclassified microbes. All of which made it ideal for a tall reed-equivalent plant to flourish. Her chest and trousers were painted thick with the sludge as she slithered forward through the prickly strands. Then she was right up to the edge of the lake, elbows in the water, parting the last of the reeds. She hadn't activated her force field skeleton yet; if the riders had even a modest sensor system on the raft, they'd spot it.

Her retinal inserts zoomed in to give her a clear image. It was in fact two rafts. The main one, with the hemispherical tent on top, was firmly anchored with four thick ropes leading down into the water, one at each corner. Docked to it was a smaller raft whose deck had a high railing. Four horses stood on its rough planks, placidly munching through the contents of their nosebags. A ferry rope stretched away from the main raft to a tree above the shore and ran through a couple of iron hoops secured to the deck of the smaller raft.

Not a bad hideaway, Paula acknowledged. The onid couldn't swim—that was very clear in the original report—and the thick woods shielded the gang from casual human observation. One of the men walked out of the tent, dressed in jeans and a yellow t-shirt. He carried a bucket in one hand. A belt holster held a rapid-fire automatic pistol. It would probably decimate the onid herd but didn't pose any danger to her, not in a force field.

The man went down to the other end of the raft, where some badly made wire cages were strapped to the decking. Paula was surprised to see that each cage contained a baby onid, squatting miserably in its own excrement, fledgling upper limbs squashed against the galvanized wire. The man opened the top of the first cage and scooped a flaccid olive-brown marak root out of the bucket. He dropped it into the cage and the little onid grabbed it eagerly, gnawing at the mushy pulp with immature teeth.

"Why, oh why?" Paula mumbled to herself. It was almost rhetorical. Everything she'd seen, all the factors of the investigation, were coming together in her hyperactive subconscious as they always did.

She drew a small kinetic gun from her belt, wrinkling her nose as the movement burst yet more bubbles in the sludge. Her e-butler reprogrammed the enhanced explosive tips in the bullets, dialing them down to their absolute minimum. She took aim carefully on the ferry rope where it was secured to the tree. Her e-butler fired the gun, avoiding the minute motion of her finger squeezing a physical trigger, which might throw the aim off a fraction. She needed accuracy for this. A maser or x-ray laser would have worked and was completely silent, but again she didn't want to risk sensors picking up the shots.

The bullet hit the trunk and detonated with a tiny *thuck*. Her amplified hearing could just make it out, but only because she was listening for it. The man feeding the captive onids certainly didn't hear it. The rope fell into the water with barely a ripple.

Paula shifted her aim, the targeting grid centering on an anchor cable where it went into the water. *Thuck*. A small plume of water burped up and the cable went slack.

She got two more anchor cables before the man raised his head, glancing round with a puzzled frown. Refusing to rush, Paula lined up on the last cable, slicing it cleanly.

The man was peering over the side of the raft now, trying to work out what was wrong. Eventually he let out a grunt and bent down to haul up one of the anchor cables. Paula couldn't help chuckling at his classic expression as he held the frayed end up to his face: ape examines pretty colors of hologram projection.

He started shouting in alarm. Three more men and two women came out of the tent. More shouts reverberated over the still lake as they discovered all the anchor cables were cut. Surprise turned to anger. Paula started wriggling backwards, retreating into the trees. The next stage was going to be the slowest snare in history. They'd realize that eventually, and when they did so anger would turn to fright. That was when they'd get desperate.

She waited patiently, a single eyebird hovering in the cover of a tree at the opposite end of the lake revealing the raft's inching progress. It wasn't a large amount of water which the streams brought into and out of the lake, but the current was steady.

Sure enough, when they were forty meters away from the mouth of the stream, the gang on the raft brought out their weapons. Paula catalogued two old military-grade maser carbines, a hunting rifle, the automatic pistol and a couple of pump-action shotguns. She began to walk along the stony streambed towards the lake. Her force field skeleton activated, cloaking her in the dimmest of purple shimmers.

"There!" One of the men bellowed and pointed as she emerged from the darkness of the overhanging trees. She stood at the mouth of the stream, dripping slime into the water like the original swamp monster. Every gun they had fired simultaneously. They weren't very good shots. Those beams and bullets which did strike her were easily deflected by her force field. It rarely even flared blue.

The horses on the smaller raft began to whinny, tossing their long necks in panic and jostling each other. The raft wobbled alarmingly.

Amid the barrage, Paula calmly drew her janglepulse and shot the flank of a horse with a low-level pulse. It shrieked and reared up, front hooves cycling in the air before crashing down, tipping one side of the barge below the surface. Then the poor frenzied animal jumped through the rail into the water and began swimming. The other horses charged after it. Mud and water churned up around them in a filthy slush as they made their way toward the lakeside, angling away from the glimmering purple figure at the head of the stream.

The raft drifted onward, dragged inexorably by the current. When it was twenty meters away Paula shouted: "I am Investigator Paula Myo. You're under arrest: please throw your weapons into the water."

"Fuck you, bitch!"

"Uh huh," she grunted as the masers opened fire again. Phosphorescent sparkles shivered through the air about her as the shotgun blasts reached her. She raised the kinetic gun, cranked up the explosive tip to full and fired straight into the tent.

She'd been completely wrong. A plyplastic tent turned out to behave exactly like a balloon. When the bullet detonated, the whole thing burst apart with a bright violet flash. Fluttering strips of shrinking plastic whipped savagely at the gang members, ripping clothes and lacerating exposed skin. The yells were more from shock than pain and the damage was mostly superficial. Paula used the janglepulse on maximum power to shoot the man who'd fed the baby onids. He spasmed, and collapsed unconscious onto the decking. The raft was only fifteen meters from the stream mouth now.

"Throw down your weapons," she repeated. "I won't ask again."

They hesitated, then one by one they let their weapons drop into the lake.

PAULA LAUNCHED A COMDRONE, which shot up to a two-kilometer altitude. From there it established a link to Lydian's diminutive cybersphere, allowing her to make the call. Twenty minutes later the Farndale executive hypersonic was landing beside the woods in a downblast of air that sent a wild cyclone of grass and leaves swirling. Gary Main hurried down the airstairs to stare at the sullen captives standing beside Paula and Dino.

"What happened?" he asked.

"They aggravated the herd by grave robbing," Paula told him. "That's why the homesteaders have been attacked. The onid didn't know how else to vent their anger at the violation. Any invader is a target for them, they can't distinguish between us."

"Graverobbing? What the hell is in an onid grave?"

Paula and Dino exchanged a look. Paula held up one of the dozen bags they'd recovered from the raft. Gary gave her a surprised glance when he felt the weight, then opened it tentatively. "Shit!" He pulled out a nugget longer than his thumb. "That's gold."

"The real, raw thing," Paula confirmed.

"Every herd uses a different totem," Dino said. "This herd had the misfortune to pick gold. To them it's nothing, a different kind of rock. To us…"

Paula waved at the Kajara range dominating the horizon. "There must be some rich veins of ore up there, and the nuggets wash down from the mountains. The whole area around their burial ground is laced with streams."

Gary shook his head at the nugget. "So they just grab the closest shiny thing, huh?"

"Yeah," Dino said. "I'm speculating, but these bastards must have been out here prospecting for minerals and found a stream with a couple of nuggets, or maybe they saw an onid carrying one back to their burial ground. After that, simple human greed kicked in."

"Poor them," Gary said. "So do all the herds along the mountains use gold?"

"Certainly not the next few along," Dino said. "But if it's prevalent, others will use it."

"Damn. I wonder how much ore is up there? We completely missed that in the geological survey. Not that preliminary satellite scans are ever particularly detailed."

"I'm sure Farndale will rectify that soon enough," Paula said. She removed the bag from Gary's grasp. "In the meantime, we need to keep this quiet. I'll take this gang back with me to Paris and the prosecutors can charge them with endangering the settlers. It means they can be kept in isolation for the immediate future."

"Sure," Gary said. "That fits in with my brief. So will the herd stop attacking us now?"

"We'll take the totems back," Dino said. "That should satisfy them."

"Take it back?" Gary gave the bags a startled look. "You're going to give it to the animals?"

"It's the only way to stop the homestead raids," Paula said.

"Someone else is going to find out what they've got soon enough," Gary warned. "There'll be a stampede of prospectors out here. They'll bring heavy machinery into the mountains. All other considerations will get shoved aside."

"I'll talk to Wilson Kime," Paula said, "see what we can work out."

"Your call," Gary said.

"That it is." *For now, anyway*, she added silently. "Get these prisoners away to the capital now, then come back for me. I shouldn't be more than another day here."

PAULA AND DINO RODE across the grasslands, heading straight for the herd's valley with no attempt to conceal themselves. They led three of the horses from the raft, laden with the bags of gold. The seven baby onid freed from cages bounded along beside the horses.

"I know what the onid have," Paula said as they entered the forest surrounding the valley. "I know how they saw the eyebirds, and how they knew about the tracker."

Dino gave her a startled look. "What?"

"Process of elimination. Besides, I have it myself." She held up her hand as her e-butler activated the sensor mesh. The silver threads of the OCtattoo gleamed in the bright sunlight. "They can see electricity. Terrestrial bees have something similar, don't they?"

"A magnetic sense," Dino said. "Of course! That fits everything. They can sense metal like the nuggets. Hell, it might even be why they can always find marak roots—the tubers have a high iron content. Damn!" He grinned happily.

Paula was still smiling as they came out into the open. The baby onids started to hoot enthusiastically. Before long every adult in the valley was heading for them.

"Just keep going for the burial ground," Dino said as the herd swarmed round the horses. This time they didn't pick up stones, but they still circled quite fast.

When they reached the mounds at the base of the cliff, Dino got down and unhitched each of the bags, cutting them open so that the nuggets spilled across the ground. The herd rushed in to claim the nuggets, clutching them close and then running off to find an open grave.

Paula was amazed to see them scamper past the closest desecrated mounds; each onid chose instead a specific grave for the totem it carried. "They know which grave each totem belongs to," she said.

"Their ancestral identity is everything to them," Dino said. "We saw that right from the start."

"That kind of memory must count for something. Surely they must be classed as proto-sentient now?"

"Possibly."

The replacement process took over an hour. "I have a theory, too," Dino said when only a few nuggets remained. He picked one up, holding in his other hand a flashgem. They'd been popular in the Commonwealth years before: artificial crystals which stored photons directly, then released them at random to produce elegant sparks. The onid that came to reclaim the nugget hooted softly, staring at the gentle sparks. It reached for the flashgem.

Dino withdrew the bauble and proffered the nugget instead. The onid reached for the flashgem again.

Dino persisted for a while, denying the onid the flashgem each time until he finally dropped the nugget at the onid's feet and stood up, pocketing the flashgem. The action agitated the onid, but it eventually picked up the nugget and rushed off to find the grave to which it belonged.

"What are you doing?" Paula asked.

"Suppose one of the herd dies and they can't find a nugget for its totem?" Dino asked. "After all, the water is washing them down those streams the whole time. They're not static. There's no guarantee."

"So?" Paula asked. "They wait until the rains wash down another batch."

"No. The graves and the herd are everything to the onid. I think they do it differently."

The last totems were retrieved and carried off to the graves. "Watch the one I offered the flashgem to," Dino said.

Paula saw it scrabble soil back into the mound's hole. When it was finished, it scurried off to the base of the tall cliff and disappeared into one of the fissures. "Ah," she said. "Good reasoning, Dino, I'm impressed. We could make an investigator out of you yet."

"Yeah, in ten lives' time when I'm so utterly bored with everything else."

The onid reappeared, carrying a new nugget. It was large. The onid had to use both its forelimbs to hold it.

"Well, what do you know," Paula said. "A genuine cave full of treasure. Thank heavens the raider gang never found that. They'd own Lydian by now, probably half of the continent to boot. How much do you think is in there?"

"Enough," Dino said. The onid hurried over, and Dino gave it the flashgem in return for the new nugget, which was half the size of his fist. He produced another flashgem. The onid raced back to the fissure.

Paula leaned forward, resting her hands on the front of the saddle. "Just how many of those flashgems have you got?"

"Not enough. I need to bring a crate back here. Will you give me that time? Please?"

"Dino..." What he was saying was completely out of character. Then she thought she saw tears in his eyes. "What do you want that kind of money for?"

"What would have happened if the asteroid which wiped out the dinosaurs back on Earth had missed?"

"Er..."

"Would they have evolved into sentients eventually? Would they be the ones who'd just fought the Starflyer War?"

"That's a rhetorical question, right?"

"Actually, no. It's a romantic question. They had millions of years to develop rationality, and failed. We, on the other hand, have been around in our current form for only about fifteen thousand years, depending who you listen to, and already we're here, two hundred light years from Earth. But this is a decisive moment for the onid. We're their extinction event, Paula."

An onid bounded up, carrying the biggest nugget they'd seen. Dino smiled ruefully at it and swapped the precious metal for another flashgem. "How about that. I'm the new Peter Minuit."

"Who?"

"Peter Minuit, the director general of the New Netherlands province. In 1626 he purchased some land from a tribe of the Wappinger Confederacy, allegedly using trinkets and cloth to a total value of sixty guilders. It was the best land deal the human race has ever known."

"Manhattan Island," Paula said.

"Correct."

"So you want to buy the Kajara Mountains."

"And all the onid lands surrounding them. Buy them, lease them, whatever deal I can strike with Farndale."

"And then what?"

"I'm sure the gang had worked it out as well," Dino said. "That's why they'd captured the baby onids. See, the onids' value extends a lot farther than some ore in those mountains. Don't you see? They're walking metal detectors. And better than that, they use the skill intelligently. They're at least as bright as a terrestrial dog. Having seen what we've seen here today, I'd say smarter. I believe I can justifiably argue for them to be given proto-sentient status."

"That's good," she said, trying to sound supportive.

"No, no. They're at the cusp right now. The gang was going to take those babies away and breed them, just like humans did with dogs. And they'd have concentrated on all the wrong traits. An acute magnetic sense would've been prized above everything. Intelligence, an independent streak—those traits would've been the first things breeders would eradicate. Do you understand? Humans have an economic incentive to meddle with the potential of other species. Every wilderness homestead on every new planet will want to own an onid. They can do everything a dog can, with the added bonus that they'll find anything valuable in your land. An effective nontechnological sensor, one you can keep expanding for zero cost through procreation."

"Are you sure they're proto-sentient?"

"No. And that's what makes this such a terrible crime. They might never make that climb out of proto-status, and we can't know because it won't happen for another ten thousand years. But that's it, Paula. With *shits* like that gang flooding across this land and stealing the herds, they never will. Definitely. I have to stop that, Paula. I have to protect the onids' one fragile chance to evolve naturally."

"By buying the Kajara? What will you do, set up some kind of protectorate?"

"Yes. They threw the Native Americans off Manhattan Island. I'm going to do the opposite. This will be a Manhattan in reverse. I'll keep them safe here. It will be an enclave where evolution can run its course, without any interference."

Paula watched the herd. They were dispersing from the burial ground now, except for a persistent five or six who hung around Dino in the hope of more trinkets. That in itself seemed to Paula a sign of basic intelligence. "That sounds very admirable." So much so, it appealed to her instinctive sense of order.

"Will you help?"

"Yes. I'll talk to Wilson. I can at least get you that time to come back and trade your trinkets for gold. And I can support any application to change onid status to proto-sentient."

"Thank you. That's a good start."

"On a very long road," Paula warned him. "I hope you know what you're doing. This isn't going to be easy."

"Change never is. That's what makes it so worthwhile."